*The sorceress sat at her loom
and began weaving.*

As she wove she sang, a clear song which pierced like crystal blades, and in a little while an air sprite came to her in the form of a bird. It was white and palest blue, with a spreading lacy tail, the colors and patterns of a clear winter's day. None but she could see it.

"Child of the air," she said, "there is a message I would have you take for me to Rothevna the Prince of the Children of Lir who dwells in the Veiled Isles, and to the bard with the gold-strung harp who has the love of Gudrun Blackhair. And these are the words . . ."

"For lovers of magic, history, and/or swashbuckling adventure, *BARD* is an exciting novel about an earthy and genuinely likeable Irish hero."

—*Science Fiction Review*

BARD III:
The Wild Sea

Ace Fantasy Books by Keith Taylor

BARD
BARD II
BARD III

BARD III
THE WILD SEA

KEITH TAYLOR

ACE FANTASY BOOKS
NEW YORK

This book is an Ace Fantasy
original edition, and has never
been previously published.

BARD III
THE WILD SEA

An Ace Fantasy Book / published by arrangement with
the author

PRINTING HISTORY
Ace Fantasy edition / June 1986

ISBN: 0-441-04915-X

Ace Fantasy Books are published by The Berkley Publishing Group,
200 Madison Avenue, New York, New York 10016.
PRINTED IN THE UNITED STATES OF AMERICA

PROLOGUE

The key will be taken,
the well will be opened . . .
—Barsaz-Breiz

"Gudrun Blackhair has returned."

Men said it all down both sides of the Narrow Sea. The Jutes of Kent said it with violent curses, and looked to their spears and their new king. When he heard the news he did not smile again for a full day.

Watchers on the white cliffs saw a ship pass by, a long swift ship bearing the emblem of a raven with spread wings on its crimson sail. Blackhair was flaunting. It was for show, that sail. She had two plain gray-green ones for business, but it was not in her mind to sneak home. Let them all know!

Two lesser, slower ships accompanied her. She sailed at their pace rather than the full, magical speed of her darling *Ormungandr,* and so the news was allowed time to spread.

A huge, costly brothel in Ratuma city, called the Dolphin and much frequented by seamen, vibrated with the news for days. Men cursed Gudrun Blackhair again, or spoke of her with grudging admiration, and one man who began a song about her was knifed by someone else who took exception to it, although whether he disliked hearing her name, or thought the song showed insufficient respect—it alleged she did lewd and downright reckless things with her sword—none bothered to inquire. Those whose function it was to do such things disposed of the corpse discreetly, and im-

1

pressed upon the slayer by means of a thorough beating that his custom was no longer required.

"Aye, she's back."

The Hastings and the South Saxons settled in Britain were cheerful. They had no particular quarrel with Gudrun Blackhair, and it tickled them to think how their Jutish neighbors to the north and west would receive the news.

In a fishing village on the Gaulish side of the water, the three ships were beached for a night and stories were exchanged. When the vessels departed in the morning, the fisher-folk knew that Gudrun's companions were Danes from the northern lands, under their chieftains Njal the Sea-Gray and Pigsknuckle Hromund. They in turn knew the name of the new king of Kent, the squabbles of the local counts and vicars and other such gossip, all as it should be. The Sarnian pirates had lost men to Urbicus the wrecker, which was not as it should be, and Gudrun made a vow to do something about it.

"Before or after we return to Sarnia?"

The question came from her second in command, a sardonic one-eyed Spaniard named Decius. The red jewel he wore in his bereft socket flashed as he spoke. His captain cast a puzzled, half frowning glance at him. His manner had changed somewhat since his sword-brother Ataulf had died in northern waters. He was either advocating utter recklessness or mocking hers.

"After," she replied.

Her lover turned from the shield-rail, brown of hair and otter-lithe. His harp rode on his back as she usually did.

"And the welcome there'll be!" he said. "They have all been thinking us dead, rumor having slain us nine times and wishes a thousand. Shall we surprise them?"

"I had rather," Gudrun Blackhair said. A smile crossed her vital, large-featured face. Most men considered her less than comely or else much, much more. To the bard she was the most beautiful woman ever to breathe air. "It would be easy if we had not *Whale's Sister* and *Wayfarer* with us. As it is . . ." She shrugged. "If we do surprise them, the fault will be theirs." She looked at her lover. "Bragi, let me hear that song about King Oisc again, I beg."

The bard, known as Bragi in that company, but whose true name was Felimid mac Fal, agreed. "I've added a verse or two since the last time," he said.

The leather bag came down from his shoulder. His harp rose into his hands. A merry, insolent tune flew across the water.

"There lived an old king by the gray northern sea,
Aparain dubh o hi ho,
There lived an old king by the gray northern sea,
And the bloodiest pirate in Britain was he,
Ro hu il o ho!

"In Britain" was acceptable to his hearers. Gudrun Black-hair did not live in Britain. The harp laughed; Felimid sang on, mirth in his voice.

"Had he been as long in the reach of his arm
Aparain dubh o hi ho,
Had he been as long in the reach of his arm
As long in the tooth and deficient in charm—
Ro hu il o ho—

"He might have reached forth and gone plundering
Gaul,
Aparain dubh o hi ho,
He might have reached forth and gone plundering
Gaul,
Without stirring his buttocks from Thanet at all!
Ro hu il o ho!"

The ship *Ormungandr* flew on. The word spread. In Baioca, that city's bishop heard it, thought of the rich churches in his care and his proximity to the sea, and offered a prayer.

Across the water, in his stronghold of Wiht-garabyrig on the island the Romans called Vectis, a prince by the name of Cynric cursed loudly. Then he ordered a ship made ready to sail.

In the hard stone fort of Grannona, which guarded the

mouth of the Seine, the word was also repeated. The commander's battle-harness suddenly felt three times as heavy to him, and he posted a stronger watch, which his men stood with only perfunctory grumbling. They had no wish to be surprised by one of Gudrun's notorious, fire-swift raids.

The alarm sounded frenziedly in the chill autumn dawn one morning, clanging and chiming as a brawny arm plied an iron bar within its cast-iron circle. The garrison tumbled out of bed to man the walls, prepared to fight. The hardest of them felt something as the long shape of *Ormungandr* slid out of the fog, its serpent-head glaring.

"Ahoy, Grannona!" came the hail. It was a man's voice, clear and strong, seeming to come from several places unmuffled by the fog—the tone of a trained bard. "I am Gudrun Blackhair's spokesman, and I give you her greetings. New-returned to these waters, she would not be discourteous and ignore her old friend Quintian. It's her hope that you command yet, and that your lungs take no harm from the fog. Alas, she cannot be stopping to visit you now. Another time, maybe."

Laughter roared from the great ship's benches. In a swirl of fog, the serpent-head with the disconcerting live glow about its carved eyes was gone. A strain of harp-music and a snatch of song drifted back.

> *"To sit at his board within range of his breath,*
> >   Aparain dubh o hi ho,
> *To sit at his board within range of his breath,*
> *Was to know why his henchmen went fearless of death,*
> >   Ro hu il o ho!"*

Quintian let out a slow, exasperated, relieved breath. A joke. One of her jokes.

He said wearily, "She's back, the bitch."

I

The man who stands at a strange threshold
Should be cautious before he cross it,
Glance this way and that:
Who knows beforehand what foes may sit
Awaiting him in the hall?

—Hávamál

Sure-footedly and with care, Felimid mounted the cliff path. Above him climbed Gudrun, with white cloth wrapped around her calves and a square of the same pinned to her back so that he would not blunder into her. He needed the help it gave him, although he saw well in the dark. The night was squally and thick with cold rain. The path would have suited ibex. They felt their way, suspended in rocky space.

Felimid knew what would befall if he slipped once. Still he felt content, light of heart and sure of reaching the top. The murkiness around him now was like clear daylight to the indecision that had plagued him through most of the summer past, the fretting tumult of not knowing fully what he wanted or what he was prepared to give for it—and his present state of mind, also, was clear daylight by comparison.

What he wanted most on the ridge of the earth wore white cloth and climbed a yard or two in front of him.

And he had her, as she had him.

Though none could see him, Felimid the bard smiled. Wind struck him in dangerous gusts, the elementals in it shrieking their mischief as they wielded long gray lashes of rain mingled with high-blown spindrift; and he could not stop smiling.

"Sst! Lover, we are almost there. Best you wait, for there ought to be guards. I will call to you."

"Right," Felimid answered, his pride not at all ruffled. If there were guards, it made sense for Gudrun to approach them, since they were her men to command. Any other who met them suddenly in the dark would have to do his talking with a metal tongue. That, Felimid was ready to forego.

He waited some time. Without the exertion of climbing to warm him, he began to shiver, despite his long sealskin jacket and the tunic and heavy shirt beneath it. Squirming closer to the rock face, he envisioned himself bathing in hot spiced wine before a huge fire, and not wishing to be selfish he placed Gudrun wallowing and streaming in the same restorative tub.

"Bragi!"

He'd taken that name upon leaving Britain, to conceal his identity and spare friends of his serious trouble, and had long since grown used to answering when it was spoken.

"Constant as ever, I haven't gone away. What is it, *acushla?*"

"What? You can speak louder, Bragi, as loud as you will. No one's here! The path is not guarded! By the gods, do they not remember how I took this isle for my own, from the scum who held it before? Do they think the same cannot happen to them?"

"I'd not be knowing what they do think. My eagle, let's ask them."

"Yes!" Pitched to be heard above the sea-noise and hooting wind, Gudrun's voice was angry. "Let us do that, and now!"

They stood on the smaller part of cliff-girt Sarnia, the southern part. As the island had been Gudrun's pirate base for years, and Felimid had been there but once before, she walked ahead. While it was barely a quarter-mile to her hall, night and cloud, rain and veering wind, made it seem a greater distance. She was swearing continuously by the time she found the courtyard with its familiar stepping stones across the mire.

"'Ware the midden," she advised. "It's to your left there."

The main door of the hall, opening upon the foreroom, had been shut and barred at sunset. Gudrun did not think of trying it. The door opening into the yard, by which servants came and went, was a more unobtrusive way in. Although it too was shut, a dagger-blade slipped through a crack allowed her to lift the bar. There had never been a need to construct her hall as an unbreakable fortress. The island of Sarnia was very nearly that in itself.

Once they had entered, smells of wine, ale, food and sweat, simmered in the warmth of trench-fires, swirled around them to contrast with the salt chill they had brought in from the night. They heard laughter, a Frankish battle-song raucously bawled by six voices, a gleeful shout of "Rip up his belly, Medard!" clattering, grunting, banging, whoops, grating metal, and bets offered and taken. Shedding their hooded sealskin jackets, the pair walked into the riotous hall.

Torches and fire lit a confusion of seven score men and forty women, some drunken, all wild. The wolfhounds from Felimid's own country, the scarred tables, the racks of weapons, were as he remembered, as were the pelts of a white bear and an enormous red ape which hung on the wall behind Gudrun's chair. It seemed to Felimid that the place smelled worse than it had that other time, but he'd just come from the clean, cold night, and maybe his nose was over-delicate. In any case the warmth was too welcome for him to think of leaving.

Two brawlers writhed on the floor, one on his back, the other astride, straining to gut each other with knives. Gudrun moved through the press of gleeful spectators, shouldering one aside, giving a second a quick neat elbow strike to the ribs, and seized the uppermost fighter. He roared a curse as Gudrun, with a noise of effort, flung him aside. He hurled himself at her so swiftly and blindly that she had to break his nose before he recognized her.

The pirate fell on his backside, startled and bloody-faced. Gudrun placed a foot on the other brawler's chest and shouted, "Be quiet, you roaring goblins! I have come back, and I will be heard!"

The clamor did not die at once. Awareness of Gudrun Blackhair's presence spread as men nudged other men, pointed, spoke, ran from knot of preoccupied gamblers to sextet of half-oblivious singers, and generally took joy in bringing word to the ignorant.

"Blackhair?"

"The lady—"

"She's back, by the Nails!"

Two other men were fighting atop a table. The bare-armed Frank gripped the short axe for which his tribe was named, the *francisca*, while his adversary swung and jabbed with a war-club. Catching sight of Gudrun, the latter stopped in astonishment. The Frank promptly tried to split his skull.

Felimid seized an empty pewter flagon and threw it straight and hard. The flagon's thick base met the shaven back of the Frank's head. Missing his stroke, he dropped limply on the edge of the table and tumbled to the floor.

The youth he'd been fighting had altered his expression in the meantime, though not for any such trifle as almost having been brained. Utter amazement, once he believed what he saw, changed to utter delight. He was perhaps seventeen, and thought Gudrun Blackhair the next thing to a goddess.

Felimid knew him. None the less, he'd have rendered him senseless instead of the Frank, had that been called for. They could renew their quarrel another time, if they even remembered its cause.

By ones and twos and groups, the pirates heard the spreading news and turned to stare. The noise died. Gudrun surveyed them, gathering their gazes to herself. She took her foot from the prone man's chest and allowed him to rise. Without a word, her unbuckled sword-belt looped about her forearm, scabbard in hand, she walked to her chair, behind which hung the splendid trophy pelts.

She did not immediately sit. Jumping to the high table, she spoke an instant before their fascinated attention would have been lost.

"You keep a miserable watch," she began. "Wherever Heimdall learned his trade, I can see it was not here! Listen, you sea-robbers! Had I been a foe, and had I chosen to bring fifty men with me instead of one," (Felimid, lounging against her tall chair in the background and missing little, smiled confidently) "you would none of you have seen morning. I could have burned you in this hall. Hugibert? Stand forth. Are you shy?"

The bard's smile widened. She was handling the situation well, and should have, considering that she had led men like these successfully for five years. Hugibert was the man she had left in command on Sarnia when she set out on her northern voyage, a big, tow-headed Frank whom the bard vaguely remembered. In waiting to be named he had lost a certain initiative; he should have greeted his leader at once, whether she was welcome to him or not. In fact, especially if she was not.

He came forward, walking too carefully. Yes, that explained it—if it needed any explanation other than dullness. He was drunken and had not marked their entrance. By Cairbre the god-harper, the man who had roused him and set him moving, his drinking companion, was none other than Pascent, the former merchant skipper! Interesting.

Hugibert blinked, swaying. His eyes focused poorly, and a patch of his hair gleamed sticky with mead. No doubt he had lowered it to the table and placed it unknowingly in a pool of the stuff.

"Lady—" he said foolishly.

"And you are the man who should have placed guards! Hugibert, you know how I took this island from the wreckers, by coming up the cliff path just as I did tonight, and there was not a wrecker alive when I had finished. What I did, another could do, and you are a fool. If you had no care for yourself, you might have had some for your comrades. The gossip I hear is that you lost some men needlessly this summer, also. What is the truth of that?"

"It was Urbicus," the Frank answered hoarsely. "That damned wrecker lord!" He swayed again, mightily drunk. The contrast between him and Gudrun Blackhair, bright-edged as a new sword and magnificently clad, was not lost on any man there. From her intricately stitched purple boots to the short Slavic vest embroidered with swans and trees, she displayed proof of a successful voyage. Her bracelets

and the gold chains looped across her chest announced it
even more clearly.

"Urbicus, was it?" Gudrun said. "We will settle with him
before winter draws in. You look like the men who can do
it, and I've brought three times fifty with me who are also
outstanding fighters." At mention of that considerable number, some men who had been disposed to be bumptious
grew thoughtful. As they realized that Gudrun had not said
precisely where these men were at the moment, they grew
more thoughtful still.

"As for what else I have brought, I can show you gold
from Bornholm, the plunder of a Wendish temple, a ransom
from Edric the Fat for his brother-in-law—yes, I captured
Vithils himself!—and the ship *Ormungandr* wholly refitted,
among other trifles," she went on. "You may see it in the
morning; the weather is too foul for carrying it here tonight."

She paused while they digested this, and the bard walked
forward, to lean on the table whereon Gudrun stood. He'd
remained in the background long enough, he felt. He too
had worn his best finery under the sealskin jacket now
discarded, and for the same reason as Gudrun: to advertise
the success of that summer's voyage and the desirability of
having such a leader.

"It's all true, so," he confirmed to the smoky hall, his
eyes stinging. "The lady has not said the half she might;
there is the little matter of her saving the Dane-king Helgi
from death, and winning his friendship, and gambling with
a dwarf for her heart, and fighting a water-godling in enchanted caverns. I'll also be telling you later, perhaps, of
the pike larger than a whale and the worst and greatest of
all sorcerers on the ridge of the earth, that she met and
undid. Let's drink to her fame!"

The Saxon youth on whose behalf Felimid had hurled
the flagon so accurately was first to cheer. Many joined
him—but many who were seeing Gudrun for the first time
were silent, some indecisive, some skeptical.

"Yes, drink to my fame," Gudrun echoed. "Then drink
to this man! I had not come back from the Baltic alive, but
for him. Let you all know too that I am his love and he
mine. If you do not remember Bragi the singer, you will

know him in future! Last of all, let us drink to Urbicus the wrecker and the death he will soon have as our gift!"

The applause was uncertain; too much had been flung at them, too quickly. Only those to whom Gudrun Blackhair was a demigoddess able to do no wrong (and these were not few; perhaps one man in three) roared their utter acceptance. Others looked askance. Gudrun's avowal of love was startling; the thought of the three times fifty men she had brought south was disconcerting; the loot she described was tempting. Then, of course, there were the new pirates who had not known her before.

The inevitable dissenting loudmouth who assumed the role of spokesman for all appeared. Treading out from the crowd, heavy, big-bellied, pockmarked, with a nose like a strawberry, he wore his hair drawn up in a horsetail tress atop his head and spoke with a forest accent so thick that he could barely be understood.

"Gudrun Blackhair, are you? You come slutting here and tell us drink to this and that! Earned your fine clothes on your back, no doubt! I always thought you made your name too easily, hag. I'm sure of it now."

"I could hang you," Gudrun said fiercely, "but I will give you your own choice of ways to die. Sword? Spear? Knife? I cannot believe something as ugly as you is married, but if your wife is blind, I will see she is not misused once I have widowed her."

The challenger roared with mirth. Poor fool. Gudrun sprang from the table and drove a knee between his thighs. Felimid flinched, as did more than one other man who witnessed it. However, the assault was meant to anger, not to disable. Gudrun might have wasted an hour goading the oaf to take her seriously by other means, and she was not so patient. Gudrun Blackhair's way was to deal swiftly, always.

"Get up and fight me," she commanded. "How will you do it?"

The strawberry-nosed man hardly heard through his pain. Hunched forward, the cords under his chin pulled tight, he croaked, "By God's eyes! I'll beat you ragged for that, you hell-sow."

"Beat me? You? Nothing so mild. You are in a death-fight, fellow, kill or die. That is how I answer words like yours! Name your weapon, or by Ull's bow I will take off your head now!"

Her sword shone bare as she spoke.

The Frank was too furious to be amazed, or to jib at fighting a woman. Still bent over, he said through a clenched jaw, "Hand-axes and shields."

"Och!" Felimid said involuntarily. Despite his vocal scorn of Gudrun, the man had plainly heard enough of her not to make it a sword quarrel. With a spear she would also have a certain reach, but the short-hafted Frankish axe meant close quarters unless she decided to risk all on throwing it. Gudrun was tall, wide-shouldered and strong-armed for her sex, and even stronger than she looked. None the less, the man carried considerably more weight of solid brawn than she.

Gudrun did not hesitate. Her sword, Kissing Viper, slid back into the sheath, and she gave it to the nearest man. Standing unarmed, she held out her hands for the weapons named, as if it was unthinkable that they should not be given at once, upon her gesture. They were.

"When you are ready, pig-eyes," she said.

The man slowly straightened, as the agonized sickness of a blow to the genitals passed. Seldom had he found himself facing a death-fight so suddenly and unceremoniously; indeed never. Yet he did not mind. The insult of that sudden nauseating blow called for a death.

Felimid felt a wild, swelling pride in his woman. This was right, however crude; it felt right. She might have ordered the man hanged, or scourged out, and perhaps she would have been obeyed—but then the new men, who did not know her, would have doubted her ability to answer her own insults, maintain her own name. And she would have had to go to greater lengths to prove it. These were men without place or lawful lord. They followed only the strongest.

Axe crashed on shield. The burly Frank hooked his weapon over the rim of Gudrun's shield and heaved to drag her off balance. At the same time, he smote at her neck with his own shield's edge.

She was not there. She made no attempt to resist his heave, the greater weight and brute strength he could summon. She spun away, ducking below the shield as she went, and instantly rushed back at him, venting the ear-splitting scream of an angry hawk.

She rammed her shield at the Frank. For an instant both shields locked together, grating. Her adversary cut at her neck, the same target twice in a row. Gudrun was quicker. Bending one knee and straightening the other, she thrust herself swiftly aside. His axe kissed her flying hair.

She struck back, and broke his hip.

He toppled sideways, his shield pulling free. The fat-enclosed eyes Gudrun had mocked flew wide as he saw his fate. Then she killed him.

Few things could have been more quickly done. It had started, and now it was finished. The bard let forth a sigh. Although she no longer worshipped Odin with blood sacrifices, she was Gudrun Blackhair still. She could axe a man without knowing his name. Having finally made up his mind to accept it, he did not shy from the disconcerting truth—but it did not delight him, either.

"I lead," she said, raising the short axe. "Does anyone else dispute it?"

"Blackhair!" the men who were hers to any extremity responded. When they boomed it the second time, many more of those in the hall joined in, and the last shout of "Blackhair!" was raised by all present, save one. The exception was Pascent.

Gudrun gave back the *francisca* and shield. Abalaric, her sightless cupbearer, waited by her seat with her favorite winter drink of hot spiced wine. She took it thankfully, and drank part of it down.

"Ahh!" she sighed. "From Odherir* itself." She looked curiously at the blind Goth. "You could not have made this since I entered the hall, Abalaric, could you? There has not been time."

"I've made it every chill night for a month, lady," he answered, "in case you should appear. Some did not like it . . . but there were those who backed me."

The cauldron containing the mead of the gods.

"True heart," Gudrun said. His blindness was the work of a Frankish duke who had once captured him, and Gudrun had avenged that blinding. "I want their names later. Those who supported you, I mean. Those who opposed do not matter." She turned to the bard. "Let's do some merry drinking, Bragi, and maybe have a song. This is my isle, and everything here is yours, from myself to the wealth of the mines. You were here only once before, and there is much to see."

"Swarms of bees, seagulls, soft music of the world, a gentle humming; wild geese, barnacle geese, shortly before Samhain, music of the dark torrent; apple trees of great bounty, the red, ramparted cliffs. And innumerable weapons shining," Felimid added, a sardonic extempore period to the idyllic phrases that had gone before. "Yes! Let's be drinking for there is only one good Roman god, and his name is Bacchus!"

He shared Gudrun's hot spiced wine and went on to the thick mead, thinking from time to time of Decius and the rest, camped until morning on the lesser isle of Brechou in the chilly fog. The plight of them moved him so greatly that he drank to their endurance, and lamented their disinclination to mount cliff paths on such a night. Then he had to drink again, lest contemplating such dreadful things should make him sad. If the drinking had failed to repel sadness (it didn't) there was music, and singing, and exchanging news, and seeing who could tell the wildest lies concerning the summer's action. Felimid used all these methods by turns, against the slight chance that the insidious Celtic sorrow might possess him after all. Thus any squalor he might have found in the hall dissolved in a strong, warm fog of mead, honey-colored across his vision, much more agreeable than the fog outside. All in all, he and Gudrun did not seek her bed until a few hours after midnight.

Neither went with a gait entirely steady; still, they had each other for support.

II

"Question me; I am a poet and tale-teller."
—The Second Battle of Mag Tuireadh

The flamboyantly rich chamber had been aired and warmed, and women had made the bed afresh, while Gudrun caroused. They had worked quickly, aware that if she entered it and found it unfit to inhabit, someone would smart.

Felimid glanced about him. The room was sizable, for his lover did not like to feel confined. Tapestries hung on the walls and juniper boughs had been spread on the floor, some of them crushed flat by a couple of large chests standing just where they had been haphazardly placed. A rack of bows stood against one wall, a fletcher's bench and stool nearby. A metal bowl filled with glowing charcoal hung by chains from a tripod. A neat soldierly pallet of furs and linen had been made up on the floor.

"I generally sleep there," Gudrun said, stumbling a little. "The shut-bed, yonder, I do not use . . . except on the coldest winter nights. It cramps me."

Her spirit more than her flesh, Felimid guessed, and made for the pallet. Down from his shoulder came his harp in her worn leather case, to be laid safely on the lid of a chest. From around his gracile waist came the belt which upheld the sword Kincaid, and he leaned that weapon against the same chest, where Gudrun's slightly wider blade soon accompanied it. Chuckling softly and a little foolishly, Gudrun unlaced his tunic, fingers straying across his chest. Their breaths mingled in a winy haze as he kissed her. Her mouth tasted hot with costly spices.

15

Suddenly she tripped and tumbled across the pallet. Felimid swayed for lack of balance, caught his footing again, and regretted his now empty arms. Well, there was a ready cure.

But Gudrun was tugging at her boots, the splendid, enchanted boots she had won in the *vodyanek*'s underwater palace, and cursing them roundly.

"Miswrought Wendish beetle-crushers! Troll-clogs! Oh, Bragi, drag them off for me!"

She leaned back on her elbows, black hair stranded across her wine-flushed face. He removed them, and then Gudrun finished drawing off his tunic, and before long they lay naked together with the bedding drawn snugly around them, their bodies warming it.

"Ah!" Gudrun cried. "Your hands are like ice! What were you doing, the while I risked my vitals in that death-fight, Bragi? Fondling a frost giant's daughter?"

"And why would I be about any such thing as that? *Your* flesh is warm." Felimid rubbed his palms hard on his thighs, then slid them over Gudrun's sleek ribs—sleek because she was well fed on what her sword had won her, and for no other reason. "Is that better, now?"

"Mm, somewhat." She clasped herself close to him, sharing warmth. "Bragi, I'd as soon not love just now."

"Then we'll wait. Are you sleepy?"

She shook her head. The thick hair of her brushed his skin. "Not as yet. A little weary." She had captained a ship through untrustworthy waters all day. Then she had climbed a steep cliff path for hundreds of feet in murk, sharp wind and rain. Lastly she had killed a man in single combat and held wassail for hours. "It's good to be with you thus. There has not been enough of it."

"Not enough," he agreed. The warmth in the bedding grew. "But there will be. A winter's worth of it, Gudrun."

"Aye, winter. I hate it. The death of the world. No faring on the sea."

"Because of storms," he said knowledgeably, having always assumed as much when he thought about it, which was seldom.

"Storms!" Gudrun said. "Why, I have fared out in summer gales laughing, and my men had no more care, and we have ridden where we would in the storm's despite. It is not wind, thunder or lightning that makes us stay in harbor, Bragi, nor cold either. It is the blinder, the giant who walks without feet and puts out the sun—fog! I will chance a storm gladly before I run a fog bank, especially in these waters. Although I have heard the *Ormungandr*'s eyes can see even through fog," she added thoughtfully.

Felimid hoped she would not experiment. He changed the subject.

"Well, this the winter will do, it will give me time to work your saga into the most finished shape it can have while you live, and make a few ballads also. Your wager with the dwarf king, that business with the water-godling and the nine ghosts, your sacking of Svantovit's temple . . . there's matter for three, without looking further. Indeed, it's not dearth of material is the trouble," he mused, "but if I sing them as they happened, none will believe me beyond this isle."

"I have heard wilder things told, and seen them believed."

"As have I, Gudrun, and sure I know what story-tellers and poets are. I should. Why, it's the custom of my people to end any tale which has been long repeated with the words: 'Now that is the story as it was told to me, and if there's a word of a lie in it, be it so! It was not I who invented it.'

"When I hear that Cuchulain sprang over three ramparts in one hero's leap," he went on, smiling with skeptical delight in the darkness, "and fought three bands of nine men, slaying eight of each nine himself alone, and then leaped out of the fortress again, and him carrying Emer his betrothed, her foster sister, and a great weight of treasure too—then it's my belief that *someone* has lied.

"Even if I kept to the unadorned truth where your deeds are concerned—and it's much to ask!—folk will always change the story they hear for one that suits them better. Always. What would Sigifrid Fafnir's bane be now if the singers had not remade him? A fool who lost a kingdom to the Huns because he couldn't keep his hands from an ally's wife!

"You they'll remake in other ways. Poets will sing of you to Saxon, Frank and Dane, wishing to anger none. And your great disadvantage is that the singers and hearers will be men. It's likely they will forget how you rescued King Helgi from the Wends, but remember your shame at a jarl's hands. They may remove that jarl from the story and replace him with Helgi. They may make you Sigifrid's lover, or mother, or invent some long, doleful captivity for you to suffer among the Huns, or change you into some northern Aoife . . ."

"Stop!" Gudrun said, her head spinning with more than wine. "Why, that oaf Sigifrid was dead a lifetime before my mother bore me! And who's Aoife?"

"A hellion who cursed her children into the shape of swans, and herself became a demon. Although another of the same name was a great warrior queen. She met Cuchulain in single combat once, and broke his spear and sword, but he gave her defeat by a trick he had planned beforehand."

"I'll believe that!" Gudrun laughed. "He must have known he could not beat her fairly, then?"

"Perhaps." Felimid kissed her mouth. "Haven't you prevailed by trickery a time or two, yourself: I have. Whatever, it is the second Aoife you call to my mind, but it is the first whose nature the bards to come are apt to be giving you. Or belike they will make you a goddess, a demon, a giantess or some other thing uncanny."

"Because I am a woman," she said bleakly, "and they will not believe a natural woman could do what I have done."

"Among your northern tribes, that's just how it would be, I'm thinking. Now in my land it would be different."

"Different, how?"

"Why, fighting women are accepted in Erin. Cuchulain was mighty with the mighty, but he needed craft to prevail against Aoife, and it was another fighting woman, Scathach of the Shadows, who taught him his battle-skill; *all the arts of war and all the feats of a champion,* the story declares. And it's not in stories only that they are found. My own foster-mother Lacth was a renowned fighter in her youth, and taught me to handle weapons. My father once met a woman in Cumbria who rode to war with the horsemen. Also, it's the law that a woman who holds land in her own right must give battle service accordingly, in Erin. And high among our goddesses stand the Great War Queens, Morrigu, Macha and Badb Catha."

"I remember you spoke of them once before. Crow goddesses, are they not?"

"Badb Catha is, and all three are shape-changers. Sometimes they and their attendant spirits—an ill crew!—are known as the *badb* all together."

"That is good, then." Gudrun tried to snuggle even closer to him. It was scarcely possible. "I no longer serve Odin of the ravens, so I must either take the wings off my helmet and cease to show my raven sail ... or turn to your war-goddesses. This Erin of yours sounds a good land for a fighting woman to live in."

"It's the best of lands," Felimid said simply. "I left to avert a feud, and I might have gone back two years since. I can't regret the paths that took me further away, since they led me to you, but someday I will return. Some not too distant day."

"I might even go with you," Gudrun said. "Someday. But first there are other worlds I would see. What do you know of those, Bragi? It's said in the north that there are nine, joined by the limbs and roots of a great tree."

"Well, there are more worlds than nine, many more. Some are perfect, it's said. *Weeping and treachery are unknown in the pleasant familiar land; there is no fierce harsh sound there, but sweet music falling upon the ear.* There are also the lands of death, and a world of goblins, and another of elves ..."

"Alfheim," Gudrun murmured.

"... and the Land Under the Waves, the Land of Youth, and more without names that any man knows. It's as if they had unseen walls between them, and in those walls, magic gates that are sometimes open, sometimes shut. At Samhain they all stand open, even the gates between life and death, and on that night the dead often come home to greet their kin and old loves. But they must depart before dawn."

"And these gates? Where may they be found, how known?

It matters, Bragi! This is why I desired so strongly to have *Ormungandr* refitted in the Land of the Dwarves! That ship can sail between the worlds with a full crew if I but know where to make the passage, and when!"

"Surely," Felimid said, without great enthusiasm, "but which world? I have no notion of how to find my way among them. I can't tell you which gates lead where. I take it you'd not care to find yourself riding the black water off the shore of Hel."

"The goddess's daughter, the mare who came to your aid when Koschei held you in bondage? (Long may he rot!) She knows such things."

"True for you. Myfanwy knows, none better. I had the right to call her ... once. She owed me a debt and had promised to come when I needed her, but now that debt is discharged and I've no more claim on her. I cannot summon her as I would a serving-woman!"

"For this purpose, you do not wish to," Gudrun said. "Do you?"

"Why, not overwhelmingly." Felimid liked the thought of a long, lazy winter by crackling fires, with plenty to eat and drink, no seafaring, little chance of an attack by foes, and Gudrun beside him. The summer had been eventful enough.

He wasn't apprehensive. Worry served no purpose, and he didn't think that even Gudrun could find an otherworldly Gate and take her ship through it in twenty nights. If he hadn't miscounted, it was no longer until Samhain.

"Sluggard!" Gudrun accused, though not sounding deeply irked. The bard wondered if that was good or bad, and what fiery dreamer's scheme she was forming. "One summer of brisk roving and you are minded to rest! This Cuchulain of yours would tear the sod in disgust!"

"Very likely. But then Cuchulain's one ambition was to die before his first hair turned gray. It's not mine, my love. And there's this to be said. The unseen walls dividing the worlds grow thicker now with each generation that passes, and more Gates close forever, to vanish from our knowledge entirely. Most of all it seems to happen where the Cross-worshippers gain ground, so Britain and Gaul hold less

promise for you than Erin. The Cross is rooted only lightly
in that soil as yet, and most of Erin's Gates remain."

"Oh, let be," Gudrun said. "You are too eager to have
me go to your land, Bragi. You speechify, you grow earnest.
I've said that maybe I will... but for now my plans are
other."

She yawned, stretching luxuriously against him. Then
she relaxed, and was asleep in moments.

It was so sudden that the bard felt deflated. It was doubtless useful to a pirate to be able to sleep and spring from
sleep at short notice, but he had begun to think she might
change her mind about not coupling that night; indeed, he'd
been about to suggest it.

Ah, well. The day had been long for him too. Perhaps
it was better to sleep first and love afterwards.

As for Gudrun's plan to sail to the otherworlds, there
were dangers in that which few would risk save in utter
ignorance. Which seemed to be just his lover's state. There
were places of fantastic beauty beyond the ridge of the earth,
yet there was also the danger of not being able to return,
or of finding that a hundred or a thousand years had passed.
Well, they should see. Yes, they should see.

III

Morning had come, and rays of honey-colored light slanted
into the chamber. Flinging the covers aside, Gudrun went
to open the shutters, letting in gusts of wind with a broad
spill of radiance. She never flinched from the raw air that
burst around her nakedness, but only cried "Hoo!" as she
hooked back the shutters.

Felimid gazed at her with delight. Smoothly, powerfully
muscled she was, as tall as himself or maybe a quarter-inch
taller, with shoulders as wide as her quintessentially female
hips and a limber waist indented between. Her black hair
blew. For a moment she stretched, braving the sting of the
autumn wind and even seeming to enjoy it. Then she came
back to the pallet, to roll in next to him.

Felimid threw the furs and linen over her, passing his
arm around her in the same gesture. Then he sought her
mouth to kiss. He felt such hungry, urgent desire it was as
though he had not kissed a woman in his two-and-twenty
years. Nor had he, ever, with passion this strong and spe-
cific, with his pulses singing *this one, this one, this one
only,* as they did now. And Gudrun returned his passion,
fully and gladly returned it.

"It's better each time," she murmured. "Better."

"And for me, too," Felimid said. "Aye, the skills and

power of a poet can be learned by one, and the pirate trade
by one, but love is a thing must be discovered by two—
and that I didn't know before."

"Do not gull me too far. You must have had a hundred
women, if the way you gathered them on Mors is any measure."

"Hardly so many," Felimid said, kissing her eyelids, "and
light encounters, all. For none of those girls would I go on
such a voyage as we made!"

This was what Gudrun wished to hear. They kissed,
embraced, licked, bit and played for some time, gentle and
rowdy by turns as the mood seized them, and at last coupled
again, so energetically that all the bedding was shaken aside.

It *was* better each time. Years before, Gudrun had been
ravaged by a jarl and most of his men, treated like a common
spear-captive until she was half-dead before she had escaped. She had not lain with another man until now.

Yet she would not ask to be humored because of that. If
dread still haunted her, she met it as she met everything,
bursting fiercely into it and through it, kicking the past
behind her as she raced into her tomorrows. Mating with
her was violently intense; it left them both sprawled on the
wrecked pallet and the juniper-strewn floor, panting, gasping and quivering.

"I must rise," Gudrun said at last. The autumn light
slanting through the room showed that the morning was far
advanced. "Decius and the others ... will be restless on
Brechou. If I am not present to tell them all is well, they
will demand to be shown and my stay-at-homes will take
it ill. They may carve and slice each other like hams."

She called for water and cloths. She walked unsteadily,
Felimid noted, grinning; but when he placed his own feet
on the floor and ambled around the chamber, taking an apple
from a copper bowl, his knees were also inclined to wobble.

Soon enough they were both groomed and clad. Felimid
looked from the window as he finished his apple. The chamber was at the top of a square wooden tower rising at one
end of the hall, to command the southeastern view. Felimid
saw grass, furze, a few bare trees and some structures he
did not recognize.

"Gudrun, what are those yonder?"

"Mines," she answered, glancing out. "I found them here when I took the isle. The wreckers never troubled to work them and I would not have troubled either, but Decius brought some miners across to delve the earth and pay me a seventh part."

"Ah. What is it they dig?"

"Silver and amethyst. This isle abounds in it. See, here is a piece."

She touched a three-foot wooden stand with closely spaced prongs at the top. A head-sized lump of silver ore rested upon them, with masses of rich purple crystal appearing to grow through it and out of it.

"I've more of it that doesn't much please me to wear," Gudrun said carelessly. "I like garnet better."

None the less, she clasped on bracelets and a collar wrought of the silver and amethyst she dispraised, for they went well with her boots, blue silk breeches and Slavic vest. For lack of other garments, the bard had also put on his clothes of the night before; the diamond-patterned shirt, light green breeches, moss green tunic and buskins of soft horse-leather, all made by the same dwarves who had refitted Gudrun's ship.

Lastly he buckled on his sword for swagger and respect, and settled the harp of Cairbre on his back because he went nowhere unless she accompanied him. Thus resplendent, they went to the hall. It was the way all feasting halls are the night after a huge carouse.

"None here will talk other than in grunts for a while," Felimid said, surveying the squalor.

"It seems not. Come, let us go to the Hatchet's Edge. If it is not guarded I will have strips of someone's hide. Decius should soon be crossing it."

The Hatchet's Edge was barely half a mile distant. Someone had given the name to the narrow isthmus between the southern part of Sarnia and the larger, northern part. Cliffs dropped forbiddingly on both sides of it, and although a hundred paces long, it was barely two wide at the top.

Twelve bareheaded, bleary-looking men guarded it with shields and spears. Looking to the green plateau beyond the isthmus, Felimid saw a second, larger band appear. Decius led it, a compact figure conveying an impression of purpose.

"I might have known you'd reach the southern bay, even in that little boat," he greeted his leader. "How were you welcomed?"

"Not ill, except by one." Gudrun laughed. "We will not have to feed him through the winter! Now, Decius, we must go softly. The foodstocks on Sarnia will last us the winter, but we have not enough for Njal and Hromund's crews. If I suffer them in the hall and they learn that, we may have trouble, and most of my fellows are still sotted drunk. Rouse enough to serve me for a ship's crew. Make sure Hugibert and Pascent are among them, and halfway sober. We will confer on Brechou, and you . . . make what you can of yon refuse."

"Can I work miracles?"

"I who know you am aware that you can."

The Spaniard's agate eye flashed in the sun. "I will douse them with ice water, since you have such faith in me. There are now two monks on Brechou, by the way, lady. They came by in a boat seeking you. They say they bear a message from Cynric the atheling."

"What, Cerdic's son? The man whose British wife we all remember?"

"None other."

"You have a long head, Decius. Does this strike you as strange? I can think of messages Cynric might wish to send me, but scarcely through a monk!"

"It puzzled me, too. I have thought, and it still puzzles me. Will you see them?"

"Yes," Gudrun said, deciding swiftly as usual, "and before I take counsel with the captains. The message may be something we should take into account."

"The Second Coming, maybe," Decius said.

Half an hour later they stood on the isle called Brechou, hearing the waves surge in the curious caves beneath it. Felimid had not pictured the monks in any particular way before he saw them. They were Celtic monks, of course; he knew no other kind. Since each monastery tended to make and follow its own rules after the example of its founder, they varied greatly. Some were ascetic to a mad degree; in others, the monks might marry and live with their

wives and children. They might be gentle or furious, learned
or simple, of mean or royal birth.

These monks carried themselves like well-born men. The
first had a square young face with eyes angling downward
from inner to outer corners, giving him a mournful but
shrewd and skeptical look which might not be at all con-
gruent with his nature. His companion was long-legged,
with mouse-colored hair and—to judge by his stance and
shifting gaze—had expectations of being eaten alive. Both
had their heads shaven forward of an imaginary line across
the tops of their heads, from ear to ear, with their hair
growing long at the back.

Of high degree or not, they stared at the pirate woman
for a moment. Many men did that. The second monk even
blushed as he recovered.

"Be welcome in the name of the brave chieftain who sent
you," Felimid said, in the Cymraeg tongue. He assumed
these men were British. "You stand before Gudrun Blackhair, the lady of Sarnia, whose fame runs from Spain to
Jutland. I'm Bragi, her spokesman. Sit and drink, if you
will."

"My gratitude to you and God for the offer," replied the
first monk. "I am Yrieith son of Durthach, and this my
companion has taken the name of Samson with the monk's
vows. And neither of us may sit or eat or drink until we
have discharged the errand on which we have been sent."

"It sounds weighty," Felimid agreed.

"Weighty enough!" the monk called Samson answered
with awkward rage. "Cynric holds our master hostage for
our obedience, a man of more holiness and learning than
Cynric's heathen soul is equal to encompass—"

"Softly!" Felimid said. "Softly. Before your tongue leads
you further astray, I must be telling you that I am heathen,
as you so sweetly put it, and the lady in addition. Maybe
your brother Yrieith should do the talking."

"I shall, with your leave," Yrieith said. "Yes. The nut-
meat of it all is that the atheling wishes to parley with your
lady, and his ship rides now in the Bay of Black and White
Sheep, on the mainland east of Angia."*

*Jersey.

"And what's the matter, and the cause, and the occasion? The lady does not run even to the bidding of kings' sons. Have you a notion what it is he's wanting?"

"It's not unknown, though it would be unsafe to speak of it freely in Cynric's presence," Yrieith answered dryly. "His wife has vanished, and he seeks her. It's in his mind that your lady may know where she had gone."

"Vanished? The princess Vivayn?"Felimid was startled. "Indeed, now that is of interest. I begin to see. The lady once abducted Vivayn and held her to ransom. Cynric believes she may have done it again, and his heart is heaped up with furious anger. Have I the right of it?"

"Truly you have," Yrieith said. "If your lady would perform an act of charity, I ask her to meet the atheling. He may slay our master if we bring him a refusal."

"How long is it since the princess was seen by Cynric?"

"It's all of two months, and Cynric has made been seeking her surreptitiously for that time, but has made no open search for the sake of his pride. And he believes that if your lady had captured Vivayn the Perfidious again, he would soon have received news. But none has come to him."

When this was translated to Gudrun, she was astounded and then mirthful. "By Ull's bow!" she said. "Again? The young stag is careless with his doe! Well, I had nothing to do with it this time. I see no purpose in meeting him ... unless he wishes my help in finding her. But I think he would be too proud to ask it."

The monks assured her that Cynric was prepared to pay a rich ransom for Vivayn again, provided she could be found and brought back discreetly. The Dane shrugged, still not greatly interested.

"I have never been one for achieving things in secret," she said, "and I am not discreet, and I do not care kittiwake droppings whether Cynric can keep his wife or not. But I may take the trouble to find her if he pays a fat ransom. Bragi, how if I send you to negotiate the matter? Will you go? Not directly into Cynric's arms. I would not trust him so far. Have him meet you in the bay midway along Angia's southern coast."

"Indeed, I'll go," Felimid answered impulsively.

The details were soon settled; he would be at the bay

named in three days' time, in the afternoon. Gudrun would not be there herself, but would send her spokesman, a skald named Bragi with power to dicker and agree as if he were Gudrun herself.

Having got what they came for and eaten a hot meal, the monks were eager to depart. They were anxious lest Cynric should lose patience and begin whittling their holy, learned master. Felimid watched the sail of their skillfully handled boat dwindle.

If Vivayn had disappeared, and none knew how, Felimid was ready to wager she had left her husband on her own initiative; in a word, escaped. He had met her. Five years before, her father Natanleod had ruled a kingdom in southern Britain, but sea-wolves led by the half-Jutish adventurer Cerdic had defeated him in battle. Cerdic had killed Natanleod, made a drinking cup from his skull and married Vivayn to his son Cynric. Because of this her fellow Britons had named her Vivayn the Perfidious, which in Felimid's view was like blaming a hare for accepting the taloned clasp of a hawk. She had been fifteen when the Jutes swarmed ashore from their war-boats, and nobody had asked her consent.

However, she was not helpless. A sorceress with remarkable powers of casting glamour, she took lovers to her bed when it pleased her, assuming the appearance of her friend Eldrida to do so in safety. The bard remembered her as remote, dispassionate of mind, passionate of body, highly intelligent and tricky. Not that he deceived himself that he knew her well. Their meeting had been too brief.

Of one thing he felt sure. She was unlikely to be found if she did not wish to be found.

He promised himself that he would have Gudrun tell him the detailed story of Vivayn's abduction and ransom, some winter evening. For the present there were things of more moment. Gudrun dealt with one of them there on Brechou, without further delay.

"I have a raid in mind," she said. "One last raid in the fortnight of good weather we may have left to us. This is a rich man. His household is great, so he will have laid in winter foodstocks, and we will require more than we have.

"Besides, I owe this man vengeance. He is a wrecker, lower than an octopus, and as unclean. During the summer he destroyed a ship filled with my men; am I right, Hugibert?"

"Aye," Hugibert said, looking uncomfortable. He'd been thinking of those men as his men, not Gudrun's, until he lost them to the wrecker's craft and sorcery; and if they had not drowned he would have been more ready to challenge her on her return. As matters stood he lacked sufficient support. "We'd sacked a villa close to Ratuma. Sea demons broke their ship apart at the cape, and nearly did the same to mine."

Big Njal, whose hair had early gone gray to give him his nickname, looked sharply at the Frank. "Sea demons, you say? Do you mean nicors?"

"Not nicors, friend." Gudrun showed her excellent teeth in distaste. "Nicors are foul and troublesome, but only mindless beasts when all is said, and they cannot leave their fens and lagoons longer than minutes. These other beings live in the sea's black depths. They love to drag seamen down to their ooze. Still, they are cowardly and seldom attack even in numbers, the way nicors will. They wait for an advantage, like wreck or tempest. But they think, and they can work magic, and although they do not breathe air they can leave the sea for an hour or more even without their magic. With it . . . I do not know."

"Right!" Hugibert added. "Urbicus has made a nest of them his allies. The son of a mare's a sorcerer himself. They share the work of wrecking ships, I suppose. The demons get pleasure and the flesh of drowned men, while Urbicus gets their goods, gear and cargoes. He could never call demons to assist him if he weren't a sorcerer."

Pigsknuckle Hromund was the other Danish chieftain who had come south with Gudrun. He blew an outward breath like a horse. "Pwrrh! Well, I wanted a good raid . . . but this? Won't the demons sink our ships?"

"I think they would," Gudrun answered, and her smile was wicked. "Because of that, I am not for striking from the sea. We should attack from the landward side."

She had spoken loudly, so that all could hear, not the

chieftains only. These were free men. They had a right to
hear the plan hammered out and have a part in making it.
Afterwards, when the plan was made and due to be carried
out ... then, of course, the chieftains led their crews, for
good or bad, and were to be obeyed.

Pascent, a tawny-haired, dark-eyed scoundrel bred in
southern Gaul, with a violent temper and guile behind his
bluster, expressed qualified liking.

"I don't know yet if the plan will work, but that much
sounds good. By God, yes! I used to be a trader. There are
a dozen or twenty wrecker lords on these coasts, and this
Urbicus is the greatest. The greatest and worst, a devil's
bastard! I'd love to have a part in the destroying of him."

"The loot would be rich," Hugibert allowed, "but the
men might fear Urbicus, lady."

"The men are there. Ask them!"

"Unless he's mighty beyond credence, we can defeat
him," Felimid said. "There were nine wizards against us at
Rugen, and three hundred picked fighting men, and Gudrun
prevailed with far less than the strength she has here at
Sarnia. So Urbicus himself, I would say, is little to be
troubled about.

"Yet I'd gladly be enlightened on one other matter. He's
a mainland lord and a subject of the Frankish king, I understand. Then won't the Frankish king and all his forces be
against us after Urbicus is destroyed?"

Njal and Pigsknuckle, the northerners, looked thoughtful
upon hearing that; but Gudrun, Pascent and even Hugibert,
a Frank himself, all showed amusement. Pascent guffawed
outright.

"Hugibert?" Gudrun said. "Will you answer Bragi?"

"I will well!" Hugibert said, grinning. "You may know
something of magic, Bragi, but you're ignorant of how
things are in Gaul. The counts and district vicars be rivals,
jealous each of the other. They were a bickering lot even
under one strong king like our mighty Hlodovech.* Now,
he's been dead a year. He left four sons. By Frankish law

*usually known by the Latin form of his name, Clovis.

they all succeeded to the kingdom, and rule it jointly—but there's no faith or trust between 'em. Each wants to be sole king of the Franks. Thus, along with their own quarrels, the counts must decide which king to support."

"If they did not scour us from Sarnia in the old king's time," Gudrun said with assurance, "they will never do so now."

Pascent nodded, though not with pleasure. He would have liked to see Gudrun's pirates washed ashore dead, with all their ships broken, so long as he wasn't among them. He hadn't joined Gudrun willingly, except in the sense that he might have chosen to drown instead. He hated all pirates with a bitter hatred. The bard knew this, and Pascent knew he knew.

However, pirates and merchant sailors were one in their cold contempt and loathing for wreckers. If Gudrun intended to make an end of some, Pascent was with her that far. Yet he hoped no less eagerly to see the day that she came to her own end.

"I'm for it," he declared.

Others were not. Many were afraid of the wrecker lord's magic. Ignorant, they thought that a man skilled in magic could simply do anything he wished.

"The sea 'ull swallow us!" someone said.

"There be ditches and walls around his castle on the landward side!" one Gaulish peasant shouted. "And scarps and ravines to pass before we'd arrive! How shall we master those even if Urbicus's magic fails him?"

"His magic is only strong upon the sea!" Gudrun answered. "For the rest, I have some of my own. Follow and I will show you how I deal with little obstacles!"

She walked down to the rocky shore of Brechou, where the waves broke and thundered. Spray flew past her. Between Brechou and Sarnia, making two channels, lay an islet about a furlong from end to end. The nearer channel sucked and surged and boomed. Sunlight slanted a little way into the chill, green-gold water.

"In a minute I will stand on that isle with dry feet and all my bones whole!" Gudrun boasted. A lock of her famous hair blew free in the wind, which pressed her breeches close as another skin to her legs. "The first dozen men to follow me shall have a triple share of the booty when we sack Urbicus's house. Now see!"

She stamped three times with her right foot.

At once a bridge of gray stone grew from the shore in front of her, arching across the water. In five heartbeats it linked Brechou to the islet. Gudrun threw up her sword exultantly, caught it by the hilt, and sped onto the bridge. Within a minute she stood where she had promised, and a dozen men with her.

When she returned, she stamped her left foot three times. The bridge dissolved upon the air like mist in the wind.

"Let me hear no more talk of scarps and ravines," she said.

IV

Though a man has fallen from his dignity, it does not lessen the honor-price of his wife, who retains the best she happens to have; so likewise, if the woman falls from her obedience, it does not subtract from the honor-price of her husband, who retains the best he happens to have.

—The Senchus Mor.

Pascent rubbed his chin and narrowed his eyes. The mellow autumn sunlight made his russet moustache look brassy. He was sailing in waters he'd always avoided as a trader, even though it had meant going many miles to seaward; the reefs, tides and ship-swallowing whirlpools of the region were deadly. He silently thanked God for the two men from Aleth he had aboard, with their comprehensive local knowledge.

"So this is Angia," Felimid said, looking innocently at the rocky headlands and bays. "A fair place, too. Gudrun's protection must be worth a few cattle to them."

"A fair place," Pascent mimicked, his ready choler rising. "Pah! The rocks around its shore are ship-gutters, and I hope they've made an end of Cynric. That would console me for being here."

The bard said mildly, "He's not such a bad fellow."

"Better than his damned father, maybe—a bare trifle better. But likely that's because he's still in Cerdic's shadow and hasn't had a chance to grow to his full wickedness yet. Why, he's younger than you."

"A babe, surely," Felimid agreed peacefully. He was

33

feeling as pleased with life as the captain felt disgruntled. Such lightheartedness was a little perverse, since he sailed to meet a man he had made a cuckold. It had happened half a year before, and to Felimid the memory was pleasant. To avoid Cynric as though abashed or afraid would have turned it dingy.

Cynric didn't know, of course—or so Felimid hoped.

"And you know him," Pascent went on accusingly.

"I've met him. I was looking for passage out of Britain and hoping to find it in Westri. An enemy of mine came along to demolish the hope within a couple of days, but I'd gone hunting with Cynric in the meantime. That may not be enough to make our speech amicable this day, considering why he has come here, but at least he should remember me."

Pascent laughed harshly. "Then if he cuts your throat with ours he'll do the thing knowing your name! That's mighty civil. I tell you, I'd rather cut his first. I would, but he probably has a Jutish war-boat with forty pirates in it. We'll have to outrun him."

"Captain, we are not here to cut throats or to run, and that is part of what makes this sail so pleasant, your grousing aside. Is there nothing at all you find good?"

"Aye. The weather, and the thought of making an end of this damned wrecker Urbicus. The b—the lady's right. He's lived too long."

"The weather," Felimid said with gentle determination, "is glorious. I could hardly founder a ship myself on such a day, supposing I were its master."

Pascent muttered something which sounded like, *"God prevent it!"* and which Felimid ignored. The afternoon held the lazy, fulfilled warmth of the last fine weather before winter comes, when harvest is done and butchering need not begin at once, when no work is urgent and it is allowable to lie abed until the sun has risen high. At just this time of year had Felimid been born.

With his bardic sight he saw many things the sea-wise but mundane Pascent did not. Sprites of the air drifted by, not troubling to take the distinct shapes they could assume when they wished. They flowed, tumbled and whirled. The sea appeared alive and seething to him in a way that it never had before. He felt its huge inchoate power through the ship's timbers, in the soles of his feet, his loins, his spine. It was not unlike the glory he felt when his body joined with Gudrun's, and without thinking or weighing the thought he knew the two were akin.

He happened then to look to starboard. Miles off, a moving cloud-shadow crossed the water, which looked pale tan and stippled. In another mood, Felimid would have let his landsman's gaze rove past it, looking but not troubling to see. Now he sharpened his sight to look in that way known to bards and Druids.

Where there had been nothing but oddly-hued water, he saw bays, gold- and brown-leaved woods, a flock of un- known birds, and a fountain like a tall silver tree springing from the highest point on the island. He saw other islands, and the roof of a great house, its shingles bright as birds' feathers, and below it a porch with crystal pillars, shining in the sun. In front of that house on the sea were two beautiful ships with sails and rigging unlike any others he had seen.

"Captain," Felimid said, pointing, "will you tell me what is yonder?"

Pascent looked, grunted and spat into the water to lee- ward. "Shoals," he said laconically.

Then Pascent thought no more of it; but Rhychdir, one of the men from Aleth who knew the local waters, had heard the question. "Lord, what did *you* see?" he asked, looking troubled.

Felimid did not tell him everything. "Why, I thought I saw houses rise out of the sea, and a ship gliding like a swan."

"Cloud-shadow," Pascent said with conviction, and thought, *helped by your crack-brained barbarian poet's fancy, my lad. You and your bitch will have us riding dra- gonflies to storm Heaven yet.*

Rhychdir looked almost frightened.

"There!" Pascent cried suddenly, pointing the other way, towards the decidedly real island of Angia so close to lar- board. They had come to their declared rendezvous, the largest bay on its southern coast, and there lay the Jutish war-boat Pascent had predicted, with thirty oars to the Sarnians' score, and forty men to their two dozen. A white shield of peace hung from the mast.

Pascent put more faith in his lesser ship's swiftness, lightness and nimbleness. She was a Pictish vessel, one of several such in Gudrun's fleet, ideal for scouting and sudden small raids. He turned her high bows for the Jutish war-boat and hailed it.

"Captain," Felimid said mildly, "it is for me to be speaking here." Then he called across the narrowing gap of water, "Greetings to you, Cynric, champion, holder of Vectis-isle, son of Cerdic, the renowned king of Westri! I come from Gudrun Blackhair and speak for her. Is the hunting still as fine in your father's kingdom?"

Cynric's eyes opened wide. His broad hands closed on the shield-rail. "By Odin, Felimid of Erin! How do you come to be speaking for that—"

"—lady of Sarnia whose fame compares with your own," the bard finished, his compliment holding a barb Cynric could scarcely, for his honor's sake, show that he recognized. Cynric had prowess and had led raiding expeditions, but he was barely twenty and still, as Pascent said, in his conquering father's shadow. Gudrun stood in nobody's. She was more famous in her own right than was Cynric, and the bard thought his neatly reversed reminder fair payment for whatever insult Cynric had been forestalled from uttering.

"May I be boarding you?"

Cynric stepped back from the rail with a broad gesture of welcome. Golden ornaments glittered on arms otherwise bare. "Aye, come, Felimid! There are many things I am eager to hear from you!"

"You fool," Pascent snarled, low-toned. "He'll take you captive, demanding the return of the wife we haven't to give him. Then he'll gut you and Blackhair will hang me—living by my stones, in all likelihood."

"I think not. Take me close alongside; I am not going to parley with Cynric bawling from bowshot distance. This I promise; if he does take me he will not keep me long. If it comes to that you may tell the lady I said so."

Felimid unbuckled his sword. In a boat with forty sea-wolves, Kincaid could not serve him. However, he settled the harp in her leather bag more firmly on his back. She had taken him into places, and safely out again, where an escort of fifty warriors would only have precipitated a battle. Until Gudrun Blackhair, she had been the only darling he loved intensely.

Cynric spoke an order, and several shields were taken from the Jutish rail. Felimid judged and timed his leap across the water almost flawlessly, landing in the shieldless gap, and Cynric caught him lest he spoil it by tumbling head-first among the thwarts.

"This requires some explaining," the atheling said. He sounded reasonable enough, although he did not smile. "You were bound on Tosti's track when last I saw you. I heard later that you met him again and he did not survive. Now you represent Gudrun Blackhair! How does that come to be?"

"Briefly, lord?"

"Briefly will do the first time, and you can be more lengthy later if I think it worth hearing." Cynric smiled in his short tawny beard, a young man of Felimid's height but broader of chest and thicker of limb, and good-natured in his way although a born predator. "Tell."

"I did slay Tosti, yes. He was too eager for my blood and the craving undid him. He was foolish; I had great luck. But then King Oisc felt bound to avenge his henchman. Agents of his tracked me to London. They learned I meant to leave Britain on a merchant ship called *Briny Kettle*, took word to Oisc, and what next I knew, he was chasing me down the Narrow Sea in his ship *Ormungandr*."

Cynric laughed, envisioning it. "The deck must have been covered with dung! Well, I know what happened next, since Blackhair possesses *Ormungandr* now, and she had Oisc's body sent home to Thanet. She appeared like a sudden squall, as she makes a practice of doing, won the battle and spared you—because you're a bard, I suppose. Is that right?"

"Entirely right, lord. Myself and two others were the last survivors of Oisc's attack. She spared us all."

"Then it could be said that Oisc's death was your fault. He was my grandsire, you know," Cynric added almost casually, watching the bard as he spoke.

"Yes, lord," Felimid agreed, doing his utmost to keep from the corner of his mouth the gentle sardonic quirk for which Cynric—if he saw it—might well kill him. "I know."

It was a dreadful professional disadvantage in a bard to take a mocking view of fabrications.

"Come aft," Cynric commanded, striding that way so that Felimid must either follow or stand talking to the air. Follow he did, although he declined to tread obediently at Cynric's heels. He allowed the other to go well ahead and stepped after at his apparent leisure, looking about the Jutish war-boat appraisingly and nodding a little, as though he found it well enough as second-rate vessels went. This was hardly a pose. After *Ormungandr,* nigh any other vessel was second-rate. Still, he watched the hard-muscled rowers without seeming to do so, lest one should decide to trip him for his demeanor. He remembered none of them from his brief time in Westri, but Cynric had been his father's guest on the British mainland then. This crew would be Cynric's own men from the isle of Vectis.

The atheling turned to face him in this greater privacy. His gaze had suddenly become a steady, devouring thing.

"You know why I am here," he said, "and unless you satisfy me, you may find it less easy to leave this ship than you did to board it."

"The princess Vivayn has vanished, I hear."

"You hear? You know!" Cynric growled. "Three years ago, Blackhair raided Vectis and carried off Vivayn. The ransom was a helmet, war-shirt and sword made by the dwarf Glinthi. She received them and sent back my wife. Yes, and she will pay for that affront one of these days! But if she was responsible once, why not a second time?"

"I follow your reasoning, lord. It's true that there can be very few who would dare. But this thing Gudrun Blackhair did not do. I've come from Sarnia, and the princess Vivayn is not there. Now perhaps I would not be above lying to you, had I a reason or did Gudrun wish it. However, if she had carried off your wife again, do you think she would be hiding it? It's not her way!"

"Also, she spent the entire summer in the north and has only now returned. If you haven't yet heard of her deeds there, by Cairbre's fingers, you will erelong! She has been too busy since May to come within miles of the princess Vivayn."

"You were with her?" Cynric demanded. The heat of his stare increased.

"From the Narrow Sea to the Baltic," Felimid said, waxing oratorical, "through raids, sea-fights, parleys, truces, feasts, bargainings, and sacrifices—" He paused, struck by a bitter memory. "—and all the long way back again. We were separated once, but that was deep within the Baltic, and for less than a month. She was traveling by land all that while, and her ship was elsewhere."

"The truth?" Despite his offensive words, Cynric looked more frustrated and baffled now than threatening.

Felimid removed his own look from the atheling's heavy, leonine stare. He answered, "You must make up your own mind, lord. I've said what happened—and if Gudrun Blackhair had done this thing, do you think she would conceal it?"

"No," Cynric sighed at last, on a large outward breath. "No. I believe you. Unless . . . might one of the captains she left behind have done it, by stealthy cunning, and plan to have all the ransom himself? The Frank Hugibert, for one?"

"I cannot say no," Felimid admitted. "If you will send me word should a demand for ransom come, I'll learn if Hugibert or another Sarnian is behind it. I who know Gudrun can say that she would deal harshly with a man who so cheated her. My advice to her in such a case would be to send home the princess as a courtesy."

"Take care!" Cynric gripped Felimid's arm, glaring at him. "I won't be gulled or humored. If that hellcat has not taken my wife, I need no help from Sarnia to get her back. And tell her from me—"

"Which her is this, lord?" Felimid made his voice convey polite inquiry. The bruising grip on his arm he appeared to ignore.

"Gudrun Blackhair, you bare-faced wordsmith! Tell her from me that I have not forgotten the debt she owes me. One day I will come to demand it." He released the bard's

arm. Reddened still, he added, "I've nothing against you
save your impudence. Therefore I'll warn you; do not be
with her then. A lark netted in company with crows is likely
to have his neck wrung with them."

This was sound advice, and well-intentioned even if,
from Cynric, a bit vainglorious. But it came too late.

"Now you had best leave my ship while you may."

Felimid did so, by means of a second leap across the
water. This time he was springing to a ship he knew, and
required no help as he landed, but steadied himself by grasping a line and letting his bent knees absorb the shock—a
faultless bit of acrobatics which pleased him greatly.

"He's somewhat angry," he said thoughtfully.

Pascent chuckled. "Is he now? I piss from a great height
upon his anger! Anything to keep us here longer?"

"No, I think not."

The captain gave a series of orders which were only half-
intelligible to the bard. His summer on the sea had not made
him a seaman. He turned his gaze southward again, to the
islands which Pascent had seen as shoals. Nothing had
changed. They were there, veiled by glamour which only
the bardic sight could pierce. Islands hidden but evidently
peopled.

The Children of Lir, he said to himself.

It was more than the name of a nine-parts-false sorrowful
tale. Lir was the sea. His children were the merfolk, as
Felimid's own ancient forebears were the Tuatha De Danann, children of the earth-mother Danu. Both peoples had
been glorious in beauty, highly skilled in magic; both had
lost their preeminence in the world to upstart tribes, and
magic was fading.

Rhychdir stood beside him. "What is it that you see
there?"

"Why, Pascent told me that nothing is there but shoals,
and should I disbelieve him? What is it you think may be
there?"

"Only shoals," Rhychdir admitted, "now. But once there
were islands with cattle and a fair town, until it sank beneath
the sea. It's said that sometimes that town can be seen yet,
and that the sight is a presage of wickedness."

"Well, then, set your mind at rest," Felimid said. "There is apt to be wickedness with or without the sight of phantom towns. If you are not ready to have your part in it, you should, maybe, go back to Aleth."

What lofty advice you give, he gibed inwardly, *now that you are firmly pledged to Gudrun. You never had one misgiving your own self, surely.*

"When I go back to Aleth, I'll be rich," Rhychdir said. "I left in the first place because I was poor."

"Good," Felimid answered vaguely.

Shall I tell Gudrun of this wonder? If there are otherworldly Gates on or under the sea, the Children of Lir will know. Those islands, that harbor and house, are no phantoms of a destroyed past. They are real now!

Suppose she finds her otherworldly Gate? If she passes through it, she may not return. Nor may I if I go with her.

Of a certainty, carved in marble, that's not what I desire. I wish her to go to Erin with me. She seems to be thinking of it . . .

No, he decided. *I will not tell her.*

V

*"Why didst thou strike my horse, by way of insult,
or by way of counsel to me?"*
————The Dream of Rhonabwy

The hall had been well cleaned. Slaves had cleared the
floor of the summer's covering, mingled with litter, and the
great doors stood wide so that the place might air. Meanwhile the pirates had moved to the larger, northern part of
the island, where rude barrack-buildings stood.

"I'm not for spending the winter in a place that stinks
like a grave-mound newly opened," Gudrun said bluntly.

Neither was Felimid. They were both well born, and
although Gudrun's housekeeping fell short of meticulous,
she having preferred to hunt and sail since she was small,
some of her early training had stayed in her marrow. Boat-
loads of rushes and sweet herbs were already being landed
to floor the hall afresh.

Gudrun had sent spies to the mainland to gather news
under the cloak of that harmless task. She had marked Urbicus the wrecker for destruction and intended to move soon.
Indeed, she would have to defer her wild justice till the
spring if she did not move very soon.

"You should have asked Cynric if he would care to join
us!" she laughed.

"He'd have said no. And taken my head off by way of
emphasis, I shouldn't wonder. The poor fellow's pride is
hurt."

"No!"

"Ochone, yes! I'm thinking he knows in his heart that
his wife has left him and has not been abducted. If he does

42

not, why, he believed me too easily when I told him that you knew nothing of the matter. He accepted my word and hardly blinked."

"You think she has left him? Of her own will?"

"She's a sorceress, or at any rate, a witch," Felimid answered. "She'd not be easy to capture against her will."

"I did it once," Gudrun said reminiscently. She laughed again. "I lifted her like a ewe while her lord was off raiding. I remember her well. Yes, and I remember her serving-woman, too. One of Cerdic's many bastards, and showed it by her spirit! She rushed my ship and got aboard while the men hung back! One of my warriors held her fast and prepared to cut her throat while she cursed us all.

"The next I knew, Vivayn had a knife and the point was pressed hard against her heart. 'If that girl dies,' she said to me, 'your boar-pig yonder will have cost you my ransom, for I'll split my heart like an apple while Cynric's men can see it! Come. If I am your captive, it fits my rank to have an attendant of my own.'

"I was interested to see what she would do. By Ull's great bow, my lover, I was so interested I nearly did refuse her! But I think she would have done it. I see her now, with that red hair almost to her feet, the broad sax in her hand and her knuckles spiking pale through the skin.

"I asked what she would have. She said, 'Your word. Eldrida lives if I live, is treated as I am treated, and goes home if I do.'

"I said, 'Done!' She dropped the sax. Then she sat down as though her own subjects were rowing her out for her pleasure. She looked aloof as a cloud. She could not have been seventeen then."

She suddenly heard herself lauding another woman to her lover, and what was worse, saw lively interest plain in his expressive face. Although she didn't know it, her own face was yet easier to read; her feelings could not have been more obvious had she kicked herself.

"A notable captive," Felimid said. "Well, the matter is one for her and Cynric to settle between them. Mmm . . . he promised, so, to return and settle his account with *you*, someday."

"He!" Gudrun cried. "He! He is a whelp with more pride than his deeds justify as yet. He—well, Tiumals?"

The man she addressed was one of her remaining Gothic fighters. Through splayed brown teeth he said, "Envoys have come from that muckworm Urbicus, lady. They crave peace and bring a gift."

"Peace?" Gudrun echoed. "Urbicus hopes for that too late. I will hear his messengers, though. Fetch them, Tiumals. I will see them before the hall, in the open."

"Aye, lady." Tiumals left.

"This is grist to my particular mill, if I am your spokesman," Felimid said.

"*If?*" Gudrun was startled and almost offended. "I make water on the word! Of course you are! I said it. You accepted the place that first time we lay together. There are no *ifs* in it."

"Then what is it you'd be saying to these envoys? Or have me say for you? They are here to handsel peace and you will not have it, therefore you cannot accept their master's friendship gift. Shall I reject it?"

"A sender of gifts is a suppliant. Bragi, I will not promise friendship or peace with that corpse-eating octopus! I am obliged to get justice for the men he drowned, and that means blood, not wergild. Also, I must get his winter foodstocks, and those he will no more yield than we can do without. I do not reject their overtures outright, but I promise nothing. By the time Urbicus knows what to make of that, we will be walking over his smoking threshold."

"Indeed. Well, I am curious to see what sort of envoys this fellow sends. If he's as treacherous as you have told me they will have double tongues."

The cold salt wind cried through the sky. Clouds tumbled, and a few small drops of rain struck. Waves boomed at the base of Sarnia's cliffs.

The envoys approached, and Gudrun turned to the bard in some umbrage. "Bragi! Do you see? Two of them only! Urbicus must wish to insult me."

"Or perhaps he guessed that you'd be for hanging them, and reckoned two men enough to lose. Hmm. That's a horse they bring with them."

It proved, specifically, to be a bay gelding of about thirteen hands. *More swift than enduring*, Gudrun thought, noting its light legs and slender body. Then she observed its trappings as it came nearer, and she frankly goggled.

She did not hear the short hissing breath Felimid drew.

The bay wore a large gold rose on its brow-band. Golden bells rang in every lock of its mane, the saddle-cloth was stiff with glittering bullion, and every buckle and spacer in its harness was gold. Uselessly but spectacularly, the bit and shoes were of gold, and when the bay gelding twitched its tail, dozens of golden bells announced their presence at that end. The accoutrements of Svantovit's sacred horse, which Gudrun had seen at a certain Baltic temple, had been rather shabby by comparison.

The two envoys might well have been brothers, finer figures of men than she would have associated with Urbicus. Both were tall and strongly made, with brown hair and shelving foreheads above deep-set eyes. They wore short tunics, breeches tied at the knee, and flapping mantles.

"Lady," said one of them in Latin, "we bring the greetings of the lord Urbicus, whom the powers protect. We bring his greetings and his entire respect, no less than your valor and prowess deserves."

"Indeed now," Felimid said, his voice flowing with honey and equally surrounded by bees, "that's mighty discerning of your master. As the lady's spokesman, I concur, and accord, and agree; and I think he may see her prowess with his own eyes, someday. Since he's so filled with respect for her, let him come to Sarnia and declare it himself. The lady and every man here is ready to receive him as his standing merits."

Gudrun glanced at him, wondering. His face was pale. He held his hands a little too deliberately away from his sword-belt. She had learned to read such signs.

The same envoy spoke. "Some of the lady's men were drowned by the shore of our master's estate, it is true. The lord Urbicus was not the cause. He wishes to meet the lady, Gudrun Blackhair, in peace and satisfy her of it, and as proof he sends a friendship gift; this horse and all it carries."

Gudrun spoke Latin only haltingly. However, she understood it well enough. To Felimid she said skeptically in her own Danish tongue, "I suppose ships have foundered or broken near Urbicus's home by chance, but not the one that concerns me. I have the account of the men in the ship which escaped. Demons and sorcery caused that wreck, Bragi!"

"Well can I believe it," he said, staring at the bay gelding.

"Yet it's a handsome horse," she went on, puzzled by his manner. "If you fancy it, you shall have it. Go, mount and try it. A blind woman could see that you yearn to. Nor am I much of a judge of horses."

"Not of this one, I would say."

The man holding the bridle scowled as Felimid came near. The gelding stamped and neighed. Felimid clucked softly, running a firm hand over the beast's neck and shoulder. A sheen of fine sweat appeared on his face, now almost white.

"Beautiful and swift as the wind, but no stayer, I judge," he declared in a normal voice. "If I ride him for a little, I can tell you more."

"This is a friendship gift from my master to the lady," the first envoy said sharply. "It is hers only."

"Gudrun Blackhair's friendship is not so easily had, and least of all by a wrecker," Gudrun answered. She did not understand fully what was happening. None the less, she meant to support her man until she found out. "Do what you think best, Bragi."

"Lady! This is—" The envoy controlled himself. "Well," he said with an affected shrug, "some of whom one would never think it are shy of horses. It's for you to leave it to another if you wish, lady."

"*Shy?*" Gudrun echoed. "Why, I will ride this nag around the island while you run at its tail!"

"No, Gudrun!" Felimid cried. "Draw your blade! *Look!*"

Kincaid was in his hand as he spoke; Kincaid, Ogma's sword, one of the ancient treasures, thirty inches of sleek blue steel with edges able to part a dangling thread of wool. Felimid sent the lean, nimble weapon hissing across the horse's throat. Then, spinning, he hocked it with another drawing slash in what looked like one continuous movement.

"The envoys!" he screamed. *"Beware, they are demons!"*

The bay gelding went down, struggling, gurgling blood—to Gudrun's sight. Yet she had learned to take seriously the things Felimid saw which others did not. She acted instantly. Her sword Kissing Viper came out as one of the envoys attacked her.

The other fled. Felimid ran after him . . . after it.

Its feet were mostly webbed taloned toe. Thus it flopped and lumbered a good deal. The glamour upon it had disguised even its gait; Felimid caught it with no trouble. It turned with the fury ascribed to trapped rats.

The bard was not there to be raked by its claws. Knees slightly bent, he circled the creature. Light shimmered along Kincaid's edge.

The creature sprang again, but never looked as if it would touch him. Its movements were too clumsy on land, and it presented little danger now that it was exposed. Tan in color, with curious blue patches, finned and scaled, it opened a squarish fanged muzzle in silent malignity and glared from golden eyes. Pink external gills lifted and spread beside its neck, layer upon ruffled layer. The effect was leonine.

It attempted once more to seize him with its webbed fingers. Felimid cut through its manelike gills and half its neck with one skillful stroke. It fell, flopping in pain. Setting his teeth, Felimid struck again and removed the head completely.

Its blood ran black and thin, smelling like vinegar.

"I needed two strokes as well," Gudrun said. "You told me these are demons. Are you sure of it?"

"I used the wrong word. The ignorant call them sea demons, never having met real demons. However, they were not men. How do you see them now?"

"As men, dead men. Bragi, I know you can see the truth behind illusion, I know that, yet—are you *sure?"*

"Study them in anything that reflects, Gudrun. It will show them as they are. These are not men, or any children of earth-mother Danu, I swear."

Frowning, Gudrun cleaned her sword and held the blade at an angle, peering. Its steel was very bright. The pattern within the metal, worked there when the several twisted strips and rods were beaten together, distorted the image. Still, Gudrun saw enough.

"Your eyes are worth your full weight in gold!" she declared, a bit pale. "Why did you slay the horse, though?"

"That's false, too. *Eac uisge,* it is—the water horse— the kelpie. It's a thing made of seaweed by magic and given the semblance of a horse. Had you mounted it as *they* wished, you would not have been seen again, I'm thinking. It would have wound you fast in its tendrils and plunged into the sea with you."

Gudrun reddened, paled, and swore fiercely. "I want another sight of this thing!"

It lay where they had left it. To Felimid it was a horror, a mass of clumped, knotted, braided seaweed with no more than the general outline of something four-footed. It had the oval fruit and long brown streamery leaves of bladder wrack, yet somehow it was different. As they approached, it moved again, reaching its tendrils towards Gudrun. Felimid felt a thrill of wild horror.

"Burn it!" he said sharply, in the same moment that his lover said, "It still lives."

The pirates now gathered about were puzzled, and voiced their puzzlement. They, and Gudrun, still saw the kelpie as a bay horse. They had also seen it as a dead one until their leader returned. Despite that, none was amazed to witness its sudden twitches. They all supposed it had not been quite dead after all. A large animal is not easy to slay with a sword.

Kelp is less easy still, being less alive to begin with.

"Burn it?" Hemming the Saxon echoed. "An axe-blow or two will serve."

"Then strike and see, friend, strike and see," Felimid said.

Hemming did so. His deceived senses told him that he split a wounded horse's skull, and that brains and blood were on his axe as a result. The "horse" continued to wallow and stretch towards Gudrun.

"Njord!" she gasped, invoking the god of ships. "Njord! Bragi, you are sure that this is a thing of seaweed?"

"As I am that Urbicus's envoys were not men, Gudrun.

The glamour should end at sundown, if you can be patient so long."

Gudrun looked into her shining blade again. It reflected a tangle of crawling kelp. With a deft stroke of Kissing Viper, she sliced off a strand. To her staring men it was as though she had cut a lock from the bloody gelding's tail. Curious, she picked it up and examined it. It felt as well as looked like horsehair to her.

Suddenly it twisted around her forearm. One of the acorn-sized bladders clamped a sucking mouth to her skin. When she tore it away there was a tiny spurt of blood.

"Njord!" she said again. "Bragi is right; burn that foulness! Nail it to the earth with stakes if you cannot make it bide in one place otherwise. Fence it in with hurdles, too."

Hemming said with fervor, "Aye, lady." He began naming men to help him.

Gudrun walked aside with Felimid. "Vampire-weed," she muttered, looking at the tiny red circle on her skin, from which a thread of blood still trickled. "I have heard of the stuff. I never saw it until now, though. Once in a northern corner of Spain, I heard a tale repeated of how, long ago, there was an infestation of it along those shores until some hero destroyed it. As I remember, there were sea demons in the business, too. Ah! Had I mounted that horse, that—what did you call it?"

"*Eaĉ uisge,*" Felimid answered. "Yes. I'm seeing that vision, too." *Gudrun engulfed, entangled, smothered, her blood drawn out by ten thousand little sucking mouths—* "We cannot make an end of Urbicus soon enough!"

"Tomorrow we sail," Gudrun assured him, smiling. "He knows I have returned, and fears me. That's plain. He well may. Our last raid before winter sets in will be a good one. Men will talk of it!

"Now I must gather the men and tell them what Urbicus tried to do, and laugh him to scorn for failing, and tell them how weak his magic must be. Afterwards I will take a sweat-bath; I have told the women to prepare one. Join me, Bragi?"

"Surely."

The next day they sailed for Gaul.

VI

Ale have you brewed, Aegir, but never
Will you give a feast again:
My flames play over all you possess,
Already they burn your back.
                              —Loki's Flyting

Felimid's war-harness was a lamellar tunic of gray
walrus-leather, strengthened in places with whalebone. He
had obtained a similar helmet and boots from the same
craftsmen, the red dwarves of the north who had refitted
Gudrun's ship. Seldom had he worn war-harness before,
and never owned any until that violent year, but in Gudrun's
company it was foolish to be without it.

Then he had abandoned it, given it to the nearest man
when he left Gudrun in anguish after her mass sacrifice of
men to Odin. When they were together again and she no
longer worshipped the battle-god, he had thought it beneath
him to ask for the harness back, so he had staked his other
possessions against tunic and helmet and won them back
instead. Now he wore them, in the ship which slid through
the sea like a snake through fine oil.

From Sarnia to the mainland was less than twenty miles.
Yet there could be more danger in twenty miles in those
devilish waters than in a hundred elsewhere. Local pilots
such as Rhychdir were worth the gold Gudrun paid them,
and a good one was in Njal's ship and another in Hromund's, and they were the masters on this run, as those far-
ranging skippers knew.

"*Ormungandr* sails nearer the wind than any other ship

I've known," Rhychdir said. "But we cannot leave the others," he added regretfully.

"Ah, you will learn the utmost *Ormungandr* can do yet," Felimid consoled him. "The lady's more eager to know it than any other."

One thing the enchanted ship could not do, though, was carry more than eighty men. Gudrun Blackhair needed many more than that to attack the wrecker stronghold. Therefore her ship idled along while *Whale's Sister* and *Wayfarer* kept pace, staying so close that if all three had run out their oars they might have meshed like interlocking combs. Behind them darted and flitted two Pictish vessels, with Hugibert in command of one and Pascent of the other. And they drew nearer the shore of Gaul.

Fear crawled into the bard's soul. He would have broken his harp and cut out his tongue before he admitted it. Still, it was there. He wasn't too much troubled by single combat, or the common risks a man took by traveling alone. He trusted his harp to secure him a welcome, his wits and horsemanship to carry him out of danger if it did threaten. Mass battle was something else. Little depended on a man's own wit and skill in such random confusion. He could lose an arm or half his face to a sword-stroke meant for another, be felled accidentally by a man on his own side. Visions of wound after wound, each more ghastly than the last, appeared to him. He clamped his long smooth jaw against an urge to heave.

It was Gudrun's fault! Before he met her, he had fought in one mass battle. One. Since then he had fought in—how many?—four or five, it seemed, all in half a year. Her fault, her fault...

His walrus-leather corselet felt heavy as stone. Beneath it, sweat crept out of his skin, feeling dirty. He lifted his head, seeking to jerk himself out of this sudden pit. He must look gray. Cairbre and Ogma, if only the sea were rougher! Then he would have an excuse, and could bend over the side and void his stomach. It might help.

Dragging himself out of himself, he concentrated on the men around him. They murmured, and the tone was not promising. He recognized it. Fear. Listening to their words,

Danish and Celtic, he caught the frightened gist.

"Sorcerer—"

"—turn us all to fish when we come against him—"

"—sea demons—"

"Aye, this Urbicus is—"

Fear. Not his kind of fear, the dread of disfigurement or maiming, but fear none the less. He was not the only one. The knowledge in itself gave Felimid strength. He lifted his shoulders, inwardly thumbing his nose at milksop terrors, and moved to Gudrun's side. She didn't look quite herself, either. . . .

"Hel take this idling!" she burst out. "Come on, my bullies, man the rest of the oars! We cannot wait forever for snails of the sea. We will reach the shore and be roasting plundered cattle by the time they catch us."

Gudrun now, impatient and angry, giving foolish orders. Even a lubber like Felimid could tell that *that* one was silly.

"Gudrun," he said urgently, "countermand! If you love your honor and your men! The Danes don't know these waters. It's *Ormungandr*'s eyes see rocks and shoals, *Ormungandr* who swims as if alive from currents, treacherous eddies, *Ormungandr* who guides them. If we leave them, it's lost they are!"

Gudrun stared at him, but he withstood her stare and refrained from saying more, although with difficulty. At last she nodded. "Belay!" she called. "Leave it as 'tis."

Yet the men continued to murmur, and Gudrun continued to look wild. Felimid, his head buzzing, turned to Decius the Spaniard, that pillar of sardonic good sense . . . turned to him in time to surprise him in one-eyed malevolent glower aimed at Gudrun.

"Ataulf didn't die because of her," Felimid said on impulse.

Decius started. "And who said he did?" he snapped.

Forseti! the bard thought, invoking a northern god of law and reasonable dealing he had lately discovered. *It's as though we were all drunk! Or is it, after all, only me? Na, na. I swear something is far wrong.*

Something, yes. Fear in him, fear in the pirates, reckless impulse in Gudrun, and maybe unadmitted resentful hatred in Decius, because of his dead sword-brother. Something was touching them all, something that seeped and dissolved, that could be clear or dark, sparkling or filthy, depending on its source, but something that always removed sharp distinctions . . .

Water magic. The opposite of air.

"Let's turn back!" someone squealed. "It's madness to fight a sorcerer. We'll drown and feed fish!"

Others agreed. An hour earlier they would have thrown him over the side in disgust. Abaft the mast, two men lifted their voices and then their swords, their eyes like those of wolverines. The bard, struggling again with dread of certain wounds, saw one of the Pictish ships leave sailing on a reach and turn away, to run southward before the wind. Morale was toppling like a cliff undermined by the sea.

Vaguely he saw Decius speak to the fearful ones, and Gudrun strike the weapons of the quarreling men apart. Yet trouble was breaking out elsewhere like pustules. Emotions both weak and violent were running wild, and the two kinds equally destructive.

Felimid's harp was in his hands—he had drawn her forth instinctively, for comfort—but he did not know how to use her to counter this sort of graveled folly. Water magic was not his forte. Unless in small ways, on the ridge of the earth . . . bodies of water like streams and lakes . . .

Besides, to his own shame, he felt tempted to let this thing proceed, so that Gudrun's attack should founder and fail.

Enough. You're a man, aren't you? And her man. Do something. You cannot make things worse!

As though to confirm it, a man toppled across a thwart near him, head welling blood.

The bard looked to the overcast sky. Air elementals rode the wind as usual, strong and reckless today. An idea came to Felimid. He struck the harp.

Brassy, jangling, insolent, the notes flew up. In that moment he was not playing his best, but the air spirits loved music, and they listened.

"Come, free ones, play a game with us!" he said in the archaic speech of bards, the professional jargon which contained, it was said, a heavy spicing of words from the language of the Tuatha De Danann, lost for a thousand years, for the air spirits knew all languages. "I'll wager you cannot stop one of our ships reaching yonder shore. Not one! If I win, follow me across the land and do me a favor at my destination." He thought of that destination and his stomach turned. "And win or lose I will give you a fine song."

They hooted and boomed. "And if you lose, flesh and bone? What then?"

"Then, clearly, I taste a deal of salt. It's a challenge, lords of the sky, for mere sport." *Life or death for us all!* "I sing well. Still, if you think yourselves too weak..." He affected to shrug. Nothing was urgent to air spirits. They were fickle and wild and none could tell what they would do. But Felimid had affinities with them.

"Your challenge is taken!"

Felimid laughed with sudden elation. *Now, Urbicus! Now see how your slimy enchantment does against men who have real matters to busy them!*

"Fine! Splendid!" He pointed to the fleeing ship. "Now that one would evade the game, I am thinking. You might chivy him back."

Then he put his back against the mast, braced himself solidly, and sang.

"A great tempest on the ocean plain, bold across its
    high borders,
The wind has arisen, wild winter has slain us!
It comes across the great fierce sea,
The spear of the wild winter season has overtaken
    it.

"The deeds of the plain, the full plain of the ocean,
    have brought alarm on our enduring host;
But for something more momentous than all, no less,
What is there more wonderful than this incomparable
    tremendous story?

"When the wind sets from the east,
The mettle of the wave is roused;
It desires to pass over us westwards to the spot where
    the sun sets,
To the wild broad green sea."

The wind spirits swooped. Some were giants, the changeable pale colours of rain, snow, and cloud, whom only Felimid saw, while others were vast insubstantial birds whose wings boomed and cracked. They brought a wild squall that rattled the five ships like dice in a box. Seamen on the verge of hate, terror and mutiny confronted emergency and sprang to work.

Felimid sang louder.

> *"When the wind sets from the north,*
> *The dark stern wave desires to strive against the*
> *southern world,*
> *Against the expanse of the sky*
> *To listen to the swans' song.*

> *"When the wind sets from the west,*
> *Across the salt sea of rapid currents,*
> *It desires to pass over us eastwards,*
> *To the Tree of the Sun to seize it,*
> *To the wide long distant sea."*

Ormungandr bucked like a horse; bucked and slammed. The steersman desperately worked the rudder-oar. Men adjusted brails and sheets while wind-driven water flew over them. The sail above Felimid was drenched; his brown hair darkened and his laughter soared. Men glanced at him and made signs against bale, thinking him crazy, and then put him out of their minds.

It was ten miles to the mainland, and they slaved until their muscles cracked for each one. Sometimes, briefly, the ever-shifting wind drove them in that direction. Then it turned against them once more. It roughened the waves to a hideous chop, aggravated the tide, spun and struck the five ships at the whim of happy devils.

> *"When the wind sets from the south,*
> *Across the land of the exiles from Britain with their*
> *long spears,*
> *The wave strikes the islands;*
> *It reaches up to the headland of Caladh Ned*
> *with its mantled, gray-green cloak.*

"The ocean is full, the sea is in flood,
Lovely is the home of ships!
The sandy wind has made eddies around Inbher na
da Ainmech;
The rudder is swift upon the wide sea."

It was not at all. The rudder-oar jarred and bounced upon the wide sea, which if it had been any wider would have swallowed Gudrun's little fleet entirely. And Felimid's eyes saw curious murky hues in that wide sea, swirling and mixing. Things like thick bubbles rose from the depths to burst near the surface. They spread colors like those of infection. As fast as they appeared, the squally tumult of the surface swept them away.

Felimid did not know if anyone else spied them. He did not think he would have spied them himself, even a year before. Now he was coming to know the sea somewhat better; the sea without, and the sea within. The sickly, infectious hues were not there to the body's vision. They were a manifestation of some enchantment, spread and propagated through the sea, which aroused . . . somehow, and Felimid did not begin to know how . . . the most debased, fatal, suicidal passions, so subtly at first that men were gripped by them before they knew.

The influence might still be there, but it wasn't working now. The pirates had no time to entertain it, any more than a man can be jealous or suspicious of his wife while running away from a bear.

Gudrun's ships lurched on, hunting the sheltered beach which lay somewhere ahead. Men plied oars which failed to bite in the heaving water, and sails were worse than useless. Near the beginning of it all, the bard had indeed groped his way to the rail and emptied his stomach, scarce noticing. And it did seem that the vile yellow fear had left him too. In a mad way he was happy.

"It is not peaceful, a wild troubled sleep,
With feverish triumph, with furious strife,
The swan's hue covers them, the plain full of sea-
beasts and its denizens;
The hair of Manannan's wife is tossed about."

When at last it ceased to toss, three ships had been dragged ashore in the blessed shelter of a beach and their crews slept like the dead. *Whale's Sister* and the Pictish raiding ship under Pascent's command came in battered the next morning.

"What happened?" Gudrun asked the bard quietly. "What did you do?"

"What happened is hard to give a name," he said, "except that we'd all have been killing and deserting each other within an hour, had the weather not given us common cause again. It was some enchantment of the wrecker's, working I think through the sea. But how is beyond me."

"You saved us all, didn't you? By nearly killing us! I do not want to remember what I thought, what I felt—and it is the same for all here, I hazard. What we left of each other, his sea demons would have finished."

"I'd say so." Felimid had the faraway look he wore when dreaming or cogitating. "Now, we've seen air magic from this cur. Nothing but air magic can make the illusions that disguised his sea demons, and it's in my mind that they themselves worked the water magic sent against us yesterday. It's mighty rare for the same man to be equally skilled in air and water sorceries, and now it's land we'll be crossing to reach him. I cannot believe he's proficient in earth magic as well."

"You mean he can do nothing more?"

"I'm guessing, to be truthful. But I think it a sharp guess, and I'll go first against him to show my trust in it."

He lay with his legs outstretched and his torso half-raised on the prop of his bent elbows, the autumn sunlight on his chest. Gudrun had gone down on a single knee beside him.

"If you go first you will go beside me."

"As always," he said.

She regarded him for a moment. There was no question that he was comely. You would admit that even if you didn't love him. Yet there was something incongruous in his looks. His forehead and long, prepossessing jaw were clearly defined, but between them the limpid eyes and snub nose gave a guileless, childlike impression that seemed at the same time appropriate . . . and deceptive. The appearance beneath the surface? The illusions of faerie?

Gudrun Blackhair wondered.

Suddenly she grinned and fisted his shoulder. "As always! Better look to your harness, Bragi. I know you. You were more concerned that your harp had taken no harm."

Shortly, after a meal of salt fish, bacon, and tack, washed down with mead, Gudrun addressed her men.

"You know what comes now," she said. "We march hard to the wreckers' hold, a place called Coriallo, built on sailors' bones. Fifty men must stay with the ships, and since you latecomers are too weary to march at once, I am choosing you."

"What?" Pigsknuckle Hromund snuffled through hairy nostrils, as though scenting a downright insult to his manhood. "We be more than fifty, Gudrun, and I for one am equal to a piddling march of—what?—fifteen mile! I will not stay behind."

"As for me," Pascent said, "I desire to cut some wrecker throats, as any decent mariner would."

"Oh, Njord of the Ships!" Gudrun swore. "I like your sentiments, but fifty must stay and that is not debatable. We settled it before we left Sarnia. They must have one undisputed leader, too, lest these local codfish mount an attack. Count heads, then!"

The late arrivals did, and there proved to be sixty-one of them, drenched and red-eyed, the skin worn from their palms.

"Eleven may come," Gudrun allowed. "Eleven of the strongest, for you must march in war-gear, then fight when we reach Coriallo. And Pascent—Hromund—one of you stays. Settle which one, quickly."

"I'll fight you for it, Gaul," Hromund offered at once.

Pascent cursed, but without his usual heat, and spread his hands in concession. "If you want it so much, heathen, go."

Thus it was arranged. Fifty men had remained on Sarnia, and now fifty remained with the ships, while two hundred marched for the wreckers' hold. They cut straight across the northern corner of the peninsula, a distance of some five leagues, as Hromund had said. Since they did not march in a wholly straight line, it turned to six.

None disputed their passage. Gudrun's two hundred pirates were an army by the measure of the time and place, although a single Roman cohort of former times would have laughed at them. Gaul no longer had standing armed forces, and by the time a host able to resist them could be raised, they would have departed.

"None but the district vicar is close enough to do anything," Decius explained to the bard as they tramped along. "For years he has colluded with Urbicus, and he could maybe raise half a thousand men . . . if he dared do so without the Count of Baioca's sanction. And then we'd go through them like a plow through sand!"

He smiled grimly as he said it. Whatever hidden bitterness he might feel against Gudrun, in whose defense his sword-brother had died, he was balanced and ready again, committed to the present raid.

"What of Urbicus himself?" Felimid asked. "How hard will his men fight?"

"Like mad weasels, I don't doubt, since they know what to expect from us. Yet they are wreckers, scavengers by trade, not fighters. Cutting the throats of men washed ashore, helpless, is about their mark. We will clear them from the world once we get to them."

They continued through the raw autumn weather. Gusty winds kept pace with them, buffeting them, sending the red leaves flying. There were bursts of cold rain and odd fusillades of hail.

They had no trouble finding shelter at their halts. It was a country of little hills and short streams, its villages set among apple trees and cattle pastures. The people fled at Gudrun Blackhair's coming, so that houses and barns lay empty for her men's use. First, though, the people freed the beasts penned for butchering, and drove them off. These did not scatter far, and the pirates gorged on freshly slaughtered beef.

Gudrun marched at their head, marched in her shirt of silvered mail weighing two and a half stone, marched with her sword Kissing Viper at her hip, a round shield on one arm and her bow in her other hand, burdened and sweating like her men. On her feet she wore the enchanted boots she had won from a water godling on a tributary of the great river Oder.

They took a few lumbering, creaking farm carts with them, filled with gear they would perhaps need. Then they came to the rocks which warded Coriallo on the landward side.

"This river runs into the very harbor," Decius said, as they camped by a stream the night before they were to attack. "There are some steep paths on the way, though none to compare with our Sarnian cliffs. I think we will not be late to the feast."

Coriallo had been a port in the days when men fought with weapons of bronze. Phoenician traders had stopped there, maybe, said Decius, and Pytheas looked across to Britain from its harbor-side and listened to rumors of Thule. Later it had become a Roman station, a customs-house, or else a little, insignificant part of the Saxon Shore defenses. Felimid listened while his meat sizzled over the fire beside him, as interested in this glimpse into Decius as in Coriallo's long past. He had known the Spaniard was wellborn. Signs of Roman breeding he may have thought long buried showed in him regularly; he had been noble. Now it appeared that he had some learning too.

Gudrun felt less interest in what Coriallo had been. Her anger against what it had become was too hot. Her only questions were for Felimid.

"This crow goddess, the War Queen of your tribe, Bragi . . . what sacrifices does she delight in?"

"Those bloody hags need none to give them sacrifices! They take their own. If you'd truly please them, then dedicate to them the heads of the warriors you slay with your own hand. H'mm. I know a song about them and a hero named Cuchulain . . . but that can wait for another time," he added, remembering how it ended and not wishing to make the camp gloomy. Songs of battle and war, he had found, were best appreciated when the battles were over.

"Give us the one about King Oisc, instead!" bawled Pigsknuckle Hromund. Others echoed his request, and Felimid obliged. Cheery and scurrilous, the strain rang through the rocks and came faintly even to the wreckers' ears.

> *"He never bestowed a gold buckle or stud,*
>   Aparain dubh o hi ho,

He never bestowed a gold buckle or stud,
And the ale that he gave had the texture of mud,
    Ro hu il o ho!

"*He never broke ring but the ring of an arse,*
    Aparain dubh o hi ho,
He never broke ring but the ring of an arse,
And the traders in boys wore a track through his
    grass,
    Ro hu il o ho!

"*They ceased to deliver when he ceased to pay,*
    Aparain dubh o hi ho,
They ceased to deliver when he ceased to pay,
And the mares and the cows kept well out of his way,
    Ro hu il o ho!"

"I'm thirsty," Felimid announced loudly, through the whooping. Ten men pressed drink on him. Others, who had not heard the song, wanted him to begin again, and this he eventually did, in two other parts of that lusty camp of ten score pirates.

"*Though Loki has fathered a wolf and a horse,*
    Aparain dubh o hi ho,
Though Loki has fathered a wolf and a horse,
And taken his sister Jarnsaxa by force,
The Kentish king's conduct he reckons too coarse,
    Ro hu il o ho!"

The wreckers in Coriallo heard the pirates' great shout of laughter, and shivered. Their master Urbicus heard it as he walked by the harbor, and covered his ears. Lord God! Lord God! Why had he lured those Frankish pirates onto the rocks? Now Gudrun Blackhair was upon him despite his efforts to destroy her at sea; she had a bard in her company who was wholly able to detect air sorceries and forestall them; and Urbicus had neither the powers innate nor the skills acquired to work evil against her through the earth.

He couldn't even flee in one of his ships. They lay useless

in the harbor because that accursed bard had persuaded the air elementals to plague Coriallo with contrary winds. Their interest in the prank would not last long—but doubtless long enough! Gudrun would be at his door on the morrow!

He felt sick with fear.

Once, Urbicus had been a bishop. He had abused his office to commit slander, expropriation and in one case blatant murder. Worse, in the eyes of his fellow bishops, he had deserted his flock to save his skin during an outbreak of deadly fever. He hadn't been dismissed from his bishopric on any of these grounds; but then his practice of sorcery had become too well known.

He had changed his name and his home. Since then he had driven bonds with the so-called "sea demons" (who in truth were no beings so powerful) and made a fat living for years by drowning men. Despite all this, he retained a comfortable opinion of himself and thought his present predicament monstrously unfair.

If Gudrun took Coriallo—and she would, she would!—there was only one way for him to escape. Not on the seas, but beneath it. He waded into the cold harbor water.

Taking off his necklace, a gold cuttlefish of somewhat bizarre form pendant from a chain, he lowered it into the sea.

Sea demons lurked in the waters off Coriallo that night. They generally did. Before long, three dripping shapes, their incongruously leonine heads outlined against the stars, towered above the little wrecker.

He began making swift, complex signs with his hands. The "demons" had much the same senses as fish, and one or two possessed by neither fish nor man, but hearing was not among their faculties. Only the glamour Urbicus had cast over his envoys had made them seem to hear and answer appropriately on Sarnia.

Urbicus spoke with his fingers for some time. The beings from the sea made signs of assent, their eyes glowing yellow. Then they vanished into the water.

Gudrun's pirates moved in the morning. They went up through the rocks, goading the beasts who drew the farm carts, putting their own sweating, straining backs against the tailgates on the rocky paths. Once they came to a ravine through which the river ran on its way to Coriallo. Gudrun stamped her foot three times on the brink, with due display and loud invocations, and a bridge appeared. She ruled her pirates as much by luck and personal magic as by her ruthless courage, and knew it.

The carts rumbled across. On the far side they were knocked apart. The pieces, particularly the wheels, and their contents too, were divided among the two hundred attackers. They carried them piecemeal down from the steep heights, waded through the little river, and came on towards the triangular bay. They reached the river's mouth.

The wrecker lord had abandoned his mansion. He and all his men were crammed in the small fort with its single gate and four towers, the tide swelling beneath it. Two ditches and a stone-lined earth rampart guarded it on the landward side.

Gudrun laughed aloud with pleasure, seeing it.

Her pirates gathered and grouped: big fair men from Scania and the Danish islands; the handful of surviving Goths; the savage, tattooed Franks, trousered and bare-armed; the score or so of Gallo-Romans; the sprinkling of men from Britain and Lesser Britain; the rarities and uniques like the few Picts and Zucharre; the narrow-faced Basque who could leap his own height in the air holding shield and axe. Banded in fifties, under Decius, Hugibert, Njal and Hromund, they set to work in sight of the wreckers on the fortlet wall.

Crude scaling ladders took shape. More ominously, the cartwheels, a large lopped tree-trunk, odd timbers and brine-soaked hides became a covered ram within three hours. During that time, Gudrun's arrows killed half a dozen men who showed themselves too boldly.

At last she discarded her bow and quiver, drew Kissing Viper, tossed sword-belt and scabbard aside. The bard had earlier hung the harp of Cairbre on a tree; he stood ready, in his leather corslet and helmet, a targe on his right arm and Kincaid in his left hand.

"Haaahh!" Gudrun shrieked. *"Follow me, Sarnia!"*

She began to move, a slow trot in her war-gear. Her

speed accumulated until she was covering ground at a respectable run, and she never looked back. Felimid raced beside her. Her pirates voiced a deep, roaring shout as they followed, bearing the ladders.

They covered their heads and their comrades' with raised shields as rocks were hurled from above with braining force. They flung makeshift ramps across the two ditches as spears rattled down. They reached the walls on three sides of the fortlet and raised their ladders with muscle-cracking effort. Gudrun was among the first to mount one.

She would be, Felimid thought, a bit sourly.

Because she was there, he kept pace with her, up another ladder as swiftly as he could go without falling. He wasn't quite first; there were two men above him. Now if he could only gain the wall and find Gudrun again, he and she might stand together and save each other from being killed until the gate came down.

That was where the real breach had to be made. The ladders at the other walls were not much more than distractions. The covered ram rumbled forward on its six cartwheels, over the short causeway, pushed by thirty straining men under the roof of wet hides. Hot pitch splashed over it. Its front kissed the gate.

"Back!" Decius shouted. "Swing back . . . *push!* Swing back . . . *push!*"

Again and again he called the time. Thirty men swung and drove, swung and drove. The improvised ram thundered on the gate timbers. By the eighth stroke the gate was vibrating like a drumhead. By the tenth it groaned and popped as fastenings tore loose. By the fourteenth it was booming capitulation, and the men swung their tree-trunk faster although their very teeth ached with strain and the vibration was in their hurting bones. More . . . and . . . *harder!* More . . . and . . . *harder!*

The gate burst wide.

Ten men, waiting unwillingly in reserve under stern orders ("Fail me in this and I will cut the blood-eagle on you," in Gudrun's amiable words) blew shrilly on horns. By this the men at the walls knew the gate was broken, and thankfully drew back. Some lay dead in the fortlet's surrounding ditches; a few, including Gudrun, had reached the top.

Felimid was among those who raced for the broken gate. Decius and his thirty were already within. The ten horn-blowers had followed; a hundred others poured after.

They killed their way through the fortlet and fired the wattle and daub interior buildings. Through the confusion and flame strode Gudrun, hunting Urbicus. Beside her once again, Felimid caught the jolting blow of an iron-bound cudgel on his targe, and drove Kincaid into the throat of the big-bellied scoundrel who had delivered it. The wrecker clutched the wound and stood with gore spilling between his fingers. Gudrun and Felimid passed on. Behind them the stricken man toppled at last, to die fairly quickly.

"Urbicus!" she screamed. "Where is Urbicus? You five, watch the gate! He could slip out! Find him and bring him to me!"

The tumult was waning. The bellows, the screams, the war-cries all gave place to groans and panting and the hot crackle of fire. Any wreckers left alive were being finished as quickly as they were found.

"Bring me Urbicus!" Gudrun yelled, smoky and bloody. The urgent craving in her voice filled the conquered fort. Men hunted through the four little towers from top to bottom; they searched the underground storerooms, prodding sacks and poking into open barrels; they searched every yard of the fortlet, above ground and below, nor was the task overlengthy. They came back from their search slowly, reluctant to confess the failure that showed plainly in each man's face.

"Nothing?" Gudrun said incredulously. "He's not here?"

They shook their heads.

"He must be here. Wait! He cast a glamour upon the creatures he sent to kill me. Maybe he has done the same for himself! Bragi, look at all our men within the fort. Look at the dead, too. That louse's miscarriage would not be above taking the semblance of a corpse to hide from my vengeance."

Felimid gazed at her coolly. "Gudrun, marrow of my heart, I am a bard and a grandson of Fergus mac Buthi, who was Erin's chief bard and passed to me the harp of

Cairbre. I'm not about to examine corpse after corpse for you. Pile them and burn them. If Urbicus is shamming among them, he will reveal himself. Or just pile the heads, so. The Morrigan will like that."

Although Gudrun's jaw did not drop, it certainly slackened a little. She stared at him. Then, after a long moment, she flushed carnation.

"Your pardon, lover. I spoke . . . as I should not. Well. Where do *you* suppose Urbicus has gone?"

"I wish I knew." Felimid looked at all the nearby pirates with his bardic sight. "No, their hideous faces do seem to be all their own, poor fellows, but maybe the gateway should just be guarded until I am certain."

"Are you hurt?" she asked suddenly.

"I? Nothing at all."

"Then what is that running into your boot? It's too red for pee and too thick for wine. Let me treat it."

The wound Felimid had not realized he had was a deep gash above the knee. The pain was considerable, and he endured it almost gladly in the knowledge that it was all he had received. He'd come through alive and unmaimed, and this fight would almost surely be the last for the winter, not counting minor brawls. Relief flooded through him, a warm grateful tide.

"We had better search again," Gudrun was saying. "No . . . no, there are men worse hurt than you, Bragi, and their hurts will not wait. But Urbicus!"

"I'll lead the search here," Felimid said. "And Decius can take fifty men to the mansion yonder, though I doubt he will be there. This fort is the strongest place on the harbor."

"We took it with ease."

The bard smiled. "Yes, we did."

Telling off four men to help him, he made his search of the fortlet. Perhaps he was more thorough, or had better luck, but in the storerooms he found a hidden entrance to a tiny cellar beneath them. He summoned Gudrun.

The pirate woman was in a bitter mood. The man she had been treating had just died under her hands. What she saw in the cellar did nothing to sweeten her.

The place, crudely hacked from rock, was empty. A constant sucking and gurgling came from a round well-shaft in the middle of the floor, accompanied by the smell of living sea-water. The print of a wet webbed hand was still on the rim.

Gudrun screamed in frustrated rage, shrill as a hawk. "He has escaped me! The scum, the son of a mare!"

"His demons took him," one of her pirates said. It was Giguderich, looking more cadaverous and gloomy than usual.

"His demons aided him!" Gudrun snarled. *"Demons!* Ha! If he gave those fish-things the power to live in air, he could give himself the power to live in water. He has escaped me!" she said again, furiously.

"For the present," Felimid agreed.

Gudrun mastered herself. "Yes. You are right, Bragi. A maddening habit with you! There will be another time. Meanwhile, we cannot stay here to receive Count Gontran's host. We must take what else we came for, and part! You are the best rider among us. Can you reach the ships with that leg?"

"A deal more easily than I could without it."

"Clever, clever. If there is a horse worthy the name around this bay, will you take it and tell Pascent we have Coriallo, and he can safely enter?"

"Find me the horse, and I'll bring the ships," Felimid promised.

Storehouses by the harbor contained winter stocks: grain, smoked and salted meat, apples, nuts and an abundance of fish no doubt supplied by the "sea demons." The pirates had begun loading it aboard two rather ill-kept oak coasters moored in the bay by the time a horse was found for the bard; a plain gray mare who looked to have no exceptional speed but much staying power. When Felimid left, the Sarnians were professionally ransacking Urbicus's house on the far side of the triangular bay. He wondered idly how rich the loot would be.

VII

Golden chariots on the plain of the sea
Heaving with the tide to the Sun:
Chariots of silver on the Plain of Games
And of bronze that has no blemish.
                                   —Bran son of Febal

Felimid had no trouble on his ride back to the ships, save
the pain of his wounded leg. He covered the six leagues in
a day, and saw no signs of a gathering war-host. Maybe the
district vicar was not willing to raise one on his own initiative, he thought, and had sent word to Count Gontran of
Baioca so that he might make the decision. Decius had said
that, hadn't he?

In the event, the Count had ample time to think it over.
The weather turned so foul that it was three days before the
Sarnian ships could put to sea, and then they sailed west,
well around the isle of Ridune, instead of north along the
coast. Pascent vehemently refused the second approach.

"Not even in this bitch of a devil's serpent!" he said,
meaning *Ormungandr*—and meaning only praise. "We'd
lose most of the other ships and maybe this one as well.
God's bones! That tide-race between Ridune and the cape
is just an open, hungry grave. Your haddock-buggering sea
demons gather there in dozens, chuckling. No. We go
around."

They went around, under the lash of a wind from the
northeast, hissing with sleet and hail. Then they were driven
back to Ridune, for all their efforts and for all Felimid's
wooing of the air elements with his harp. They lost one of
the Pictish ships and saved only two of her crew.

68

Pascent snarled, "I thought the winds did your bidding, harp-man?"

"Then you dreamed!" Felimid retorted, red-eyed and sleepless and desperate himself. "I speak to them, and they to me. Sometimes they do as I wish, for a song or a whim or their fickle pleasure. Sometimes! But if I could command them I would not be here." As he spoke, *Ormungandr* lifted dizzyingly, bows to a climbing wave. A hooting wind drove spray and cold rain. "I'd be riding in the cavalcade of the gods!"

"You may be yet!" Pascent told him.

Ormungandr survived. Indeed, no other ships were lost, although *Wayfarer*'s planks were badly sprung. She wallowed and leaked sadly as they came to Coriallo harbor, eight days after they had started. Their only trouble had been from the weather; Urbicus and his scaly allies had done nothing.

"You were long in coming," said Hugibert to Pascent. "We might ha' been destroyed five times while you allowed a little blow to delay you."

"Ha! Listen to him! You Frankish dog-wolf, all you had to do was squat on your backside and wait idle, after you'd killed a few wreckers!"

"Six score is more than a few. And while we were breaking into their fort, where were you? Idle on *your* backside!"

Felimid heard that exchange and marveled. Hugibert sounded positively good-natured. He and Pascent must have become thick cronies indeed.

They prepared to depart. The weather had turned temporarily fine, and a gentle favoring wind blew. Men who had sailed with Gudrun Blackhair for years nodded sagely, and told the northerners that this was what happened when you had the lady with you. Her weather-luck was a byword. There was a great deal of I-mind-the-time-when, and much convenient forgetting of times when even Gudrun had encountered storms or foul winds.

Meanwhile, Felimid and Gudrun were making love on piled sheepskins in one of the fortlet's towers. After making the last use of the place, they gutted it with fire. They burned everything else on the bay, too, especially the once-bishop's

looted house. There would be little to which he could return
if he dared come back. Then they sailed with the next tide.

"Our last raid for the year," Gudrun said as she watched
the blackened shore recede.

"A workmanlike raid, too." It was Decius who responded, richly content. "We have what we came for. Foodstocks and vengeance, the wreckers destroyed, and we're
clean away with few comrades dead."

"Not all that we came for." Gudrun's eyes glittered like
weapon-metal. "Urbicus escaped! But not for long. I'll hunt
him wherever he has gone, and have his life for those men
of mine he drowned with the help of demons! He cannot
hide beneath the sea for always."

"I am not so sure," Decius said, frowning. "There is that
story we heard in Galicia—oh, just another seaman's yarn,
belike, but vampire weed and sea demons are real, as we
have seen. The story had it that a magician who wanted to
do so could *become* a sea demon. At the cost of abandoning
air and light he might then be immortal."

"And if that be life." Felimid leaned indolently upon the
stern-post. The breeze prowled through his smooth brown
hair. "If Urbicus does *that,* it will be a worse punishment
than any we could visit upon him. Even should he learn
eventually to like it."

He envisioned the cold dark belly of the sea, where
nothing was but ooze, rock and grotesque fish, where creatures called demons lived on what fell from the sunlit upper
waters. He made a wry face.

"Let's be vigilant," he added. "The creatures may attack
us. If I were Urbicus, I'd urge them to do so! He can't
return to Coriallo while we flourish and remember him."

"They are not nicors, whose bellies command them and
who have no wits," Gudrun said. "Indeed, they strike me
as cowardly."

"Something in that," Felimid agreed. "Maybe I'm mis-
taken to think of a direct attack. Still, the sea is our road
and they can always reach us through the sea. They have
shown us! I wonder if we should not try to find allies who
are also of the sea, but more to our liking than demons."

"When you know of any, Bragi, tell me."

He did tell her. He waited until they were in Gudrun's hall again to open his mind completely. The place was now aired, with new rushes and sweet herbs spread thickly on the floor, and altogether more pleasant than it erst had been. Felimid was glad. He didn't like squalor.

"Those allies I mentioned," he said. "I think I know where we might be finding them."

"I would doubt that if another man told me, but from you I must believe it. Say further, Bragi."

He told her what he had seen when he spoke with Cynric, and what he thought the sight signified.

"My head upon it. They appear to most men as shoals, but they are islands where a tribe of the Children of Lir do dwell, hidden by glamour and illusion, turned sideways to the Sun. That was my guess from the first. Now and again, since, the winds have told me more, when they chanced to be blowing from the south and I chanced to be giving ear. That wasn't often while we sailed against Coriallo, mind. I'd seldom the time or attention to spare. But I know more now than I did."

"The winds told you," Gudrun repeated uncertainly. She did not doubt that such things could be. She only wondered if her lover was joking.

"True as your mouth is warm."

He tested the aptness of that simile. Gudrun cooperated, and turned the kiss into a lengthy one, but when it ended she showed that she had not been distracted.

"What are the Children of Lir?"

Felimid drew a steadying breath or two before he answered. "I can explain that or I can make love to you. Not both."

"You can make love to me all night long, and I hope you will," Gudrun answered, forthright as a fire. "At present I had better be the pirate, and you my news-monger, the Ratatosk squirrel. Tell."

"The Children of Lir. Yes. Well, they are a race. Lir is the sea, and they are his people, just as my ancient forebears were the people of earth-mother Danu. Call them mer-folk. But not fish-spawn of the black depths! They have true human form. They breathe air and their blood runs warm as ours. They are cousins to the seal and the dolphin, and if any folk could tell you what Urbicus is doing now, they would be the Children of Lir. Their aid against him would be an excellent thing to have." He ended thoughtfully, "If there be any getting it."

"You favor trying?"

"So much as that . . . I am not sure. Maybe we'd find it simpler to go to them than to leave again. If they veil their islands with glamour, it is because they wish to be secret."

"Right!" Gudrun affirmed with vigor. "And if they wish to be secret, it means they are weak. I do not think they would deny *me* anything I care to ask."

"Then you will go to them?"

"Surely! What did you believe I would do when you told me this?" Gudrun checked her enthusiasm suddenly. She looked keenly at the bard. "You have known it—how long?— since the day you talked with Cynric. Why did you not speak before?"

"Oh. There was Urbicus to be dealt with. For all I knew, one or both of us might die. I reckoned the Children of Lir could wait until the wreckers were well settled."

He said it lightly, carelessly; a bit too much so. The pirate was no fool. Sudden comprehension flashed from her eyes, her face, the poise and ready tension of her whole figure.

"Had we killed Urbicus with the rest, you would not have told me this, ever—would you, Bragi?"

"Well, no. I had decided not to when I came back from my parley with Cynric . . . *your* parley with Cynric. In truth I'm sorry I had to change my mind. But since Urbicus remains at large . . ."

"*Vermin eat Urbicus!* You are my spokesman, my skald, my courier, my herald—and more than that—and you deceived me! You kept a thing from me you knew I would wish to know! *Why?*"

She was furious, formidable, a vessel of danger, and fifteen inches from him. Withal, she was amazingly like a hurt child. For both reasons, it was a time for clear truth. He said quietly:

"Because you are Gudrun Blackhair, and I do not want the Children of Lir destroyed."

"Destroyed?"

"Sure, that was my word. Destroyed. Is it such an un-likely word to connect with you? I know you've slain some whose deaths left the earth a sweeter place. The mer-folk, though . . . more than three hundred spears, I think they would fear their dwelling-places becoming known in nearby Gaul, and particularly to the church. For the church withers and destroys all magic as fever withers life. Despite all your high confidence, my darling, I think the Children of Lir can defend themselves against you. A bishop with curses and relics would be another thing."

"But the Children are no kin of yours!"

"But they are. Their people and mine knew each other well of old, and now a few scraps and fragments of marvel are our last heritage. I want to see them. I know they may not feel the same way towards me. Just the same, I hold it worth the risk.

"I'd not be too high-minded to bluff them, cajole them, hint at exposure if we must come to that. But really to do it? Betray them to the Cross-worshippers? I'd sear my tongue first, and see all your proud ships burn, *Ormungandr* in-cluded . . . and now you know."

"Now indeed I do!" Gudrun said. "Thanks for that plain speaking, Bragi. I would I had heard it from you sooner."

"Your nature isn't one for keeping secrets, Gudrun."

"Bah, secrets!" she said. "I do not believe in them! I understand it when you speak of marvel, though. Haven't I gone through the world seeking marvel? I went hungry and cold on the Jutland heath as an outlaw sooner than live a tame life. I've gone from the ice of Thule to the hot sand of the south. Now I desire to go beyond this world itself, in *Ormungandr*. You know all this.

"I have paid my way as I went with ransom and loot. There is nothing new or strange in that. Still, I can take those things anywhere, and I have proved it.

"What I do not do, Bragi, is foul my own nest. I have never raided the isles near Sarnia. I am on good terms with the lords of Angia, Lesia and Ridune, and even with the town of Aleth. No more will I offend these merfolk if I can avoid it. Less! I wish that even less!"

"Then by all means let's call upon them."

They went.

Ormungandr slid through the gray October seas. With Felimid and Gudrun were nineteen picked men. They might go with a hundred, the bard had said, and the one purpose it would serve would be to assure the Children of Lir that they were unfriendly. Gudrun had listened to him.

"Bragi!" she said now, urgently. "Those are shoals, those are banks!"

"The water's shoaling, right enough," he agreed, "but it's islands that lie ahead. I see them plainly, I tell you. They are wooded, and among the woods is a fountain like a tall white tree, and yonder a ship is coming to meet us."

The day was clear and the light like yellow wine. Gudrun said, "Cat's paws of wind on the sea, nothing more."

The strange ship came smoothly through the water, half the length of *Ormungandr,* lighter and more beautiful. Her hull gleamed silver-white and her figurehead was a brown seahorse. Her sails, shapen and rigged like none Felimid had ever seen elsewhere, were scarlet, tan and white, in a pattern like interweaving ribbons.

The men in her—

It was a moment before Felimid could hail them in a steady voice. "Fair weather attend you, children of the sea! It's to win favor that we have come, and not to irrupt, or invade, or make war—and to that end I ask that we may come into your havens. I am Felimid mac Fal of Erin, a bard of the third degree, and it's for Gudrun Blackhair of Sarnia I speak."

"Yes," came the answer, in the blessed speech of Erin. "None would mistake the serpent-ship *Ormungandr.* Now I am Olcain mac Gav, the husband of ships, and I make you welcome with my lips and invite you forward. But my honor bids me say to you that it will not rest with me whether you go back again."

The men of Ormungandr looked at each other, puzzled. "Bragi talks to nothing." "I did think I heard—" "A trick of the wind, sea-birds crying."

"It is none of those," Gudrun said tensely. "Look in the mirror, and be wise!"

The "mirror" was a bronze tray from the loot of Coriallo.

Gudrun had been scanning the shoals in its surface while her men gabbled. Because of scars and dents, it was not perfect, but it showed the reality of the scene and not the glamor. By Felimid's advice it had been polished to gleaming brightness and brought along.

Two men held it while others looked in it.

"Now take us in," Gudrun ordered.

Felimid called the stroke and gave other instructions, his bardic eyes guiding them. There were four or five of the glamor-veiled islands, the largest, where the white fountain played, as big as Sarnia though lower and much easier of access. Among them lay sandbanks and shallow lagoons of jewel-hued water; amethyst above the purple kelp, amber above the brown, emerald above the green.

They anchored *Ormungandr* in half a fathom of water, in company with three other of the sea people's smaller ships. There were shallops, long rowboats and leather-skinned curraghs riding in a bay not far distant or drawn up on the shore. In the shelter of the low woods, Felimid saw curious lodges like ribbed hemispherical tents, although more solid. A little further off rose the solar and roof of a wonderful house. Felimid had seen larger, though few that came to his mind were fairer.

"You lads remain with the ship," Gudrun said. "If Bragi and I do not return by the time you think we should—say, tomorrow midday—and you depart, it will not be I who says you deserted your chieftain. Take the head from any man who does! Tell Decius what happened, and then act as he decides. He knows what to do should you not hear from me."

Reluctantly, they agreed. Their chieftain had gone to face eldritch things before, and they knew she would not be dissuaded now.

Felimid and Gudrun went ashore in a punt Olcain had summoned. In the eyes of her pirates, those who were not staring into the mirror, the pair were wading through the shallow water to a sandbank. Gudrun saw the same thing, although she felt neither chill nor resistance below her waist.

She asked curiously, "How do they look?"

He replied with verses, in the Danish tongue.

> "Lover famed for fearless action,
>   Flustered now by sea-men's glamour,
>   Let my words eke out your vision
>   And your ears replace your eyesight.
>   Middling tall, well made and handsome,
>   Lapped in skin as white as milk,
>   Pricked with patterns green and silver
>   Are these pastors of the sea.

> "Beardless, with their long hair braided,
>   Unseen standing close to you,
>   Fare they naked but for kilts
>   Fangled it appears from fish-skin
>   Swords they bear, and spears well
>   balanced,
>   Of some white unrusting steel;
>   Near we now their gathering-hall,
>   Marvel-hunger there to nourish."

"Thanks!" Gudrun said. "By Njord, I will not get much food for my marvel-hunger if I see no more than I do now."

"It's in my mind that something can be done," the bard replied, a bit enigmatically.

The door-warder of the hall did it. This green-haired giant, a complete head taller than Felimid, touched Gudrun's eyelids and ears with his fingertips.

"Enter freely and by your own choice," he said. "The prince's truth I give to you. See and hear what is so."

Gudrun started wildly at the sudden sight of the immense men before her—and she had seen many astonishing things. None chuckled at her amazement; the Children of Lir were evidently a well-mannered folk. *They may decide to feed us to sea-serpents with our shoes on,* Felimid thought, *but they will be courteous about it.*

Well, nobody had asked them to come here.

He owned to himself, as they went through the foreroom, that he'd always wanted to come since his bardic sight had discovered this place. It was pleasant, to be here without intent to fight, without a hundred roaring killers at his back, success or failure resting on his own quickness and ability to carry a thing off. It resurrected that man of a year ago who had not answered to the name Bragi. He still existed, close under the skin of Gudrun Blackhair's lover.

They entered the hall proper, having discarded their weapons. Gudrun frankly stared. Felimid's gaze roved swiftly around the place, seizing a general impression of color, sound and structure; the partitioned booths against the wall, with their trellises of fretted bronze and hangings of sea-spider silk, the double circle of yew pillars upholding the roof, the open space in the center, soft light from luminescent globes, the faint green tinge and occasional sparkle in the air itself, shell mosaics, carvings of fish and birds, the men and women . . . the Children of Lir.

White skins. Green or brown or purple hair. The fluent movements of seals in water, hampered by little clothing.

Then Felimid halted as though struck a sharp blow. At a place of honor in the largest booth, raised against the wall on the western side, hair the color of red bronze caught his glance as a woman rose, coolly self-possessed.

"Welcome," said Vivayn, smiling.

She had not been able to resist having the first word. But she inclined her head at once towards the man in the highest seat, and said, "Prince Rothevna is the master here. He has no tongue but his own, and I doubt that you have his. My lords, pardon me. I spoke out of my turn, for these folk are known to me."

Vivayn. Cynric's missing wife.

Dazed—or perhaps not quite that—by her presence, the bard made himself turn his attention to the prince of these islands. Brown-haired and blue-eyed, Rothevna might have passed as a man of earthly breed save for his lack of hair on face and body, his great size, slightly bigger even than his doorkeeper, and the fine curling green and silver lines tattooed on his shoulders, arms, breast and brow. An older man in a long tunic rose from beside him.

"I am Idh," he said simply, in a voice cadenced like rolling surf. "I speak for the prince. Rothevna, Son of the Sea, scion of Manannan, offers you courtesy. Having pierced his illusions and come to his house uninvited, you have not the status of guests . . . as yet . . . but neither does he receive you in anger." *As yet*, the unspoken words echoed.

"For which we are glad," Felimid answered courteously.
"I stand with Gudrun Blackhair, the lady of Sarnia, Varek's
daughter. You will know of her, my lord. Myself, I am
Felimid mac Fal, known to some as Bragi, her speaker and
bard and satirist. We are here in friendship and the hope of
friendship, so."

He used the contemporary language of Erin, like Idh.
Gudrun did not speak it, and he assumed the Children of
Lir had no Danish.

"There is Danann blood in you, I think," Idh remarked.

"True for you, my lord. A deal of it; five parts or more.
And it may even be a drop from the Children of Lir. There
was close friendship between our peoples in the long ago."

"Which only the bards and storytellers remember now.
The Tuatha De Danann and the Children of Lir have been
driven beyond this world. Descendants and remnants are all
that survive here. Our strength in these frail islands is that
we are unknown." His tone crashed suddenly, like a wave
breaking over rock. "We mean to continue so."

A hiatus followed, while Idh interpreted the gist for his
prince and Felimid relayed it to Gudrun.

"If they would continue secret," Gudrun said, "the best
they can do is help us against Urbicus."

"It's that I am about to be saying to them, but whether
they will accept it or not is another matter. Cairbre and
Ogma, do you observe the smile on Vivayn's face? She's
enjoying herself."

"And why not? I captured her once. Yet she takes no
part. Go on, Bragi! You can persuade these folk if any man
can."

Her confidence filled him with pleasure. He said to Idh,
"The *secret* was told me by a simple fisherman, my lord.
That there is a thing or two uncanny about these shoals
appears known to many."

"True," Idh conceded. "Yet that is all they do know, and
they avoid us. The common belief is that once a peopled
town of the earth-folk flourished here, then sank beneath
the sea, and makes phantom appearances to this day. This
is better than having it known that there are peopled isles
here *now*."

"What is it you are avoiding, my lord?" Felimid asked gently. He scrupulously did not say "fear." It wouldn't have been wise, and besides, he was not at all sure the word applied in this situation. He sensed that these Children of Lir had motives he did not yet understand—and which, perhaps, they did not intend for him to understand.

"We avoid the world as it has become. This has been our place since the Narrow Sea was formed, and we hold it. Not with illusion only. Were the Frankish kings to send a fleet against us, we could scatter and sink that fleet. They would not even see us."

The Frankish kings, or another.

"The powers of a Son of the Sea are mighty," Felimid agreed. He accepted the yellow wine a young man poured for him in a delicate, goblet-shaped shell. "They might wither at the touch of dead Rome, though . . . and the dead relics of dead saints of the all-deadening Church. Suppose the Frankish king sent those against you, in the hands of bishops? Now we are not Cross-worshippers, Gudrun Black-hair of Sarnia and I, but we have an enemy who was once a bishop. We've put him to flight, as you'll doubtless be knowing, and we think he has taken refuge with his allies, the spawn of the black depths. However, he may choose to scuttle back to his mother the Church and try to ingratiate himself there. One way would be to betray the secret of these isles, for certainly he knows it. As it's in my mind that you know him."

"Urbicus the wrecker," Idh said at once, his voice freighted with scorn. "Ally with you against him? I can answer you that suggestion. *He* is no threat to the Children of Lir. Not all his wiles can lure our ships or captains to destruction. Nor has he dared to try.

"But there's plenty to interest the pirates of Sarnia in this hall. *They* might be a threat if they knew what is here. So they shall not know."

Felimid did not like the way the conversation was going. He gave Idh his most untroubled, guileless smile and said, "I'd not disturb your peace of mind for gold, my lord, but you have just disturbed mine a bit. You are too late to prevent it. The men of Sarnia do know, and they have their orders in case none of us return. They do not need the bardic sight to perceive this place as it is. They only need numerous mirrors . . . and they can even enlist the aid of bishops if they must."

Idh's beardless, old-eyed features seemed impervious. "So? You may have sentenced the men of Sarnia, one and all, to death. Does it not occur to you that we could ally ourselves, not with you, but with Urbicus and the Cold Ones? Sunlit upper waters or black depths, it's all the same sea, Felimid of Erin."

Felimid's blood thickened in his body. Therefore he wore his face with assurance and said gravely, "I'd not be acting suddenly in your place, my lord Idh. Three hundred spearmen are likely to swarm ashore here inquiring why. As for the Cold Ones, those spawn of darkness, they did little to help Urbicus when we came to Coriallo. I'm thinking they are cowardly or faithless. They may be both! Now none has ever heard of Gudrun Blackhair or the Children of Lir breaking faith, once it was pledged."

"True," Idh acknowledged. "I assure you there will be no hasty dealing here. You will bide among us, that is all. We will see what your sailors in *Ormungandr* do. If they leave for Sarnia, we may well let them go. If they come intruding ashore, blind as they are . . . well, the sea has hidden better bones than theirs. Either way, the prince will decide what happens after that."

"What is he saying, Bragi?" Gudrun asked.

The bard told her, succinctly.

"By Njord of the Ships!" she yelled, flushing. "I'll bide here at their command, will I? While they decide what to do with my men—*my men!* Not Gudrun Blackhair!"

She made three swift steps toward Rothevna. The seaprince sat motionless, calm as a statue. From a corner of one eye, Felimid saw a supple, undulating brown shape dart across the floor. It surged through a booth, up a level to the prince's chair, and seemingly in an instant, Gudrun lay on the floor with an otter big as herself nuzzling her throat. The creature had no air of viciousness; its breath was sweet, as Gudrun was well able to judge, and its whole posture and expression conveyed a nature amiable, cocky, vain, disposed to frolic. It wasn't even showing teeth. However,

Gudrun was fully aware that sharp teeth were there, just
behind the whiskered lip that tickled her throat.

"Suppose we eschew fighting," Idh suggested.

Then the prince spoke, and every other sound in the hall
hushed at once.

"The Son of the Sea wills that your lady be kept apart
from you," Idh said. "Her recklessness may cause trouble.
Also, it's best that you have no reason to speak in Danish—
or Jutish!—which none of us understand. The British tongue
is acceptable, and you are free of the hall so that you do
not forfeit that freedom as she has done."

There didn't seem to be much to say to that, or do about
it. Two men in scaly kilts led Gudrun away, and not until
she was out of sight did Felimid notice that he had dropped
his wine. He was offered more, and took it, scarcely heed-
ing.

VIII

*"Aye, lord," said his men to Matholwch, "set now
a ban on the ships and the ferry-boats and the cor-
acles, so that none may go to Britain, and such as
come hither from Britain, imprison them and let them
not go back, lest this be known." And they determined
on that.*

—The Mabinogion

"We seem to share a predicament each time we meet,"
Vivayn said.

She was and was not as he remembered her. The startling
beauty, combined of a fine-boned perfect oval of a face,
eyes like gray crystals, white skin like a healthy child's, as
fine, fair and smooth, and faintly smiling dark-red lips (all
of these factors united, coordinated and given a theme by
her relentlessly clear intelligence) was unchanged. She had
kept her cool aplomb. Felimid had seen it shaken; but a
knife held at her throat by a demented berserk had been
required to effect that. Certainly she seemed composed now.

What had altered was her detached, remote, indifferent
air. He remembered well how that had intrigued, and an-
noyed, him. True, their first encounter had been brief, and
this was only the second. None the less he sensed a new
force and involvement in her.

"Indeed, princess," he said, responding to her remark.
"But are we precisely sharing one now?"

"I think we are. And what is this matter of titles to me?
We have lain together, and we were even almost killed
together. That ought to confer the freedom to use each
other's names."

"My pleasure, Vivayn."

He ate a morsel of smoking whale's flesh, cooked in a strange sauce. The food varied from fish soup to venison, honey to seaweed, oysters to apples and nuts, with various meats, fruits and relishes the bard did not know at all. Some dishes, such as a whole three-foot octopus cooked in cream, he was glad to ignore. Vivayn availed herself of it cheerfully.

"I heard that you had vanished, and it was in my mind that you'd done so by choice," he continued. "Now I suppose I know how. Cynric is not pleased. He thought perhaps Gudrun was responsible again; I convinced him that she wasn't."

"His honor is involved," Vivayn said sardonically. "Also, my sorcery was useful to him. He will marry some Jutish chieftain's daughter who will give him sons, and be more content with her. And perhaps admit to himself occasionally that he finds her dull.

"Yes, the Children of Lir aided me to leave Vectis. I wanted to be taken to Lesser Britain. I have kin there. I thought the sureties I gave and received were enough to guarantee that they would keep faith; but as you see, they haven't." Vivayn looked around the hall, with its jewels, carvings, frescoes, and golden seals rolling on the floor instead of dogs. A naked, yellow-haired girl of two years rode one, squealing gleefully. The prisoner's clear gaze returned to Felimid. "Well," she said, "I have been wrong before."

"You're taking it calmly!"

"No, Felimid. I'm taking it in very bad part indeed." The pure voice hummed like a harp-string lightly plucked. "I mean to let my gentle, beloved hosts know it in due course, too. I didn't escape from the Jutish kingdom in order to be constrained by others. However... there's little to be gained by open display of anger. It didn't achieve very much for Gudrun."

Felimid risked a quick sentence in the Jutish tongue. "Working together, we can leave here... perhaps. But Gudrun comes too."

"Naturally," Vivayn said, in the British Celtic dialect they had been speaking. "And there are others whom you know. Here, Eldrida, see who has arrived."

Eldrida, too? Yes, it was she of the yellow braids and deep-breasted, sumptuous body, Vivayn's close friend and companion in mischief, and the gods knew how she had been able to keep Vivayn's secrets for years, for reticence wasn't in her. The narrowness of her gray-green eyes was purely a matter of the configuration of her eyelids, not an acquired sign of calculation or suspicion. She sat laughing on the bard's knee and kissed him warmly.

"Felimid of Erin! Yes, Vivayn, I had heard he was here, and Gudrun also! And captive like us? Well. It might be worse."

She winked at him. Clearly she was not reconciled to staying either. She slid the pleasant rounded weight of her bottom off his lap and sat more decorously beside him. She wore a gown of strawberry wool, broidered on the neck, sleeves and hem with yarn of a darker red, and fawn hose under it, as the bard had seen when he glimpsed her ankles. Sitting at his left, Vivayn went similarly dressed, though her gown was worked with twisting, intertwining Celtic patterns, black and two shades of blue; and she also wore a sable cloak lined with priceless pearl-gray silk.

The white-skinned folk of Rothevna's hall wore little more than the naked child romping with the seal. Sandals and scaly kilt for the men, two oblongs of fabric clasped on the shoulders and belted at the waist for the women, appeared to suffice them. Clearly they were not as susceptible to cold as their prisoner-guests.

Vivayn seemed to follow the trend of Felimid's thought. "They can stay in the sea for hours at a time," she said. "Olcain once swam along the bottom of a lagoon while I counted my ten fingers over. And over, and over. When he surfaced I had done fifty times and once, and he was not gasping."

"Any of us must have come up desperate in half the time," Eldrida averred. "And chilled blue, in this season." She looked at the yellow-haired child on the hall's sunken floor. "As Nye will be, if I don't put some clothes on her. And I don't suppose that seal is good-natured without limit. By your leave, Felimid? I'll soon be back."

She vanished, to snatch up the girl in a manner none who had ever lived in a family could mistake.

"Eldrida's daughter?"

"A sharp guess. She has a son some fifteen months older, and he is here too. She would not leave them; I would not leave her. She would have been the first one questioned when I took my leave."

"Yes," Felimid said, remembering. "Little Glinthi would have seen to that if no other did. He has no particular hatred for you, I think, but he'd greatly enjoy seeing Cerdic lose his one legitimate son. He'd gladly set Cynric close upon your tail in hopes of that happening."

"True. At least I've averted that. I don't wish Cynric to die, although I would shed no tears for his father. And Cynric would surely die if he came seeking me *here*. As surely as would Gudrun's men. No, the tack you followed with Prince Rothevna, that your foe—Urbicus?—may be a danger because he was once a bishop, was the most promising. Although I think even that will not persuade him."

Vivayn considered a space, gazing into some airy distance, resting her side-tilted face in her open hand, the heel of that hand fitting neatly under her jaw, the slim index finger swiftly tapping her temple.

She emerged from her reverie. "You might strengthen it thus. Say to the prince that Cynric is hunting me. It's a thing he knows to be true. Suggest that Urbicus might go to him, armed with the news that you, Gudrun and I are here, and seek to make Cynric his cat's-paw. It's by no means impossible. Cynric's sea-wolves combined with the Church's power would make a mighty danger."

"With Urbicus the go-between? H'mm, a notion. He might even dare, although Cynric would rather grease his ship's spine with a wrecker's blood than ally with him. Any seaman would, as I have been learning. But to find you . . ."

"Try. It cannot do harm."

It did no harm. However, it did no good in the sense of bringing them any closer to departing the isles of the Children of Lir. Felimid was not able to speak before the prince again. The old counsellor, Idh, did listen to him, and even agreed in a guarded way that it might be best for the Children

of Lir to trace the defeated wrecker and make an end of
him, lest he threaten their camouflage. Yet for the same
reason, Felimid and Gudrun must remain.

Prisoners for life? the bard thought. *However long, or
short that may be? No, old man. Assuredly no. I'm with
Vivayn in that.*

When Eldrida returned, it was Vivayn who risked a brief
word in Jutish, which their . . . hosts . . . had forbidden. "I
will speak to you later tonight, though I do not come near
you," she said. "You are a bard, but of which degree? Have
you the secret of the Three Strains?"

"I'm proficient," he assured her, low-voiced. He did not
ask how she would speak to him without coming near him.
He knew. Like her, he understood air magic.

"Show us before the night is out," Eldrida begged. "You
must have some new songs. You caught Tosti Fenrir's-get
at last, I heard. Word has it that you've been setting the
north by the ears, too."

"That we have!" Felimid helped her turn the talk to ordinary matters with a silent blessing upon her. "The red
dwarves, the Obodrites and the Danes will all remember us
long. I'm making Gudrun's saga, and while it's nowhere
near completion, in the meantime . . ."

He made opportunity to sing it before long; not the saga,
or even part of it, but a rousing ale-song that he had made
that first night back in Sarnia. Gudrun's pirates had been
delighted by it. He sang it now in defiance, making the
harp-strings crash and ring, raising his voice to the high
roof, hoping Gudrun heard and that her spirits were lifted.

> "Oh, Gudrun's out again, mannies,
>   And Gudrun's word is law,
>   And Gudrun Blackhair's the bravest chief
>   That ever the green sea saw!

> "Jarl Ivarr held her once, mannies,
>   And that was ill for him;
>   She drove a spearhead through his lights
>   Across the red shield's rim.

"So pour the ale that Gudrun gives
And drink to Gudrun's fame,
Then follow the black wings and crimson sail,
And glory to Gudrun's name!

"Aye, drink her health in ale, mannies,
And drink her health in wine,
For Gudrun's friends are all my friends,
And Gudrun's foes are mine!"

Some of the Children of Lir laughed, and some frowned, and a few cheered. Vivayn said ironically, "Bravo!" but Eldrida leaned across, bright-eyed, and fisted him encouragingly in the ribs.

A bard of the sea-folk came forward. His harp-frame was of sea ivory, the strings gut, and he played like the waves, the restless changing tides, the swift currents of the bright upper sea itself. He played the seasons that come and go in the sea as on the land. And then he played the black, unchanging depths, forever dark and silent, yet fertile with the silt of ages raining from above, and equally able to well up from below to nourish . . . or defile . . . the sunlit surface. And Felimid understood what Idh had said about it all being one ocean.

He would have matched that music with gifts of his own, gifts from forest, field, mountain and river, but one sharp warning kick from Vivayn deterred him. *Let them think you fit only to praise chiefs to order,* the kick said. Felimid had to admit that was the better tactic, hard though it was to feign being an ineffectual twanger and mouthpiece.

I promise you a true demonstration of what I can do later, Children of Lir . . .

IX

The graceful drake does not sleep,
he makes ready to swim,
he has neither rest nor sleep, here,
in his refuge he does not sleep.
—Duanaire Finn

Felimid lay under a down quilt, resting as did the Children of Lir, in one of the partitioned booths around the circumference of the hall. He rested but did not sleep, and his harp was placed nearby. He hadn't removed either breeches or buskins.

He went over it again in his mind. Gudrun was somewhere above, in or near the prince's big sleeping chamber that was also his sun-parlor, with its astounding glass windows. He'd have to bring her down to the hall, then. He'd also have to get their swords from the foreroom. *That* was surely guarded; one went through it to the main doors. Then they would have to reach *Ormungandr,* for there was absolutely no other hope of escaping pursuit by the ships of the Children of Lir.

Ormungandr would be closely watched, of course, for just that reason, if the Children of Lir had more intelligence than hens.

He remembered his escape from King Oisc's dun with the British girl Regan. He'd contrived that without using magic, because the Kentishmen had none either. Had he been forced to use his bardic powers against such yokels, he'd have thought he was positively lowering himself. But the Children of Lir were beings of magic themselves, and only magic could open a way out of their stronghold.

Luckily, he had it—and Vivayn had more.

"Felimid."

The voice spoke softly in the void air by his head.

"Vivayn."

He had never learned how to work air magic in quite this way; nevertheless, he grasped at once how it was done. Speech was carried through air. An air sprite, invisible and bodiless, could produce speech without lungs or tongue at the behest of a subtle sorceress.

Vivayn evidently thought—or was gambling—that this kind of air magic would prove too subtle for the Children of Lir to be aware of it. Certainly they could work air magic, unlike the water-breathing sea demons. At least, some of them could. The illusion which veiled their islands showed that. Yet its large extent and perennial nature made it simpler to create than Vivayn's glamours, which although smaller and briefer were far more finely detailed—and generally had to move about.

"You must harp slumber on the hall. Then Rothevna's chamber. I won't succumb—and I'll warn Gudrun, for she must be wakeful."

"Eldrida?" the bard whispered. "Her children?"

The sprite carried his words to Vivayn swiftly as a breeze, and brought hers back to him, freighted with humor.

"Away. I warned her to leave the hall, and they are with her. Now I speak to Gudrun, and that is the dangerous part! I'll give you word when I have convinced her. If I do."

Felimid waited, sweating. Vivayn might believe that speaking to Gudrun was the dangerous part; he would have disputed her if there had been time for debate! He reached for his harp. Touching the worn leather bag which contained her gave him confidence.

They misjudged when they parted me from a sword but left me you, Cairbre's darling.

Sooner than he had expected, the incorporeal voice spoke to him again. "She believes, Felimid; her ears are soundly stopped. You may begin."

The bard felt sudden mistrust. "She believed? So swiftly? A voice from nowhere?"

"It was *your* voice, my friend. I bade the sprite assume

it. I thought that would save time." The cool undertone
heated then, humanly distressed and urgent. "Hurry! Do
you suppose me unaware that I'll never leave these isles if
Gudrun does not? She won't lie still with her ears stopped
all night long!"

No. Gudrun Blackhair was no model of patience. Felimid
drew Golden Singer from the harp-bag. Her metal strings
gleamed. Quietly, he rolled out of his pallet, bare to the
waist but fully clad below it. He listened to the sleepers
around him. They breathed as they ought.

He glanced at the drapes of sea-spider silk that curtained
the booth. Light filtered gently through from the central part
of the hall. He saw and heard nothing—which he supposed
proved only that the sea-man who guarded him knew his
task.

Felimid played. He touched the strings so lightly at first
that the strain was a bare breath of sound. It was the heart
of a warm dark night, the touch of fur, oil smoothed into
tired muscles, the effect of rare wine; it was sleep. It spread
through the booth, seeped past the drapes. Outside, there
was a soft rattle as something fell, and a kind of rolling
thump as something else went down more slowly.

Within the booths, the Children of Lir had fallen into a
deeper slumber which nothing would break until dawn. Just
beyond the drapes, Felimid stepped over a fallen purple-
haired youth muscled like an orca, with his dropped spear
beside him. Felimid didn't doubt that the youth could have
driven it all the way through his body, granted the chance.

The luminescent yellow lanterns still glowed. They
showed the central space of the hall to be empty of guards
or other presences. Even the golden seals had gone. Felimid
left the spear where it lay and walked once around the
circumference of the hall, playing the sleep strain. When
he reached the inner door of the foreroom, he stood there
for some moments, sending the soporific, irresistible music
through the panels. Muffled sliding, rattling noises came
back to him, to his delight. He passed on.

A structure of pale orange wood, part ladder, part stair,
led to the prince's quarters above the hall. Felimid mounted
it. Deeply absorbed in playing the enchanted strain (as he

had to be to play it at all), he could not watch his back or protect himself. He simply had to risk a thrown spear from someone who had avoided the effect of his music.

Two spear-bearing guards toppled. Two lovers couching in an alcove fell swiftly asleep in each other's arms, neither one would feel complimented when they awoke. Even the bard felt somewhat ashamed, though it was surely a tribute to his power. Lastly the great figure of Rothevna, Son of the Sea, lay motionless on his bed, breathing slowly.

The bard found Gudrun in another alcove. Vivayn had dealt honestly. Gudrun sat straight-backed upright, with soft cloth crammed into her ears and her hands pressed over them. When the bard appeared, with strangeness and distance still in his eyes from playing the slumber-strain, she promptly took them away.

"Bragi?"

"I'm all right, my dear. Think of me as a little bit drunk." He smiled from his far place of the mind. "Or as though I've just been struck a fair blow on the jaw. It will pass. Now it's time that we went away."

She stared at him, awed. And Gudrun Blackhair was not easily awed. "You mean we can? With such ease?"

"We can," Vivayn assured her from beyond the alcove, "though not quite with ease. It is going to be done with vast effort, alas."

"You!" Gudrun stood, bare to the waist as her lover was, smoothly beautifully, formidably muscled under the tidy layer of woman-fat which smoothed her outlines.

"I!" Vivayn agreed. Her detached, imperturbable air had vanished. She was alive, determined and attending nothing less than essentials. "With my help Felimid came this far, but I think none of us will go much further unless we take him for a hostage."

She indicated Rothevna with a gesture involving her whole arm and a flowerlike opening of her hand towards the sea-prince's bed.

The pirate saw the worth of that suggestion at once. Ransom, hostages, sureties given and received; these were the everyday measures of her trade. "Yes, by Njord and Ull! He will have to walk. Can you waken him?"

"Nothing will wake him before sunrise," Felimid said, "or any of those who heard my slumber-strain. Nothing. He must be carried or stay here."

"Carried?" Gudrun glanced at the huge, inert form. "I suppose we can do it if we must. To the harbor?"

"Not there, if I may guide you." Vivayn's eyes shone like light-gray crystals. "To the eastern shore of the island. That is about half a mile. Eldrida and her children are there, near two large rocks rising out of the water. Can you mimic a shearwater's cry? She will know you come from me, then."

"And then what?" Gudrun demanded. "We must get aboard *Ormungandr* with him, not lug him across the isle to sit on the shore pretending to be birds."

"On the contrary," Vivayn said. "*Ormungandr* is watched closely, by those ships you know of but cannot see except by reflection. Your men may leave so long as they depart without you. They won't wait much longer, and *you* could never get aboard unseen. But I can. Then *Ormungandr* will depart, and gather you all on the way."

"My men would not take orders or even a suggestion from you."

"Ah," Vivayn countered, "but they will not be taking them from *me*. Tell her, Felimid."

"She can assume your appearance, *mo chridh*," he said, "and give commands in your voice. She has taken Eldrida's semblance before now, and put her own upon Eldrida, when she desired to come and go unremarked, in Westri."

"Pretend to be *me?*" Gudrun said, amazed by the effrontery of it.

"Forget your pride or we're all undone," Felimid said. "We must have Rothevna, we cannot take him aboard *Ormungandr* where the ship lies now, and only you and I together have the strength to carry him elsewhere. Therefore Vivayn must substitute for you to the men. She will guide the ship well. Illusions can't deceive her, remember."

"I can scarcely play you false, if that is what you are thinking," Vivayn added. "My false appearance will leave me at sunrise. If the real Gudrun Blackhair is not among them by then, your pirates will have much to say to the spurious one."

"They would that!" Gudrun considered a moment. "Eld-rida . . . you would not desert her, either. But there's more to being Gudrun Blackhair than a semblance and a voice, princess. You must have the power in you to back it. Can you take command and give orders that my edgy, suspicious killers will *obey?*"

"If I cannot, I have wasted the past four years, between me and God! My husband's men are no cooing doves. Who do you suppose gave commands on Vectis each summer, of necessity, when Cynric was away marauding? I could not do it at first, and so I had to learn, that was all. I have also learned to know one end of a ship from another . . . I'll bring your men to you. Just tell me the names of the most important ones and what they look like."

"All right, done!"

"Not quite so fast. I set a price upon my help. I desire," said Vivayn, "that you take us to Aleth in Lesser Britain, set us ashore safely, and keep silent about it thereafter so that Cynric cannot find us."

"Done!" Gudrun repeated. "Not let us *move!*"

"Certainly." Vivayn flitted ahead. Gudrun dragged on her other garments, then helped her lover lift, drag and manhandle the sea-prince into the hall below, once almost falling into it instead.

Panting, they crossed to the doors of the foreroom.

"Our swords are there yet, I think," Felimid said, letting Rothevna sink to the floor. "There were guards . . . I harped them to asleep."

"I must believe you," Gudrun answered. "None the less, I am naked without a weapon." She looked about. Seeing the prone youth who had been Felimid's watchman, she possessed herself of his spear. "So! Now open the doors, my man."

Felimid opened the doors.

Two armed warriors burst through them.

Vivayn did the best thing she could possibly have done, with no fighting skills and no time to employ magic. She cast herself on the floor, rolling into the legs of the foremost warrior so that he stumbled over her.

Felimid's only weapons were those he'd been born own-

ing. He locked his hands together and smashed them down
hard on the warrior's neck. He rolled over, dazed, but none
the less beginning to rise at once. Felimid kicked him in
the middle. The warrior dropped his spear and raised his
shield with both hands to ward himself against a third blow.
Felimid barely pulled it in time to avoid breaking bones on
the forged green metal. Then they were tussling on their
knees for possession of the small, highly maneuverable
shield, a deadly weapon in its own right.

Someone uttered a high, whistling shriek. The other sea-
man went slowly to his knees, Gudrun's spearhead in his
body, tearing his liver; down, eyes starting, mouth locked,
fighting his death each slow inch of the way, but sinking.
Gudrun tore her weapon ruthlessly out of his flesh. He made
a low, indescribable noise and fell on his side, curling up
in his agony. Gudrun stared, fascinated, for death and killing
had always fascinated her. Then she finished the man cleanly,
with a quick deep thrust in the throat, and shook herself.

Felimid was having some trouble with his own adversary.
When Gudrun's red spearhead kissed the man's throat, the
trouble ended. Vivayn grasped the other spear, the one which
had fallen, and menaced him for the other side. The bard
rose.

"I think you are taken," he said to the white-skinned
warrior. "Will you die now or live a little longer?"

"Live," the warrior said. "If I can without betrayal."

"A little indignity . . . at worst. We will not refuse some
help in carrying the prince."

The warrior thought about it, and nodded.

They found six other warriors in the foreroom, all asleep,
none stirring. Eight men had been stationed there nightlong
lest the outsiders should try to escape; a tribute to Gudrun's
reputation, as she said with real pleasure. Their spears lay
fallen at random like a game of spillikens. Evidently two
had been quick-witted enough to cover their ears and keep
them covered at the first sound of Golden Singer's music.

"Here are our swords," Felimid said.

Where sailors are, even sailors of a faerie race, there is
always cord and rope. In the foreroom they found various
short coils of it, beside folded hammocks neatly stowed on

shelves. They lashed the fallen spears together to make one strong pole, and dangled Rothevna from it cocooned in a hammock. Their prisoner took one end of the pole; Gudrun made a neck-leash for him and held that.

They had closed the inner doors on the ugly sight of the dead man lying just beyond them. Only now did Felimid consider that he was half-naked, for he had been somewhat busy. He stripped a tunic of scaly leather from one of the sleeping warriors, drew it on and then availed himself of one of the thick mantles hanging in the foreroom. So covered, he opened the outer doors.

They paused in the cover of some trees while Vivayn, in a short colloquy with Gudrun, obtained the information she had wanted and repeated it back to be sure she would not make mistakes. Then she moved towards the harbor. The prisoner was taken aback when the others started in a different direction. Gudrun said to him, poison-sweetly, "Shout an alarm if it pleases you."

He didn't.

Moving through the sparse autumn woods in the dark, bearing the senseless Rothevna while mist and drizzle blurred the world to nothing mere yards off, would have been a wretched business had not Felimid and Gudrun's spirits been so high. For their prisoner, it doubtless was. He stumbled, and muttered things in his own ancient language.

Felimid carried the forward end of the pole. He fully trusted Gudrun to control the sea-warrior. The fellow was probably obedient more from a deliberate choice to go with his helpless prince than from any fear of the strangers, but if he should change his mind and be foolish—why, Rothevna would fall with a jolt, and a swift killing later, Gudrun would clean her sword, sheathe it, and shoulder the burden.

In daylight they could have tramped the distance, carrying Rothevna in half an hour. In the wet night, on an island to which they were strangers, it took them about two. Then they hogtied their prisoner beside his prince and spent some time searching up and down the invisible shore making shearwater cries. At last Eldrida answered them—and with a much better imitation of the bird.

She welcomed Felimid with a hug and a warm, sensual

kiss, then welcomed Gudrun in the same way—which supported guesses the bard had already made.

"Where is Vivayn?" Eldrida asked then.

"Did she not tell you?"

"Vivayn? Gods! You know her! Or maybe you do not. She was a league above the earth and thinking swifter than the wind blows. She told me to go from the hall with the kids, and to wait here." Eldrida sneezed. "Not even to expect you, though it's what I did half expect, once I'd thought upon it. Where is Vivayn, though? Don't you know either?"

"We're hoping that she's giving orders aboard *Ormungandr,* in Gudrun's form," Felimid answered.

"Huh!" Gudrun said loudly.

"I'm hoping it, so," Felimid amended. "Gudrun is offended by the notion. None the less, that's the plan. *Ormungandr* should be by here before morning to take us from this shore."

"I don't like it here," complained the little girl, Nye. Stoical, or bashful, the boy remained silent.

"I don't like it overmuch either, lass," Eldrida soothed. "Just you be good and stay, and tomorrow we'll ride on a great ship."

"Don't want a ship!"

"Oh, Frey's big prick!" Eldrida said, exasperated, as Nye clung to her skirted leg like a wet puppy.

Felimid smiled and shook his head in sympathy. It was always so. These were the things his kind left out of the hero-tales. You schemed cleverly, you worked magic, you spilled life-blood, and instead of an immediate dashing escape or a tragic defeat at odds of thousands to one, you found yourself kicking your heels on a wet dark shore with a snotty toddler complaining to you.

Over Nye's querulous bitching, he told Eldrida the story.

"Will *Ormungandr* get away?" she asked at last. "There are ships with Children of Lir in them, watching yours."

"The crews have instructions to let Gudrun's men leave without her, if they decide to. Vivayn was confident she could reach the ship, and if she's wrong, we can do nothing. We have to leave that part to her."

"Aye, aye," Eldrida said impatiently. "I'd wager on Vivayn, too! But when *Ormungandr* does go from the lagoon, the watchers will take word to the hall at once, and they'll find—what?"

"The entire hall in enchanted sleep, one man's dead slain corpse with crimson upon it and red, and their prince vanished," Felimid said, growing more thoughtful with each item he declared. "Yes. They will not just sit clucking their tongues and saying one to another, *well, is not this passing strange?* They'll be after *Ormungandr* like the Fenians after deeds of honor, so."

"And after us!" Eldrida said.

"Then talk less," Gudrun hissed. "Although I think they will do no land-tracking in this wet."

"In any case," Felimid said, "we have Rothevna." With blatant bravado he sat down on the hammock-wrapped figure. "If they find us, we can just hold a sword to his throat and ask them what they plan to do about it. Don't cry, little one. Come share my cloak and I'll tell you a story while we wait for this miserable rain to stop."

Thus he passed the time until *Ormungandr* came gliding out of the fog, the eyes of the serpent-head glowing as though they could indeed see through mist and rain and the barriers between worlds, as men and the dwarves who made it said. And when Felimid hailed the ship he was answered in the voice of the woman who stood beside him.

X

*And there and then, as soon as he came to the
sea he received the sea's nature, and swam as well
as the best fish in the sea.*

—The Mabinogion

The long room had been swept clean of dust. Cobwebs
remained, shrouding the corners and angles of the ceiling.
Smoke from the charcoal braziers dimmed everything; the
rows of straw pallets, the scattered gear, the pirates honing,
mending, greasing or inspecting their weapons.

Gudrun sat on a stool, eyeing Prince Rothevna. The sea-
prince stood, indifferent to the cloak wrapped around his
nakedness and to the hostage-fetters he wore. His companion captive, Lhidaig, stood behind him in similar chains,
for since Gudrun had said that his prince must wear them,
he had demanded them too.

Felimid stood beside Gudrun to interpret.

Vivayn and Eldrida sat nearby, on a dilapidated couch.

"If we restore you to your folk," Felimid said to the
prince, "we must have your oath that you will do nothing
and allow nothing which might prevent our safe return to
Sarnia. That is the least we will accept for your freedom."

"For a man of my standing, it is too little," Rothevna
said, through Lhidaig. "No ransom?"

"Any treasures of your island would cause a deal of talk,"
Felimid told him. "I had not thought you would care for
that. Take it as a courtesy—between allies, or between
enemies, as you will."

Rothevna smiled. So did Lhidaig.

"I swear, then. I swear none shall molest you while you return to Sarnia, by my command, or by my sanction, or by my instigation, or that I have power to prevent. And if I come against you later to destroy you, I will send you word in advance. I swear by Lir."

"Free them," Gudrun said.

The hostage-fetters rattled and clanked on the floor.

"We'll depart, then," Lhidaig declared, "and in the islands there will be praise for the lady of Sarnia's fairness."

"You will depart . . . how?"

"The ships which followed from the Veiled Isles are still there, yonder. If they are not, we can swim all the way. It's no more than seven leagues, and we are Children of Lir."

Gudrun shook her crow-black head in wonder. "The choice is your own, but you need not be in haste. Eat first, if you like."

"Thanks, lady. We prefer to go now. It is not your hospitality we mislike," he said, straight-faced, "but this town. And the tide will not wait."

Felimid appreciated that. This sleazy place with its cobwebs and mildewed stucco had once been a house where people lived; now it was a place where strangers camped. Much of the town was better, much of it was no better, and none of it was what it had been when Rome was all-powerful. Yet for himself and the Children of Lir, it was worse because the very stones of the place were a substance in which no magic could flourish. That was the way of Rome. As well hope to grow wheat in the brown sea-sand.

From courtesy, Gudrun and Felimid walked out with the pair. Aleth stood on a small promontory at the very mouth of the Rance. The estuary stretched south for miles, now at slack water. Soon the tide would come in.

Rothevna chose a spot below which the water was still deep, and threw off his borrowed mantle as gladly as he had the shackles. His huge tattooed body struck the water with scarcely a splash, and Lhidaig followed. The brown head and the green broke surface again, briefly, then disappeared. Felimid did not see them again, though he could picture them sliding through the cold autumn waters, out around the tiny offshore island, out and out to where the ships rode on the sea, waiting, unseen by common mortal eyes. Perhaps they would rise now and again to sport like dolphins in the joy of their freedom.

"It is done now," Gudrun said, looking fruitlessly after the pair. "Yet perhaps I should have killed them."

"Nothing could have been worse," Felimid assured her. "Their people would surely have sought revenge then, whatever they do now. And not their people alone; I said it to you, and Vivayn said it."

So they had. "Son of the Sea" was more than a title, borne by certain lords and chiefs among the race of Lir. It was a magical truth. Manannan had been called Son of the Sea. The British godling Dylan had been known as Son of the Sea and Son of the Waves, and those waves had beaten ever since in anguish and fury against the shore where he had received his death from the hand of his uncle. The Sons of the Sea were loved dearly by the wild, surging, inchoate power which fathered them, and if Rothevna had been killed and Felimid had had aught to do with it, he would have wished to be a long way inland before the prince breathed his last.

They returned to the crumbling house. Aleth's walls and gates were as badly kept, so that a dozen places offered easy ingress. Its site was its best defense now. Twenty-odd pirates could swagger there as they pleased. Certainly they were hard men, with a noted leader, but two hundred years before, they would have walked softly or ended on crosses.

"Aegir and Njord be my witnesses, it is good that we are not raiding this place!" Gudrun said. "This estuary might kill even *Ormungandr* if it were hostile and I timed the tide wrongly. We are here for another half day as it is."

Even Felimid could see that. They had come to Aleth at the top of the tide and run *Ormungandr* ashore; now it was low water, with the serpent-ship thoroughly aground, but that should not matter. Gudrun had never done harm in Aleth. It was friendly, like the Channel Islands. She never sacked or plundered her immediate neighbors. The razing of Coriallo had been a special case at which few were likely to take real offense.

"There is still Urbicus," she mused.

In the unkempt house, they passed Eldrida talking with one of Gudrun's pirates, the Saxon named Hemming. He grinned; she laughed. The yellow heads bent towards each other, and his scarred arm slipped around her waist.

"He's making swift way," Gudrun commented.

"I'd say they both are."

Vivayn's hair was alight in the smoky camping-room. "The mermen have gone back to the sea?" she queried. "Not a satisfying business, unless for Eldrida and me. You did not get what you wanted from them, and they could not hold you."

"That is to be seen," Gudrun said. "We may have made a better impression than you think. I have shown my strength, and kept my word by letting them go free. What they do now is up to them. True enough, though, you are the only clear gainers! You are now where you wished to be. What will you do next?"

"Leave Aleth, I think. Some prosperous place much further inland would suit me better. Rothevna may decide to come back and collect me; the season would be a small barrier to him. There is also Cynric, though I need not await him before the spring, now."

She did not say, *There is even you.* Vivayn did not like to be rude, or obvious.

She spoke privately with the bard before they left. Gudrun was snatching a few hours' rest, and the Celtic language of Britain amounted to a secret tongue for the two of them, among Gudrun's pirates.

"Rothevna's fiercely secret," he remarked. "Would you be knowing why?"

"Most would suppose he does not want his islands taken and his folk dispossessed."

"Ah, Vivayn," he said. "You are playing. I know you know better. That's for children of earth like us. The clans of the sea-people never fought our ancestors for land, and they don't live on land or become attached to it in the way we do. Yet Rothevna's folk have lived on the Veiled Isles for generations, holding them jealously. I ask myself, why?"

"Can you answer yourself?"

"They retreated before the iron of the Sun-worshippers

much as the Danann did. Some at least passed through Gates
into other worlds. Maybe Rothevna's clan conceals and
guards such a Gate for the kindred on the other side of it."

"That might be."

"I did see things in Rothevna's hall which scarcely seemed
of *this* world. The timber stair leading to his chamber, now;
that wasn't made of any familiar wood. The windows of
his sun-parlor couldn't be made by an craftsmen I know.
Maybe in Rome . . . or maybe not even there." Felimid had
no definite knowledge of Rome. To him it meant tyranny
and the spreading death of magic, yet also, paradoxically,
it was a synonym for marvels. "This tunic I wear could be
dragon-leather, but not from any British dragon, and not, I
am thinking from any dragon that prowls known oceans—
though there I'm willing to be corrected. The mosaics and
murals had scenes in them I'd swear were other worldly. I
find enough there for more than a cautious might-be, Vivayn."

"I agree," she said. "I was trying you. That's close ob-
servation and reasoning for a single night."

"You were there for two months," he said, showing a
lure.

Vivayn refused it. "Now that I'm free, I find that I'd
sooner not speak of them. However . . . what sort of speaking do you think you will do to Gudrun?"

"I think," he answered judiciously, "that I'll say no words
at all which might incite her to rush back to the Veiled Isles.
That would be to press her luck. If Rothevna's secret is
what I've surmised, and he were to learn that Gudrun knows
it, I suspect he'd take it ill. He's giving some thought to
making war upon Sarnia as matters stand. And of course I
do not *know.*"

"Of course you don't."

Vivayn said it very well, eschewing any blatant ironies
of expression or an improbably demure tone. She added:

"This is the second time you have done me a considerable
favor, Felimid—or is it Bragi, now? Call upon me to repay
it if ever there is need. I mean to be very difficult to find
for any other, but a message of yours I will hear."

"That was outright stiff! It wouldn't be that your pride

hates to be indebted? Vivayn, I know that you'll repay if required, and I will take a favor from you when I'm needing one. But it gripes me to leave you and Eldrida here with two children and only the clothes on your backs. Will you at least take some gold from me? It's in my mind that you would drink poison, turn blue and die before asking for it."

"Exaggeration. I will take it with the grace a true king's daughter should show while seizing gold with both hands. You're generous . . . Bragi. I thank you."

Outside, the mighty, hammering tide of the region drove into the Rance, surging up the estuary until the steep banks quivered. Eastward, the waves broke along the wet granite shore only less strongly, and clouds pressed low over a vast rainy woodland.

XI

"She's got more lives than Hell has devils," Hugibert snarled.

"Just one, like any mortal," Pascent said.

"You say?" The Frank wiped remnants of food out of his fair moustache with the back of a large hand. Then he drank some ale, replacing the grease and crumbs with a crescent of foam. "She came back from that northern voyage when we thought she'd die. And she should have. Any reasonable soul would have. She went against Urbicus, and she should have died then, too. We—"

"Quiet!"

"Quiet?" Hugibert looked coldly at the erstwhile trader. "I'm not your dog, to shut my mouth when you tell me. Nobody's about. Your nerve failing?"

"I'm not the one who says the bitch is unkillable, you are." Pascent returned the Frank's pale-eyed stare with a resentfully hot one. "What's more, I want to see her dead as much as you. I'm not going to serve a madwoman all my days. Give me a decent merchant ship again and I'll be back to my proper trade."

"While she's alive, you daren't break your oath to her." Hugibert nodded. The honey-colored autumn light slanted through cracks in the boat-house wall, striping his face and arm. "She doesn't look like dying so far. We sent a warning to that wrecker dog, Urbicus, so that he'd know she was coming and be ready for her, with allies, weapons and sorcery, and finish her off for us, and what happened? We didn't guess she'd attack from the landward side, through those hills, so she surprised him anyway! Now she's off talking to mermen, and they may not destroy her either. I'm telling you, Pascent, the man who wants her dead is going to have to slay her himself."

"Not surrounded by three hundred men who would tear you in pieces for it—supposing you had the luck to go that swiftly."

"I'm not a fool. In a sea-fight or a shore battle, though, who's to know what hand struck which blow?"

Now it was Pascent's turn to nod. Slowly, he did so, while pouring more ale from the jug placed between them on a thwart.

"It's chancy, though, comrade. That mail of Blackhair's is the best. You'd have to chop off a leg below her wear-shirt to be sure of killing her. Of ending her captaincy, anyhow." He spat into the far shadows of the boat-house. "She's the kind of spoiled, glorious idiot who might well suicide if crippled, too. The idea's good, but you won't have a chance to put it into effect until the spring. Coriallo was our last raid for the year, and none is likely to come against Sarnia in this season."

"Unless it's Urbicus," the Frank said grimly. "He will be sure we deceived him."

"Aye, Urbicus. Him with his stinking fish! We will have to fight him like the rest if he comes."

"I don't mind that," Hugibert growled. "I'd *rather* fight him. But Blackhair . . . the lady . . . she overreaches. It's not right." A note of honest complaint entered his voice. "That northern voyage, then Coriallo, now the seafolk. If she finds them, she'll bring them down on us. It's always something new, like that voyage to Erin years ago, or that other one far south of Spain itself. Were she content with just raiding in the waters she knows, she'd spend fewer lives. She'll be the end of us all if someone doesn't stop her."

"True." Pascent rubbed his chin thoughtfully. "I am glad I didn't go into the north with her. Forty Goths she took

along, all stout fighters by the looks of them, and how many
did she bring back alive? About a dozen."

"I don't mind that. A good Goth is a dead one. It will
be Franks next time, though, like as not."

"No, that we'll prevent. *What was that?*"

He spoke the last three words in a tone so low they barely
reached Hugibert's ear. Then he went on talking, casual,
cheery stuff, even as he gestured at the open boat-house
door. Hugibert grinned unpleasantly, and went stooping towards the bows of the winter-housed ship while Pascent
nattered. Once in a while the Gaul answered himself, with
a taciturn grunt or a mumble, sustaining the conversation
alone.

Hugibert was quiet, although not furtive about swinging
down to the boat-house floor. Best to behave as though
nothing was wrong, for nothing might be. Outside, sunlight
was breaking through heavy cloud, and—by Merovech's
tomb!—someone was crouched against the boat-house wall,
listening.

It was Abalaric.

Hugibert's blood chilled. Abalaric, of all men! He was
Gudrun's cupbearer, whose sight had been destroyed when
a mainland lord captured him. Gudrun had avenged him,
and then given him an honored post and a living. He worshipped Gudrun Blackhair as he had never worshipped God,
and he owned the sharpest ears on Sarnia. Save maybe for
that damned bard's . . .

Hugibert cast a quick glance around him. Then he rushed
at the sightless man. He slipped and scrambled once on the
way. Abalaric heard, rose to flee, and was caught before
he'd gone two yards. Hugibert seized him by the throat;
Abalaric twisted free.

"You treacherous offal—!" he gasped.

Hugibert shoved him sprawling, then kicked his head
murderously. The cupbearer rolled over, stunned for a moment. Hugibert knelt astride him, gripped his chin in both
hands, and dragged his victim' s head up, up, backwards,
throwing all the power of his tattooed arms and body into
it. He vented a sharp grunt of effort as Abalaric's neck
cracked. The cupbearer's last breath rattled and bubbled in

his throat. Then he was quiet for all time.

Pascent left the boat-house, hand close to his knife-hilt, the half-obscured sun shining innocently on his russet hair and bold-featured face. He stopped short when he saw the huddled corpse.

"Christus!" he said.

"I had to do it," Hugibert growled. "He was listening— heard it all, surely. Blackhair would've heeded him, and he'd have told her, too, short of death shutting his lips. What now?"

"Huh." Pascent thought swiftly. "Did you use steel?"

"No. I broke his neck, as you see."

Pascent clapped the Frank on the shoulder. "Good man! He fell, then, something he might easily do—but from where?"

"Down the path yonder? It's steep enough."

They carried the luckless cupbearer a short way up the path, then allowed him to fall. He came to rest in a convincingly natural position, battered and sandy. Hugibert chuckled.

"He's well served for spying! He was only a Goth anyhow. Let's get away from here."

"No, comrade, not so fast!" Pascent winked. "Let's finish the ale, then walk along the shore and go up by another path. We don't wish to be the ones who find him."

"Aye. Right." Hugibert stuck his thumb in his mouth, sucking as he walked.

"What's wrong?" Pascent asked.

The Frank removed his thumb. "My grasp slipped a bit, before I finished him. He caught this between his teeth and almost ripped it off!"

"Better say that you pinched it while laying up the ships, if anybody asks."

They had virtually forgotten Abalaric by the time the ale-jug was emptied. Killing a man was no great matter on Sarnia.

"Now, what of Urbicus?" the Frank asked, belching. "We were talking of him, I recall, when that eavesdropping bit of dung betrayed himself. Hard to say what a magician will do."

Pascent agreed. "I'd want revenge, were I that man, but belike he's too much of a yellowbelly to seek it. We can only wait and see. While he's around, though, we may need Gudrun."

"Get rid of him, you mean, and then get rid of her?"

"Just so."

And without her, Pascent thought, *this band of sea-thieves will rot and break apart like ice in the sun. One less to trouble me. Why, you fool, Hugibert, without her you'll be hanging on a gibbet in a little while—or reduced to doing honest work and doing it poorly.*

Aye, but if I were to say that to you, even kindly meant, you'd be for ripping my bowels, lad. You might learn something if you took orders from me for three years. And you may yet.

Expansive, ale-blithe, Pascent walked on with his comrade.

XII

The unfriendliness was then aroused of the fishes of the deep.

—Beowulf

Abalaric's funeral pyre blazed on the Sarnian cliff-top for hours. Gudrun watched the red flame-banners blow and increase, then fall as the long mound of coals collapsed in on itself. It showed her regard for Abalaric that she would command such obsequies for a cupbearer; but then, he had been a warrior before he was taken and blinded, and a good one. Varek's daughter had not forgotten.

That his death might have been murder never entered her mind.

"I had no joy from the sea-people," she declared from her seat. "They may even ally themselves with Urbicus and his scaly demons. Their lord said as much. Well, the shame's his if he does."

"And more than shame," Felimid offered. "Depend upon it, if he does that, Vivayn will know. She's a tricksy one, but just in her fashion. She acknowledged that she owes us a debt. Now she's a princess and a kind of Christian. She could cause a bishop of the gallows-god to investigate and curse those islands, where we would gain nothing by trying. Which would mean the end of all magic there."

"If that befell, would you be pleased, Bragi?"

"I would not," the bard answered frankly. "Yet it would please me far better than being massacred to preserve Rothevna's secrets. Mind, if he does what will bring it about, he and Idh are much less wise than I think them. Less fastidious, too, if they league with fish."

109

"Let them come!" a Frank said. "We'll cut them to pieces and bait hooks with them from Baioca to Vannes!"

"In the meantime, we can mark the cross and the chi-rho on the side posts of every door to the hall," Decius said. "Likewise we can lay iron under every threshold."

Felimid did not think that would have much effect. Such symbols were only symbols without "holiness" to give them power. He uttered the word mockingly in his mind, because what Christians called holiness he tended to see as a spreading canker. Also, the Children of Lir could hold and wield iron as well as any children of earth. They never depended on it overmuch because the sea rusted it easily, but the metal did not affright them.

No matter. If the pirates felt surer of themselves for doing it, they might cut giant crosses in the turf and paint the chi-rho on their foreheads, and Felimid would not complain.

"Since we're now warded against the Children of Lir," he said dryly, "let's think of the sea demons. How would we fight if we were cold and cruel as fish, and as cowardly, and could not live an hour out of the sea?"

"The two who came here did!" Sigar the Dane objected.

"True for you, Sigar. They did, and that because a sorcerer who breathes air gave them the power, and put the appearance of men upon them. I vow by my standing as a bard, they could never have done that for themselves. Their magic is of another kind."

"All our ships are laid up in boat-houses for the winter," cried someone else. "What if the sea demons come to destroy them?"

"That's so," Gudrun declared. "The ships are our strength and weakness, both. We must guard them. Closely."

It was agreed at last that the boat-houses should be guarded by fifty men each night, and that these should sleep the following day. Felimid thought, *That is how it will be for nine-nights, and more nine-nights, while the Cold Ones wait in their black depths where winter makes little difference, and our watch will grow slack. Then they will strike, probably at Yule. They may even wait until March.*

This might have happened, had not Urbicus been eager for revenge. How he incited the Cold Ones to act so swiftly, none ever knew. Maybe he reminded them that Sarnia had once been a wreckers' lair and might be that again, if cleared of pirates. Conceivably he had promised them human flesh. Their delight in eating men had been known to whelm their caution before.

The weather continued to offer drizzle, mist, chill and the smell of rotting wet leaves. All Gudrun's ships lay secure in their winter quarters, except *Ormungandr,* whose serpent-head could see through fog; and even *Ormungandr* would not ride the waves much longer.

Felimid spent some time at the forge of Marcel, the pirates' smith and armorer. None could truthfully call him a master craftsman, for spearheads, axes and thick-bladed, serviceable knives were the best weapons he could make. For the work of a real swordsmith, Gudrun had to send to the mainland. Felimid's needs were modest, though. He had Marcel prepare a set of moulds and make a few dozen silver sling-missiles for him. Gudrun was amused to see them.

"Lover, plain lead is enough for those vinegar-blooded fish! They are not werewolves. Steel can finish them. We showed that, you and I."

"I know. None the less, there may be those among them who can't be slain so conveniently, as there are werewolves, wizards and berserks among men." The bard indicated a chi-rho symbol cut into the surface of a table. "The men have their precuations, and you've taken to honoring Erin's War Queens. These are mine. At worst, they're extravagant."

"I do not grudge the silver, you know that, my man. But I will not head my arrows with it! I trust steel."

"I'd trust my arrows, too, if I could shoot as you do. Mmm—I mentioned Erin. Once I talked of your maybe going there with me, and you did not refuse."

"I did not say yes, either."

"True. Yet I'd like it if you did. Gudrun, you maintain this pirate band on Sarnia by your courage and fierceness, but it is now what it was in the beginning—a pirate band— just greater and stronger. There is nothing here fit to last."

"Who said I wish there to be? Sarnia's a pirate nest, a base from which I can venture where I will. I like the place, yes. The trophies, the signs that I have led and conquered, they please me. But when the time is right and my fate leads me elsewhere, I will leave it. I am not Clovis or Cerdic, not one for building kingdoms."

"Nor I." Felimid smiled at her. "Glad I am to hear you say it. I know where you are planning to go now that you have *Ormungandr,* for you have told me often. You'll explore the Otherworlds."

"I will," Gudrun answered, very firmly. She evidently expected opposition from her lover.

Felimid didn't oppose her. Her determination when she really wanted something was as hard as a diamond, and unreasoning as a child's.

"Beyond Erin, if the stories say truly, there are magic Gates in such numbers that the sea must hold some mighty bewildered fish. There are islands which appear and disappear—like Rothevna's realm, and I will not answer for it that even I could find it again—and Gates to the realms Tir-Nan-Og, Tir-Tairn-Gire, Mag Mell, Hy Brasel, and others. Surely there should be more left in the western sea than here! Rome and the church have destroyed most of them."

"Peace, Bragi. You have all winter to tell me these stories, and I promise to listen. Meanwhile, by all the gods, we are likely to be attacked by monsters! They may have that filthy vampire-kelp with them, in the form of ocean horses or not."

"They might, so. We will not prevail against that with spears and swords. This hero you were hearing of in Spain, who dealt with a plague of it—how did he triumph?"

"He used quicklime, in the tale. We have none here. There is ample store of tallow, though, and pitch. That should do."

Gudrun had a strong hut built near the boat-houses. Simple and plain, with a soldier's bed of pine sprigs in it, which suited her well. Spread with a few sheepskins, it became pampered ease to the way she had slept as an outlaw on the Jutland heath. To Felimid, also, it seemed like lordly quarters, when he recalled how he had spent the previous winter. Yet it seemed pointless, too.

"You mean to sleep the entire season here, waiting for Urbicus?" he grumbled.

"I do not think I will have to. If a se'n-night passes and the demons are not here, I will go back to the hall and sleep in this hut every third night only. That is twice as often as the men stand watch on this shore. It must be so. Trust me, Bragi, the way to command a gang of hard-living, hard-drinking slayers is to show you can live harder, last longer and slay more fiercely than any of them—and never ask aught of them that you are not ready to endure yourself!"

"I'll remember," he said, smiling. "More! I'll even do things with you that I would not be asking any of the band to endure."

Gudrun threw a sheepskin at him.

They did not have to wait seven nights. They did not even have to wait three. On the second night, with waves hissing and rolling up the shore, lashed by a cold wind, and ragged clouds intermittently hiding and revealing the autumn stars, the sea demons appeared.

No signal or shouted alarm warned of their coming. A heavy body slammed against the hut's door, and as the sleepers awoke, reaching for their weapons, the simple latch was sprung, the door flew wide and a shambling thing which stank like rancid herring was with them, swinging a toothed club.

Felimid drove Kincaid through its belly. Gudrun, with a hawk's scream, half severed its head and hurled what remained of the creature into another couple of its kind striving to enter the hut. As they stumbled, Felimid slammed the door in their scaly muzzles—literally, with sharp snapping sounds of impact. Gudrun was dragging on her leather sark, clapping helmet on head and slipping her arm into her shield's grip and bracer. As a matter of course she had arranged these things where she could find them quickly in the dark.

"I am ready," she said, moving to the door. "Busk your own self now."

Groping his way to the low bed, Felimid did. Boots and breeches and the supple dragon-leather tunic he had stolen in Rothevna's hall he was wearing. His sword he had already in his hand. Now, helmet and targe...

"Help me!" Gudrun gasped. "The sea's dregs are all at this bloody door!"

Felimid set his back against it, aiding her to hold it shut.

After a few moments, in the course of which the door came
partly open once and a webbed paw shot through the gap,
to be severed at once with the jamb for a chopping block,
the pressure eased.

"Cunning haddock-brothers," the bard commented. "They
hope we'll rush out. They wait, now. Surely a couple will
be on the roof."

"Then we leave another way!"

Gudrun rushed to the hut's east wall, made, like the others
of strong wattle, the chinks stuffed with seaweed. It was
lashed to thick posts. She cut the lashings with a few strokes
of Kissing Viper.

"Help me," she said again, bending to get a grip.

Felimid laid his own sword Kincaid on the ground and
took hold with both hands. They heaved together with their
full combined strength. The last fastenings cracked and
popped; the entire wall ripped away from the hut, to flatten
a surprised demon as it fell. Felimid and Gudrun trampled
over it, swords flashing in their hands again. A demon
toppled from the tilting, slippery reed-thatch of the roof.
Felimid glimpsed him falling and gutted him like a cod an
instant after he landed.

The creature under their feet squirmed from beneath the
vandalized wall. Gudrun slashed a great wedge of meat and
gristle from its leg. Mute as a fish, it made no sound; none
of them did. Somehow that was appalling.

The creatures swarmed, lurching on their webbed feet
like crippled frogs. The bard received a confused impression
of heavy, forward-leaning bodies, wet scales, shining topaz
eyes and white fangs, but his imagination supplied all the
details he had formerly seen by daylight.

He and Gudrun fell back within the remnant of the hut.
They were protected on three sides now, and could see
unobstructed on the fourth—at least for so long as it did
not occur to the Cold Ones to push down the sagging roof
upon them.

The creatures didn't try. In the still black depths, no roofs
were built, and things never fell quickly anyhow. They
plummeted slowly, weighing less under water, and swim-
ming one had the freedom of three dimensions. The demons

were not used to the constraints of moving on land.

Sadly, they were not stupid either. As the two humans retreated before the short hatchets and cleavers confronting them, long spears—the other kind of weapon effective under water—were driven through the wall of woven branches behind. A point caught Gudrun in the back.

Its force had been lessened by its passage through the wall, and Gudrun's leather sark stopped it completely. However, the impact over her kidney still dropped her to her knees in sickening pain.

Felimid howled, "ERINNN!" and chopped two of the protruding spear-shafts through, while catching a chipped stone cleaver's edge on his targe. He stood over Gudrun, not knowing in the angry dark whether she was badly hurt or dying, and struck out raging with his lean lethal sword.

"Sarnians!" he shouted above the wave-rush and fighting noise. "Here, to your lady! She gave you gold, open-handed, free . . . *will you leave her bard to fight for her?* Come here, you lousy sea-rats!"

It wasn't finished oration. His teachers at the bardic college would have thought he fell considerably beneath his training. However, it reached the men to whom it was spoken, on their own level. They fought their way, a couple of tight knots of them, to the wrecked hut. They reached it as Gudrun rose unsteadily, grinding her teeth, and lifted a sword which for once was feeble.

Spears drove through scaly hides. Axes cut deep. Shields rammed into monstrous faces and flanks. On the Cold Ones' side, chert-headed spears drew red smoking blood from men's bodies, webbed half-hands gripped the rims of shields to drag them low, and fangs lunged at appalled faces.

"The boat-houses!" someone cried. "That's where the rest are standing them off."

"The beacon . . ." Gudrun croaked.

Felimid knew what she meant. A beacon of oil-soaked wood, shielded under a greased leather awning, lay at the top of the path leading up from this bay. Fifty men against four or seven score demons needed help. If someone had gone to light the beacon immediately when this onslaught began, they might get that help.

They won to the side of a boat-house. Inside, pine torches blazed and men could see what they were about. They had formed an unyielding wall of shields across the doorway. The mute creatures tried to break it, but went down in their black blood instead, turning the sand dark. Like things were transpiring at the other boat-houses.

With a wet slithering and a smell of salt and iodine, vampire-kelp tangled Felimid's feet. He remained standing and slashed at it. This time it was a mat eight feet wide and something less than a foot high. Men tripped, yelling, and the Cold Ones cut them asunder while the vampire-weed drank.

Little by little, Gudrun's men edged along the boat-house wall to the doorway, hard pressed by the frighteningly silent monsters whose frilled, manelike gills ruffled and spread. Four men had been dragged down and killed. Felimid dreaded being the fifth, but he stayed between the sea-things and Gudrun as her other men did, and warded her pending her recovery.

"Ormungandr," she gasped. "Curse them! How fares *Ormungandr?"*

Felimid didn't answer, because he was busy and because he didn't know. High above, he saw a sudden crimson smudge in the night, growing to a blaze. They would have help soon. Men from the long barrack-houses would arm and come running, at least eighty. It was less than three-quarters of a mile. If they survived until then, all should be well—and *Ormungandr* could wait! In that moment, Felimid didn't greatly care if the sea demons broke it to pieces.

"O-hoy, in the boat-house there!" a man bawled at his elbow. Felimid was startled to recognize the voice of Tiumals, the splay-toothed Goth—startled because, in the dark and the turmoil, he hadn't known the man was among their handful. "O-hoy! We're coming in, with the lady, you bastards! With Gudrun, you hear? Lend us a hand!"

The men in the doorway did, forcing their way outward against the tan-scaled monsters which glittered in the torchlight. The half-dozen pirates with Gudrun at their center made a last rush, and were received by the larger group, which retreated again into the doorway.

Felimid turned his head to assess Gudrun's state. He should have been looking the other way, at their enemies from the sea. Gudrun was, her sweating, pain-gray face aimed like a weapon towards the foe.

Because of that, Felimid saw clearly by the shaking torchlight as Hugibert began to drive a spear at her back, now lacking a wall and covered only by the leather sark.

The bard vented a war-yell that would have disconcerted a troll. He brought it from the pit of his outraged belly as he moved—and he had never moved more swiftly, who was noted for swift adroit movement. Kincaid parried the spearhead, knocking it aside, and an instant later Felimid's targe struck the Frank's middle like a round convex dish—not with the dangerous edge, but with its whole surface, to produce a merely sickening effect, which the bard regretted.

He was wildly angry; not just high-colored and ready to indulge in high words, not exaggerating for effect, not inflamed by the violence of the moment. He was angry in a way that meant he or Hugibert must die.

"Oh, you foul dog," he whispered fiercely. "You'll answer, by the gods my people swear by, you'll answer for this. Watch him, *a gradh!*" he said to Gudrun in a louder voice. "He tried to kill you."

Other kelpies now came against them. These were not flattish mats, but weed-masses in the general shape of beasts, about as bulky as horses and determined to break the shield-wall. Their "legs" were hidden by dangling skirts of streamery leaves. The featureless heads shoved forward, insensately butting. They looked like ghastly hobbyhorses, and no amount of stabbing or slashing availed against them. They could not feel.

"Fall back, ye heroes," bawled a man in the ship behind them. "We have a welcome for these!"

Felimid was glad to fall back. It meant that he could have his attention on Hugibert again. The kelpies followed, squelching, their nature as masses of seaweed open and undisguised. There were three.

The pirates in the ship smashed open kegs of pitch and tallow, fired them, and heaved them down crackling, in a hissing trail of smoke and fat red flames. One fiery, adhesive

mass engulfed the blank head of the nearest kelpie while
another covered haunch and flank. A second weed-thing
was saddled and mounted by a sibilating dragon force hatched
from wood, and the third reared peculiarly as its plotted
destruction came down to shatter beneath its forequarters.
This creature relinquished its vaguely animal shape and
spread out as a living wet mat to smother the burning tallow.
A last half-shattered, kindled keg fell heavily atop it to cover
it with fire. Splashes of sizzling tallow struck pirates and
gilled horrors alike.

Then the men from the barracks-houses came to their aid
at last, and the Cold Ones withdrew to the sea. Mindless,
the kelpies thrashed about, threatening to burn the ships in
the boat-house. Decius, always careful, had ordered soaked
hides and barrels of sea-water placed aboard also, lest they
should come to regret Gudrun's style of defense. Thus damage was averted.

Having time and space, now, Felimid took his sling and
hurled the weighty silver balls at the departing sea demons.
Heads broke open; brains flew. Inner organs ruptured when
he hit bodies. Gudrun ran to the ruined hut for her bow and
killed some more herself, by the flaring torchlight, though
not many. Her own men waded after them too closely, press-
ing into the water with gleeful shouts, and she could seldom
shoot for fear of hitting them. Pigsknuckle Hromund roared
that it was better than spearing flounder.

The bard challenged Hugibert the next day.

"You tried to murder her with a spear in the back," he
said, before eighty men and more. "In the dark and confusion of the fighting you tried it. I struck your spear aside
myself, and I should have slain you then! But today will
do."

Hugibert said, "You lie, you currying bastard, and it's I
will slay you because you've defamed me." He spat on the
rushes. "Unless the lady protects you. Hope for it, scut."

"Bragi's word is good enough for me," Gudrun said hotly.

"Him? Lady, he's . . . your leman. We all know that! But
what will you do?" Hugibert asked defiantly. "Noose a rope
for me, just on his say-so? I've been your man for years.
What's he? The amusement of a season! It's his word against

mine, and if he's not lying, he's made a mistake—aye, a bad mistake."

Hugibert narrowed his eyes, glared, fondled the grip of his long sword and ruffled, to make clear how bad a mistake.

"Less bad than your own," Gudrun said, "when you missed your stroke at me. I will have you hanged here and now!"

A bellow of protest came from the Franks in the hall, and not the Franks only. Decius shouldered his way forward, agate eye gleaming, dark face somber.

"No, lady," he said, deferential to her as usual, though not submissive. "No. Were he the least man here, it would not do. Hugibert is one of your ship-captains! Hang him on Bragi's unsupported word, and where does that place the rest of us? Hugibert's neck is no frailer than any of ours."

A murmur of thorough agreement went through the witnessing throng.

"That's right," Hugibert growled. "You hear that, all? You say well, Decius, and he doesn't say it out of friendship for me, either. He was Ataulf's sword-brother, and it's no secret that Ataulf and I never loved each other. It's only the truth."

"I stand to that," Pascent declared, thumbs tucked aggressively in his belt, but speaking, as Decius noted with a sharp turn of his head and a sardonic flash of his jeweled eye, only now that he'd observed how the wind blew. "Suppose one of us displeases you next? Or the bard fancies he sees us doing something naughty? Devils! It's his trade to make things up. He sees mermaids and sprites where a normal man sees nothing but spindrift. Did *you* see Hugibert try to murder you, lady?"

"I—no. If I had, there would be no need for this debate!"

"How should she?" Felimid snapped. "He thrust his spear at her back!"

"Did anyone else see it happen?"

None had. Hugibert had chosen his time well—dark, and tumult, and engagement with a foe whose nature caused astonishment and horror, while Gudrun wore only leather instead of her famous mail.

"Then it's Hugibert's word against Bragi's, as he says."

Decius looked bleakly at Gudrun. "I know whose word I would take. But I no more witnessed it than you did, lady. That makes it a matter between the two of them."

"It was my life he attempted to take, and I his chieftain," Gudrun said. "By the gods, I have something to say about that, do I not?"

"But you never saw."

"Cairbre and Ogma! All this is profitless," Felimid interjected. "I saw!" He trod forward to address Hugibert at a range of two feet. "Murder and treachery. A serpent's stroke in the back against your own chieftain. I'm the witness, I'm the accuser, and I'll be your justice besides. If you dare fight me."

"You're challenging me?"

"I have challenged you. A death-fight."

The words were accompanied by an uncharacteristically hard green stare. Decius heard and saw with approval. Although he knew the bard to be a fine fighter at need, he had thought him too amiable and lazy to push any matter to its conclusion, more likely to stand back and let it conclude itself. He had fought Ataulf when the Gothic captain provoked him intolerably—and won—but he had taken care that it did not go so far as killing, arranging the rules of the combat to prevent that. And he'd never thrust himself aggressively forward that Decius could remember. He didn't initiate, he responded. Usually.

Hugibert was taken aback by the unexpected direct challenge, too, and not so pleased to hear it uttered as the Spaniard. Yet never for an instant did he think of refusing it. He said slowly,

"I choose where and how?"

"I will fight you with one foot in a bucket so long as conditions are even," Felimid said, with a passing trace of his normal levity, "and I'll kill you if I can."

"If you can!" Hugibert echoed derisively.

He thought hard. Despite his verbal scorn, he had seen enough of Felimid's sword-skill to avoid meeting him with that weapon. They would probably be well matched using spears, but Hugibert wanted an advantage if he could get one. He thought further.

The bard seemed to like a bit of distance between himself
and blood. Sword, sling and javelin; these were the weapons
with which he was outstandingly fine. Knives, or the short-
hafted Frankish axes, might well disconcert him. Or how
about—yes!

"Bare hands," he rasped, "to the death."

Gudrun started, took a step forward. Decius whistled,
very softly. Felimid's gaze flickered. He hoped that he didn't
look as pale as he suddenly felt.

"You'll kill me if you can, will you?" Hugibert mocked,
"All right, dog. But you'll have to kill me hand to hand,
nothing considered foul. I think it's I will kill you."

"Yes? That's to be shown."

In moments they faced each other, Felimid wearing his
breeches and light flexible buskins as he had the night they
escaped from the Veiled Isles, stripped above the waist.
Hugibert had thrown off his wolfskin over-tunic; he wore
only his linen tunic and ankle-high cowhide shoes. His tow
moustache and hair shone pale in the dim daylight.

"This is between Hugibert and Bragi," Gudrun announced, her face pale under its wind tan. "Let any man
touch either, or give a weapon or other aid, or make a noise
to distract or give advantage . . . to either . . . and he dies."

Felimid wanted to begin, and to finish. Looking at the
Frank, he saw repeatedly in his mind the spear drive at
Gudrun's back.

"Now!" Gudrun said, and watched with her hands
clenched hard.

Felimid sprang on the word, a bouncing leap ending in
a kick at Hugibert's stomach. At it, not to it. He snatched
his foot back as the Frank reached to seize it, dropped to
the hall floor in a close-curled ball and suddenly straightened, ramming his head to the same target.

Hugibert was knocked from his feet, though not winded.
His torso felt tough as saddle leather. He grabbed Felimid's
hair, yanked, and aimed a short chopping punch into Felimid's eye with intent to blind. Felimid turned his head,
taking the blow on his cheek, which immediately bled. He
drove the heel of his hand up under Hugibert's chin, to lift
it, then struck the formerly protected throat with the edge

of his hand. Hugibert croaked sickly, but did not weaken. Instead he swung his head sharply forward. His crown collided with Felimid's brow, and the bard went rolling off him, his skull filled with lightnings of splitting, devastating pain.

He clawed for the Frank's hand as he went. Catching a single finger, he wrenched hard, and Hugibert grunted. In the next moment, he tried to kick Felimid's head through the doorway. The bard rolled over in time. Then he was on his feet once more.

Any reticence he might have had was now gone. The exchange of savage, merciless blows had made him know in his marrow that there was no stopping save for the death of one. He circled the Frank more carefully now. An opening, a weakness, an unwary step...Hugibert watched for the same, and discovered it. Felimid trod a little stiffly on the leg which had been wounded at Coriallo. Although not a bad wound, it was still new, still healing.

Hugibert closed with his accuser. They were both quick, well-balanced men, with trim tough muscles. Felimid had a certain experience of brawling and a whimsical, unpredictable repertoire. Hugibert, less quick-witted, had more knowledge of wrestling, and enough tenacity to serve any purpose.

He came to grips, had his grip swiftly broken, sought another, and passed an arm like a coiling snake around the bard's waist. Felimid back-heeled, none too well, and broke his fall by catching Hugibert's arm as he was thrown.

Hugibert dropped beside him, sought and found a simple knee-lock from which Felimid saved his leg with a hammer-blow of his elbow to Hugibert's kidney. He followed it by slashing his fingertips across the Frank's eyes. Then he locked his hands together and struck hard at the back of Hugibert's neck.

The half-blinded man slipped within the blow, so that it landed on the fibrous muscles of his back, and slid doggedly upward, stamping, kneeing, until he achieved a firm hug.

Now Felimid was in dire trouble. He twisted, Hugibert countered with practiced expertise, and the hug became a hold which could kill and began to tighten. Felimid resisted, probing for nerves, as his senses turned foggy.

Then Hugibert's torn thumb began to bleed copiously again. His hold turned greasy; the bard twisted free. He never knew that Abalaric had saved him when the cupbearer was ashes. He stamped hard on Hugibert's toes, exposed by the open-topped cowhide shoe. Three of them broke. Hugibert applied another hug, snarling. Felimid slid his hands over the Frank's back, gripped the flat slabs of muscle over the ribs, sank his fingers in, twisted, wrenched and wrung.

Stronger than his lithe build indicated, he was strongest of all in his wrists and hands. His fingers inflicted agony through Hugibert's tunic, while the Frank, his thin, monotonous snarling a steady noise, tightened his hug in a sustained effort to crack Felimid's ribs like old wicker.

Felimid stamped downwards again. Hugibert took his damaged foot out of the way, and Felimid hooked it, back-heeling. Then he was down on his backside, the world filled with immediate, vivid pain, his nose broken by another sudden head-butt, and Hugibert diving upon him.

He rolled aside, choking on blood. Hugibert landed across the backs of his thighs, pinning him briefly. He grabbed the bard's foot, and his wounded calf with the other hand, and set himself to rip open that wound anew.

He succeeded, to his cost. Half by luck, half by instinct, Felimid got a scissors grip around the Frank's waist. His steely horseman's thighs applied pressure until Hugibert purpled, squinting from bloody eyes. He groped, seeking Felimid's hurt calf to mangle again. His impaired sight allowed Felimid to catch one of the reaching arms. He twisted it slowly around and up, between Hugibert's shoulder blades, and went on forcing it.

The pressure of his thighs increased, though his calf hurt monstrously. He snuffled blood past the crimson pain in his nose. Hugibert thrashed, hammered, punched with his free hand, frenzied as the ligaments in his shoulder began to tear. He struggled his utmost, and it profited him not even slightly.

His shoulder-joint came out of the socket, and he bellowed, helpless.

"Quarter!"

Quarter. Behind his battered, pulpy forehead, Felimid conceived the thought that he'd never refused quarter before when someone asked it. Had he? Suppose he let Hugibert live. What then?

He saw that treacherous blow from behind. If there were others, mercy could encourage them. By nature he might be a lark, but he was flying with crows now. If he thought he would never have carrion work to do in such company, he was a fool.

He hauled the Frank to his knees by his sweat-drenched hair, bore him backwards in a short, stumbling run, and snapped his neck on the edge of a table . . . though not until the third time he tried.

He released the corpse, shaking, and spewed everything in his stomach.

If Abalaric's ghost was present, it surely smiled.

XIII

"You continue to carry from hut to hut among your countrymen certain tables on which you celebrate the divine sacrifice of the mass with the assistance of women whom you call conhospitae. *While you distribute the Eucharist, they take the chalice and administer the blood of Christ to the people. This is an innovation, an unprecedented superstition."*
—Letter From the Bishops of Tours

Rumbling and creaking along the rutted track, the three ox-wains traveled west at the beasts' patient pace. From time to time the cart-men prodded them with long goads. Mist crept and swirled in the surrounding forest among the naked oaks and the beeches, many of which kept their lustrous leaves, although these had died. It was an eerie place in autumn, the vast low-lying Forest of Dol.

The cart-man at the fore said uneasily, "Not far now, lady."

"That's good, Adlyn."

Vivayn and Eldrida, Nye and young Cerdic, rode in the one cart. They sat on sacks of purchased grain with which they planned to ensure their welcome where they were bound.

"And that is true," Adlyn whispered to himself. "Not far now to the holy mountain, and to Lansulcan—and the saint will know how to banish you."

He and his fellows had been glad to carry two young women home with them, since the yellow-haired one was very comely and the other beautiful. In such restless times it meant little that she was plainly a great lady, too, since she appeared destitute, with none to protect her. From Britain, no doubt. She wouldn't be the first lady to journey from that island in such circumstances, with the sea-wolves swarming in. A gift to five honest men.

They had approached the pair, grinning, that first evening. The grins had vanished when they heard the shocking roar of a barghest, and glimpsed its shambling form among the trees. Vivayn had appeared to tower seven feet tall, bone-thin, with a face like an exquisite skull and fire where her hair had been, a long gray knife in her bird-taloned grasp. She had demanded then if they wished her to summon the barghest closer.

There had been no trouble since.

Dimly, now, they saw the outlines of a sheer granite outcrop hundreds of feet high, startling in the midst of this lowland. They passed shorn, empty fields and thatched farmhouses, most with stake fences.

The folk of Lansulcan came to see the strangers, who gazed back with interest. A rustic lot, Vivayn thought, in their unbleached fawn linen, their breeches and buckskin or cowhide tunics, long skirts and simple jacket-bodices, and plain heavy wool mantles for both sexes. Healthy, hard-working people in no danger of starving, if remote from the outside world—and this although the town of Avranches, a bishop's see, was less than three leagues distant.

"Welcome, Adlyn," said a big, rough-voiced mare of a woman who appeared to be his wife. She studied the travel-stained newcomers, manifestly thinking the worst. "Who be these?"

Adlyn moved to what he considered a safe distance from the princess. "*That* one is a witch, or an evil fay!" he yelled, pointing at her. "She—"

The other cart-men joined him in accusing her, the result being a confused babble of barghests and hags.

"Let the saint judge her," one of Adlyn's companions advised.

"Sulghein, yes! Take her to Sulghein!"

"That sounds wise," Vivayn agreed. "If I am the things these men are shouting, you should have a saint to deal with me. Perhaps, if I am not what they say, he will strike them dumb for their slander." The cart-men looked uncomfortable. "However, I will not be taken to anybody. I can walk. Where is your saint to be found?"

"He lives on the mountain," Adlyn's wife said, and did not add, "lady."

"That's hardy of him," Vivayn murmured, lifting her gaze to the crag and letting the woman's discourtesy pass. Then she spoke to the people. Whether they believed she was evil or not, they were enjoying the novelty and drama of the situation.

"I've been forced to flee Britain by the seawolves," she said, "like you, like your parents. I am a princess of south Britain, for what that is worth in these times, and my companion is a king's daughter also." (The daughter-through-rape of a savage, self-made king, one bastard out of many, but a king's daughter.) "It is shelter and hospitality we are seeking. We bring food with us, though I am sure Lansulcan's stocks would not fail even if we had none. Your land's fruitfulness is known."

A fay, Adlyn had called her. His fellow yokels found that believable. No woman they had seen before had eyes like large gray crystals, or unflawed skin . . . and the other, luscious as fruit in a basket . . .

Men boggled and dreamed wildly, just as the cart drivers had done. Every woman in the place hated her, hated them both.

"I am Vivayn," the princess said. "And you?"

"Molofi." This time, grudgingly, Adlyn's wife said, "Lady."

"Molofi. Will you do me the kindness of leading me to the saint?"

She did not expect to be refused, nor was she.

"The mountain's holy," Molofi said, beneath its foot. "The warrior angel lives there now; Michael, the saint calls him. Used to be other gods here, but Michael drove them away."

"A very sacred place. Were you born here?"

"No," Molofi grunted, climbing. "Crossed from Britain as a girl, with my parents. To 'scape the sea-wolves, as you said."

"Like me," Vivayn agreed flatteringly.

Having spoken to a priest in Aleth, she knew a little about the holy crag. Long ago it had been sacred to the sun-lord Lugh. In the Empire's time, Mithras had been worshipped there, and now it was that other warrior-god of the high places, Michael the Archangel. Probably not much had changed except the names. Still, it crossed Vivayn's mind that the crag might have been a little less steep and remained holy.

Near the peak stood a large, well-built hut. Fathoms below, the misty forest stretched for leagues to the sea. Departing bird flocks went many-voiced overhead, in great multitudes, and somewhere stags bellowed as the clash of antlers began.

"My great lord?" Molofi called.

She was diffident, this big, rough-voiced woman. Then the saint came out of his hut, and she dropped to her knees.

Vivayn saw why, for this Sulghein had power. She felt it at once. In his blue robe, with the sacred knife hanging from his braided belt and an equal-armed cross very like a quatrefoil on his breast, he gave the immediate impression of a Druid rather than a Christian priest. His Celtic tonsure, the front of his head shaved while his hair grew long and wild behind, furthered the impression.

Vivayn knew the kind, for there were many in Britain. Founder, firebrand and priest, to these people he was also their sacred prince and probably of true royal lineage, for many monks were. In addition, he would be part magician whether he knew it or not, battle-leader when necessary, abbot and bishop combined, and of more weight in this lonely place than the authenticated bishop of nearby but worlds distant Avranches. And of much, much more weight than the Pope of Rome, who would have had foaming, horror-stricken fits at the sight of him.

"Lord," Vivayn said formally, "a good day to thee."

Sulghein said nothing, and in a moment she realized that he was waiting for her to speak further.

"I am a stranger to you, made homeless by the sea-wolves," she said. It was approximately true. "I seek hospitality for myself, a friend and her children. My name and rank—"

The saint continued to gaze at her. The color of his eyes was a very ordinary blue. The look in them was not ordinary at all. He saw angels and devils, and perhaps the future, but nothing else—and they were more real to him than the granite under his feet.

"You are Vivayn, Natanleod's daughter," Sulghein said, "known as the Perfidious. You were well enough content with the sea-wolves for years. Why do you flee them now?"

Vivayn felt anger like a white blizzard within her. Molofi's ears had stretched into tufted points, and her leathery face expressed glee, Vivayn was sure. She did not glance at her to see.

The blizzard broke around Sulghein. "It is the name fools have given me. I cannot prevent your joining them if you wish. The further from Vectis, the more they speak the word *perfidious*. My own people never used it when I guarded their farms and secured them justice with their new overlord. They may well call me perfidious now that I have left them! Either way it is my affair, and I will settle my own accounts with the devil. I am not here to be condemned or forgiven by you."

"No, lady, you are not. You will be condemned or forgiven elsewhere, as you say. My question still goes unanswered. Why did you wait four years to leave your devil-husband?"

"Had I left him before, I should simply have been taken back. I'm stronger and more cunning now than I was four years ago; perhaps even wiser. The time seemed right."

She met his gaze and held it. Sulghein said, "You may remain."

Molofi broke in, outraged. "Lord! She's...Adlyn vows she's an evil fay. His words, I swear."

"She is mortal," Sulghein said with utter certainty—and aright. "Be sure to tell Adlyn that I said it."

Molofi shut her mouth. There could not, Vivayn thought, be many men able to have that effect on her with a word.

A couple of days later, Vivayn took communion in the little thatched church on the holy mountain. She saw Sulghein consecrate the bread, which should have been done by two priests jointly, and listened to the prayer ring from his mouth.

"Qui pridie quam pateretur, in sanctus manibus suis accepit panem, respexit in coelum ad te, sancte Pater, omnipotens aeterne Deus, gratias agens..."

Two virgins in white robes carried the wine about in superb glass chalices. They might almost have been Druidesses of old. In some ways they probably were. Vivayn was not even slightly shocked.

Her blood ran suddenly cold, though, when she saw a skull in a gemmed gold setting displayed in a place of honor. A skull! Cerdic had slain Natanleod her father, and jeweled and gilded his skull in a similar way, *and made it into a drinking cup.*

Somehow she swallowed the wine.

It wasn't a barbaric trophy here, of course, but a relic of some powerful saint. Its presence carried no pagan connotations, no hint of the ancient wild magic of the severed head. Its meaning was wholly Christian.

Of course.

Still, Vivayn felt that she had achieved something when she walked out of the church on steady legs.

XIV

The monster roared, the mountains echoed;
Middle Earth was mightily shaken.
Then the serpent-fish sank back.
                              —The Lay of Hymir

Gudrun tied the bandage with a neat sailor's knot.

"If treated gently henceforward, it ought to heal," she declared. A slight frown touched her brow. "That cur Hugibert did his best to ensure that it would not."

"Now, it doesn't feel bad."

Gudrun lifted her gaze from below Felimid's knee, and burst out laughing at the sight of his face, to his irritation. His brow was one vast pulpy bruise from Hugibert's head-butts, wondrously tinted, and both his eyes had blackened. Although Gudrun had set his broken nose, it was comically swollen.

"It w-will heal straight, I think, Bragi," she said. She grinned at him. "There is not really enough length in it for a bend."

"Thanks! Cairbre and Ogma! I wasn't battered like this by Edric's Saxons, or Withhad's, or the men at Svantovit's temple!"

"No," Gudrun agreed. "You are indeed a man of great luck. But Hugibert, though he turned treacher, was one of *my* captains."

"Och, congratulations," Felimid groaned. "He was a jolly brawler, indeed."

"You proved better," she said. "You slew him with your hands, and for me. I have heard the men talking, and they all think it was well done. They are amazed; few would have thought you hard enough. And I think I have grown softer for you. I no longer serve Odin . . ."

"You regret that still."

"No, Bragi! I have never been one for looking back. I defied him to love you and that was well worth it. Is worth it! I am looking to the future, for I think he has not done with me yet, and he no longer intends well by me. I hear him sometimes, riding the gales, and dead men I killed follow him laughing."

Felimid took her gently by the shoulders. "You're Gudrun Blackhair," her reminded her.

"Gudrun Blackhair, not a fearful child? Yes. I am. But hold me."

He willingly held her, until his hands had smoothed the tension from her shoulders and back. She sighed and sought his mouth with her eyes closed, kissing him very gently, very tenderly, very long, mindful of the state of his face.

At least there was no damage to his mouth. But when she opened her eyes again she could not contain her belly-knotting laughter.

"Oh, B-Bragi! I am sorry. Your face . . . it is like a dish of b-blackberries and cream!" She hooted.

"It feels more like the site of both battles of Moytura! Were you after saying you had grown softer? Once I'm sufficiently healed I will tumble you on your back and make you howl apologies at the roof-beams."

"Boaster," she said. "I will hold you to that promise, once my back is less sore, and you will be lucky if you are alive the next morning."

She could joke about sex now. That was another change. He remembered how rawly belligerent she had been about the nature of their relationship in its early days. Nor were those so far in the past. What had it been, three months, or four?

"I will be away for a time, Bragi," she told him with one of her swift changes of tack. "The chieftain of Lesia is friendly, and I mean to invite him to my Yule feast. That is one northern custom I still keep."

"It's in *Ormungandr* you'll be going?"

"Surely! It would not suit my honor to go in a skiff!"

She ought to be safe, then. Lesia could be seen from the cliffs of Sarnia on any day the weather was not wholly blind; a strong man could swim the six miles between the islands. *Ormungandr* would make the crossing in an hour, with Lesia itself as a shield against any storms from the open Atlantic. As for other dangers, they would have to be endured when they came.

"Are you thinking of sea demons?" Gudrun asked.

"Yes. Still, they tried and they failed. It's in my mind that Urbicus will not incite them to tackle you again . . . or not with success. Were I one of those scaly corpse-eaters, I would say to him that he must prove his power by dealing with you himself, or I would regard him as no fit ally."

"The Children of Lir are braver, and their ships go unseen."

"And they half threatened to join with the sea demons. Well, you needn't go to Lesia; it's nothing urgent."

"I will go."

He'd known she would. She must defy the powers that would restrict her freedom of the sea, and he could not always be holding her hand, any more than she could always protect him. They were lovers, not snail and shell.

The next day, a crew rowed Gudrun around the northern tip of Sarnia and turned the ship westward. Zucharre the Basque, a tough, compact man who seemed ready to bounce into the air when he walked, seconded her. Most of the rowers were Franks, although Rowan, the Saxon youth to whom Gudrun was a goddess, sat among them. Rhychdir went as steersman.

The wind blew light in the clear, cold air. *Frost coming,* Gudrun thought. She stood tall in her silvered war-shirt, the leather harness she wore above it holding it close to her body. That cloth-supple mail would otherwise have shifted like flowing water whenever she moved quickly, and spoiled her balance. Even dwarfish mail was not weightless.

Her second favorite bow stood nearby, with a quiver of thirty arrows. She thought she might amuse Laban of Lesia with her marksmanship while she was there. She didn't expect to find a bowman who could shoot in competition with her; she knew of no real archers in the islands except her Danes and the few Goths now on Sarnia. Still, there might be one, some traveler spending the winter as the chief's guest.

Life was good. She found that she didn't even mind the coming of detested winter.

The sea surged and burst.

Gray-green water divided, spilling over the rising shape of something humped and vast. It broke surface, streaming, leather-brown, jellyfish-brown, decaying-blubber-brown. A coiling neck rose into sight, lifting high as an oak, with a head eightfold bigger than an elk's. Eyes as big each as a man's head showed lifeless and dull above a gape of teeth like spearheads aligned in rows. A stench like a plague-grave rolled from it.

It was dead, completely dead, long dead.

The rotting flippers moved, driving it forward.

"*Row*," Gudrun shouted, and called the time. *Ormungandr* shot forward, more alive and swifter than the thing from the black depths, the thing decaying. Its tail beat. It halted clumsily behind *Ormungandr's* stern, rolled over in a welter of creaming water and stretched its neck for the steersman.

Rhychdir saw the monstrous head coming his way, and stood fast at the tiller-handle of the great steering oar. With the teeth a yard from him, he flung himself down so that the dead jaws clashed above his head, then rolled back to take the oar again as the neck slid past, foul yards of it.

The stroke oarsman was lifted, screaming, in that mouth. His ribs crunched, his lungs were torn open, his heart burst. The jaws opened. He dropped into the sea, spraying blood.

Gudrun gripped her fury and terror hard. Screaming commands would send the men into panic; she called the orders clearly, concisely. They were tough enough to remain sane. The larboard oars rose in a ragged comb from the snarled water while the starboard rowers pulled, and *Ormungandr* turned more sleekly than the dead monster would ever do.

It wallowed and thrashed after them.

Behind Gudrun, a pliant, dripping form eight feet from nose-tip to tail-tip whisked over the gunwale, slid between two surprised oarsmen, writhed, twisted and changed form. A stupefied croak of warning brought Gudrun spinning around, sword in hand, to see the giant otter she remembered become a naked man with an otter-skin dangling empty from his hand.

"Peace, Blackhair!" he laughed. "We're friendly today. Look yonder and see."

Suspicious, she trod back to keep him and the monster in sight.

"Do not slay him, yet," she said.

Twenty white-skinned figures dove and played around the monster, wielding short heavy blades of polished flint. It vanished below the surface as Gudrun looked, with a boom of whalelike flukes, the Children of Lir diving in pursuit.

"That is Urbicus, not us," the otter-man assured her. "We have no need to raise dead dragons. We'd have chopped through your strakes from underneath—and I think the beast will come up and try to capsize you, next! Decide quickly, chieftain! Will you trust my advice? We can thwart that."

"How? And why should you wish to?"

A green-haired woman came glimmering to the surface and cried to *Ormungandr* in her own tongue.

"Quickly!" the otter-man barked. "Back water, hard!"

Gudrun hesitated.

"It's your ship."

She rapped the order. *Ormungandr*'s long ash oars reversed their motion, and the ship shot backwards as the dead monster rose into the sunlight again, the stink of its decay causing the air to quiver. Children of Lir clung to it, hacking at its flippers.

"Njord of the Ships!" Gudrun swore.

"We cannot hurt it, or drive it away," the otterman explained. "It is *dead*. We can cripple it, though, and then it will be no danger. Manannan's horses! It is clumsy even now! If you will give us steel axes and heavy knives, we can do the work sooner."

Or let the salt sea into my ship . . .

She decided. "You have it."

She passed the word down one side of *Ormungandr* while

Zucharre took the other. A dozen short Frankish axes dropped splashing between the oar-blades, and as many single-edged knives. Some of the pirates saw daughters of Lir, not sons, waiting to catch the weapons, and goggled at the wet white breasts before recovering and calling out the greetings of their choice. They reacted more by habit than serious intent, though, and the sea-women, comprehending the manner if not always the words, gave back grins or mocking gestures. Then they dove adroitly after the sinking weapons.

The corpse-monster wallowed as it turned to attack again.

"It will catch you if you flee straight for land," murmured the otter-man. "Turn close about it; circle and dodge. It's less nimble than your ship."

"Teach your grandmother to suck eggs," Gudrun retorted. "I had about noticed that before you came. Have you a name?"

"Turo."

"I think your teeth were at my throat none so long ago, friend."

"Yes," Turo said cheerfully. "You were not the best-behaved guest my prince ever had."

Then there was no time for further chat. Gudrun had to be constantly watching the sea, the corpse-monster and the Children of Lir, while issuing orders that danced *Ormungandr* around like a salmon in a river. A second time the monster dove deep, and again a sea-man rose to cry a warning which only in her lean war-dragon would Gudrun have had time to use gainfully. Even then, a great decaying shoulder struck the ship's quarter and made it lurch far over.

The horrible head came down in a cloud of stench. One pirate was crushed under the wattled throat, while the man on the thwart before him vanished into insensate jaws. Gudrun ran and sprang, yelling her war-cry, Kissing Viper in her hand. The monster lunged clumsily at her, snapping. She bounced from the flooring to a thwart, and thence across the ship, as swiftly as though her war-shirt weighed a pound.

She swung Kissing Viper expertly. A great slab of stinking meat split from the monster's neck with a greasy, sucking sound. The head lifted and came down for her once more. Jumping aside, she found solid footing and slashed a great dead eyeball across. It wept foulness over her.

In the water, the Children of Lir continued to gnaw with their weapons. The monster did not feel them. None the less, they did their work.

It reared higher out of the sea, and rested more of its carrion weight on the ship's side in its eagerness to reach Gudrun. Two oars splintered. The jagged end of one drove into the dead monster's belly, piercing deeply. The creature drew back at once.

The right flipper came away from its carcass at last. Other Children of Lir were at work on the flukes, although these were constantly moving. *Ormungandr*'s rowers took the ship clear of the dead thing, but first it snatched another man shrieking into the air, to drop him after killing him.

Like that monster pike in the Baltic, Gudrun thought suddenly. *Yet not like it. That was a wizard's sending the power of nine old priests combined. Hurt it and you hurt them. Nothing hurts this! It will not stop until it is hacked to bits.*

Then we shall destroy it!

"Make ready to ram that lich," she ordered. "These mer-folk have done well by us; now we will show them they made no mistake!"

The creature wallowed, attempting to dive. The Children of Lir drove barbed harpoons into it, with inflated bladders attached. Its rotting muscles took it down, but not strongly enough, and the white swimmers followed. Its bulk showed through the water, fathoms down.

It surfaced again. Its mutilated flukes slapped the sea. Slowly it turned towards *Ormungandr*.

The ship's serpent-prow aimed straight at the gross body. *Ormungandr* rushed forward, while Gudrun called the stroke in ever higher excitement. Water hissed below the tall figurehead, as if the serpent's mouth had a voice.

"Die, you carrion, *die!*" Gudrun yelled at the last second.

The bow crashed into the lich with a rending of thick brown hide. Dead ribs splintered inward; dead flesh broke, crumbled and toppled in stinking masses into the sea. Rowers were thrown off their thwarts. Others grabbed poles to push clear of the moving carcass. They cursed and choked in the stink. The Children of Lir worked in frenzy on the other flipper, hacking, slicing. The long neck arched; the awful teeth picked one of them from the sea like a floating apple.

Waves crashed through the ribs, sluicing them white. Gudrun stared into the noisome body cavity. Something came loose, fell outward, caught against the ribs. Another wave slapped it inward again. Gudrun had taken it for some half-rotted organ, a slimy lump of nothing in particular. The clean sea washed it, exposed it.

Gudrun saw limbs, a bald head, a figure curled within the dead monster like a rat in a desecrated body. For a lunatic moment, Gudrun thought the monster had had some luckless sailor in its belly when it died. Then the figure moved, struggling, and she knew.

She snatched her bow, strung it and shot four arrows as fast as she could draw and loose. One sank from sight in carrion viscera, one skewered a rib and broke, but a third flew between the white bars and sank into Urbicus's belly, while the fourth pierced his shoulder.

He squealed like a snared rabbit. The grisly head far above him waved drunkenly, then dropped like a stone on toppling fathoms of neck. Brine flew up in a gigantic splash.

The Children of Lir hauled Urbicus from his nasty hiding place and towed him through the waves to *Ormungandr*'s side. Red swirled from his wounds to streak the water. He yammered and feebly struggled.

The sea-monster, now only an inert body, settled slowly with waves breaking over it. The swimmers, cleansed of muck in the sea, handed Urbicus to the willing grasp of Gudrun's pirates and swarmed up the sides after him, treading on oars, grasping the shields hung along the rail. Urbicus lay in the ship's bottom, streaming water. Gudrun stood above him, smiling cruelly.

"Welcome, wrecker," she said. Her experienced eye told her that he was very likely dying. She would see that he did, in any case.

Urbicus said nothing. Gudrun then gave her attention to the Children of Lir, Rothevna among them. He seemed to bulk even more tall and wide than she remembered.

"Welcome, prince," she said in an utterly different voice. "Your aid was timely, yet I do wonder why you gave it."

The prince spoke. Turo the otter-man translated.

"We decided that he was a worse threat than you, Gudrun Blackhair. He knew far more of us than do you. Besides, he was a bishop, or had been, and the church means only destruction to our kind—and to yours and your lover's, I will mention."

"It is not the church that will destroy me."

"Ask your man his opinion, Gudrun. He's wise."

"What of you and I, prince? Had you wished to be rid of Urbicus and Gudrun both, you might have waited until one had triumphed, then made an end of the other."

"It was considered. The Children of Lir need no aid from such as Urbicus, and mine, when it came to it, was the loudest voice saying so. We will fight you ourselves if there must be war between us."

"I want none, lord." The old Gudrun would have defied him to his face and cared not what ensued. But Felimid waited for her on Sarnia. "I was forced to slay one of your folk when you would have kept me against my will. Will his kindred take wergild for him? I do not know if that is even your custom."

"The price I ask for his life is silence," Rothevna said through the mouth of Turo. "That you forget where we dwell, and aid us against any who may learn it in the future. To ensure that, let us exchange hostages."

"You have it," Gudrun said, "and my friendship with it. You are a mighty and generous man, lord."

Urbicus had lain in the bottom of the ship while the chieftains talked, disregarded like so much rubbish. Now his feet drummed wildly on the floor-timbers, and he died.

The wrecker's body was not cast into the sea, by Rothevna's request. Gudrun carried it to Lesia and had it buried deep, after the head was cut off and laid beneath the bent knee to prevent his ghost's walking. The dead sea-monster he had sorcerously animated from within drifted ashore, and broke apart on the rocks not a mile from Urbicus's grave.

He was mourned by none.

XV

*There are with the Feine seven absconders, whom
the sanctuary of God nor of man does not save, as
being unrighteous: bees which abscond; a runaway
thief; an absconder from his tribe; a man of red
weapons; a woman who elopes out of the law of
cohabitation; a woman or a man who absconds from
maintaining father or mother;—unless it be a person
who does not yield justice, after paths of theft; and
even in this case the sanctuary of God nor of man
does not save any unrighteous person if he leaves
any person behind him who was in want of his service,
to whom it is proper for him to return.*
                                        —The Senchus Mór

In Lansulcan, the shuffling feet and glances directed at
the ground, when it came to a question of who should take
in the strangers, were wonderful. None the less a couple of
farmers did offer hospitality at once. Vivayn opted for the
household of Megelin, for he seemed decent. His household
included a wife, a brother, two sons, a daughter, and sixteen
other folk, so four more, half of them young children, were
no insupportable burden.

"Are you Christians?" his wife asked severely.

"What else would a Roman princess be?" asked Vivayn,
who was of Pictish descent, and Eldrida said, "Yes," although she had never quite grasped the distinction between
Freya and Mary. The wife of Megelin looked doubtful, but
somehow could not quite meet Vivayn's light-gray eyes and
express her doubt.

"She's a bad one, the worst I've seen," she nagged her husband in bed that night. "You have only to look at her. Red hair is another name for wickedness, and the rest of her might be made of ice and snow. *Princess!* Yes, a princess who married the son of her father's murderer, and a heathen sea-wolf, not even human . . . likely she's not human herself! Who but a changeling would do what she did? You've taken evil under our roof, Megelin, and I fear it."

"Ah, bah," he grumbled. "Silly chatter. I know what began it. That nitwit Adlyn tried to ravish her and got a sharp lesson, and began to howl that she's a fay for spite. Well, the saint declares she's not, and he should know."

"The saint's too good. Also, he's a man, and a fool for a pretty face like all men, even monks! What if she's not a fay, then? Is a traitor-sorceress better? She's had dealings with the sea-wolves! Are we to forgive that?"

"Leave it, Kelda," Megelin said. "She fled the sea-wolves as we did. She's destitute, as we were. The inwardness of what happened before that is something we can't know, and kings and kings' daughters often behave ill."

"What about her companion? Two children without a father between them, and a wicked eye; that Eldrida is a trollop!"

The man sighed. Clearly he was not going to have any sleep for a while yet. "Belike the sea-wolves killed the father. It has been known to happen. Or she was kept as a concubine, or a number of the sea-wolves took her. That has been known to happen too."

"Humph. It's useless blinding yourself to facts, Megelin. She's of the sea-wolf breed her own self. *Christian,* she said! And butter wouldn't melt in her promising mouth, and I'm Empress of Rome! No man has ever had to rape that one, or do anything else to her save maybe to fight her off. You have only to look at her to know."

"Maybe that's why I made her welcome!" Megelin roared, exasperated.

Kelda did not let him forget that for the rest of his life.

While Megelin enjoyed his pleasant pillow-talk, the cartmen were drinking with some of the district's farm workers at the small water mill which served Lansulcan. The mill-wife, Brisen, made the best ale between Aleth and Avranches, they said, and for them that encompassed the world. Her three large beechwood vats were seldom idle; she hung out a green branch whenever she was brewing, and her long bakehouse behind the mill was the nearest thing to a grog-shop Lansulcan had.

Inspired by her ale, Adlyn was talking. His version of events had grown since he spoke to Molofi, despite the words she had brought down the mountain. Vivayn had changed into a crow bigger than three eagles and flown to perch on the sun; in the form of a woman again, she had summoned a barghest, gone into the woods with the monster and coupled with it; then she had forced all the cart-men to perform with her until they were exhausted, under threat of being torn apart by the lurking barghest. After some more drinks he repeated the story, and it had grown again.

"Does Molofi know this?" some skeptic bawled. The others laughed loudly, though with an uneasy note in their mirth. The strangers had arrived at an ominous time, for Samhain was very near, and everyone knew what sort of beings traveled freely on that night. Sorceries were particularly effective then.

"Ah, she's harmless with the saint about," someone else declared, and added after a moment, "Probably . . ."

Early next morning, his breath steaming in the cold, Eldrida's boy went to watch the butchering. There wasn't a great deal to be done. The folk of Lansulcan kept few cattle, but they could feed even fewer through the winter, so a small slaughter-yard had to be prepared, for common use and at a reasonable distance from any farmstead, lest it draw wolves.

The spears flashed and reddened. The beasts cried out as they died, their blood smoking in the cold. Then the dressing-out began. Cerdic's attention wandered, and he looked for someone to play with. Seeing some of the local children nearby, he joined them, stepping on a few large puddles as he approached, to hear the ice crackle.

"Hello," he said.

One answered. Soon they were being Britons and Saxons, howling in from an imagined sea, storming and defending forts, killing each other with bloodless ferocity and getting up again to fight and die as some new warrior.

Cerdic naturally played at being his grandfather, the barbarian sea-king whose name he shared. Although big enough for seven, he was actually five, too young for discretion.

Before long they were telling stories. It came to Cerdic then that he had been raised in a princely dun and crossed the sea while these children had never seen anything except the few farmsteads around them, the mill, the river and the forest. He told them about the long war-boats of Vectis and the warriors with their spears and braided hair, going out to plunder. He told them about the Children of Lir on the Veiled Isles, who swam like fish, didn't care how cold the sea was, and had green and silver patterns pricked in their skin. He jumbled the two places and tribes together in the telling, without knowing it or meaning to. They became more intermingled yet in his listeners' minds.

Inevitably, there was a scoffer. As he was telling them artlessly about Turo, who could change from a man to a large otter, a black-haired boy of about his own size said, "Oh, you lie and lie!" and pushed him roughly.

Cerdic pushed back. "None of it is lies! I saw Gudrun Blackhair, too. I was on her ship *Ormungandr*, and the prince of all the sea people was there. They robbed everything and burned the town!" he added for effect.

The other boy pushed him again. Cerdic pushed in return, and in a moment they were scuffling on the frosty ground. It was harmless. Although the other boys called encouragement to the dark lad, they did not join him in drubbing the stranger. It might have become nasty if it had been allowed to continue, but in the event, it proved even nastier when someone intervened.

Adlyn did. Seeing the black and yellow heads side by side in the panting tussle, he jerked the boys apart. Scowling at Cerdic, he demanded to know who had started it, and the Lansulcan gang were swift to cry, "He did!"

Adlyn hit Cerdic sideways, then kicked his backside harder than was needful. He wasn't in the sweetest of humors, for his head ached after his drinking bout. Again, it could have ended there. This, however, was Cerdic's grandson. He did not run.

He rose from the frosty ground and shouted with his

mouth bleeding, "You dirty son of a mare! I, I, I'll cut your head off! I'll come back in a ship with all my men! I'll burn your house down!"

They were the wrong words to use in Lansulcan, and if they were to be said at all, a boy of the sea-wolf breed who carried the name Cerdic was the wrong one to say them. Adlyn had seen homes burning and heads cut off, before he fled Britain. So had some others at the slaughter-yard, and Cerdic's young voice had carried.

"You will, eh?" said Adlyn, his voice terribly soft. "Not if you never grow to the size of a man, you little devil."

He twisted one hand in Cerdic's tunic, lifted him from the ground, and began to strike him with growing fury, forehand and backhand clouts. The boy seized Adlyn's wrist, swung up his feet and kicked him in the chest, to no profitable effect. The blows rained fast and hard until Cerdic's tunic ripped and he fell out of it to the ground.

"Let him be!"

Eldrida had come looking for her son, and found him. She ran forward, yellow hair flying, her gray-green, tawny-flecked eyes narrowed, her full mouth snarling. She halted by Cerdic, ripped a small knife from its sheath and held it blade upward.

"Touch him!" she spat. "Touch him again and I will have you in bloody pieces hanging from hooks like your own cattle! I'll have your family jewels for earrings!"

"His dam," Adlyn said, breathing hard. "I see where the little scut gets it, now."

He stepped towards her.

"Gets what? The belly to talk for himself? And where do you get it, Adlyn? From having your whole tribe behind you?"

She slashed his reaching hand, and laughed as he swore and sprang back with blood dripping.

"You couldn't take a woman even with friends to help, you gutless marvel! Found something you could manage! It's well Cerdic is not a year older. He'd be too much for you then."

Adlyn whitened, and went for her. She cut him again before he seized her arm. He twisted it until she let the knife fall with a scream muffled behind clenched teeth, then knocked her winding.

"Bitch!"

Eldrida picked herself up. She touched her son gently, finding no broken bones. He whimpered, partly stunned. She lifted him in her arms.

"Dogs try to mate with bitches," she said.

Adlyn aimed a blow at her, and felt wholly justified. He had about persuaded himself by now that his drunken version of events on the road was the true one. Eldrida gasped, clutched her boy and didn't retaliate. Discretion was coming to her, somewhat late. The cart-man struck her twice more.

"Draw my blood, will you?" he snarled. "Now I'll color your back like storm-clouds. Drag her to the fence and give me a spear-shaft!"

Having done no good, discretion departed once more. "Salute the barghest for me," Eldrida said.

That weakened Adlyn's purpose. She wasn't beaten.

On the holy mountain, Sulghein stood in a cistern of water to his neck, devotedly freezing while uttering blue-lipped prayers. As he prayed, fiery visions filled his mind. He saw the oceans rise to swallow the land. Stars fell blackening out of the sky, and sunken ships were resurrected from the sea floor with dead crews aboard. They floated despite their skeletal state and the festoons of weed they trailed. Monsters commanded them, changing form to appear as white-skinned men, then partially melting into monsters again. One leg showed scaly and web-footed, the other remained human, while their arms were likewise mismatched but on opposite sides, and always the heads were those of demons. They were sailing through the Forest of Dol to the crag of Saint Michael, and there was nowhere to hide.

"The Fomors!" Sulghein cried. "The Fomors return from the sunken lands and the sea gives up its dead! And I stood upon the sand of the sea, and saw a beast rise up out of the sea, having seven heads and ten horns, and upon his horns ten crowns, and upon his heads the name of blasphemy.... Fear God, and give glory to him, for the hour of his judgment is come; and worship him that made heaven, and earth, and the sea, and the fountains of waters!"

Below, among his people, there was pother out of all
proportion to events. Megelin found himself in the middle.
Eldrida was his guest, Adlyn had beaten her son, she had
evidently tried to murder Adlyn; all that was a sufficiently
pretty kettle of fish in itself. But the seething froth and scum
which obscured it—"He said the sea people would come to
kill us all," the black-haired boy accused. "He said he'd
bring them."

"He might, too. Cerdic's his grandfather—Cerdic of
Westri, by heaven!"

"All this is foolishness!" Eldrida protested. "It was noth-
ing to begin with but a fight between boys! Yes, my son is
Cerdic's grandson—one of them. He must have fifty such.
Is that cause for this hero to beat a little boy to death?"

"It's best that a sea-wolf's cub should never grow big
enough to bite," Molofi said.

Eldrida's hands itched for a spear. *I'll remember you said
that, hag,* she thought. But she was frightened now. *Where
have you gone, Vivayn? These are your people, of your
blood—more than I am, anyhow. Maybe you could do something with them.*

Adlyn lifted the black-haired boy to his shoulder. "Now,
son, tell everybody," he urged. "What did that cub say about
Gudrun and the sea-wolves?"

*Son! He's Adlyn's son! I really did it this time. No wonder
he wants my tripes. I attacked and miscalled him in front
of his boy!*

*Hel take that. Isn't Cerdic mine? And Adlyn playing the
loving daddy is enough to make a crow vomit....*

"Say out, Trem," Molofi urged, gloating.

Trem had lost his pleasure in being the center of attention.
Baffled by the din his elders were making, as children often
are, he yet sensed that he was likely to lose half a yard of
hide if he did not shift the blame for—whatever was wrong—
to Cerdic. Yet he couldn't see what Cerdic had done that
was so bad, either. He licked his lips.

"I s-started the fight," he said.

Eldrida sent him a glowing look. She knew that wouldn't
help. The fight was not the heart of this. Still it had been
a good thing to say.

Adlyn shook the boy so that he almost fell from his seat. "None of that! The fight was nothing; what did he say?"

"He said he came in Gudrun Blackhair's ship, and there are islands none can see with green mermen and dragons, and they're coming to burn our houses! He says he'll make them kill us."

"You see!" Adlyn said. "And Vivayn the Perfidious is Cynric's wife, Cerdic's daughter-in-law. Why's she traveling through this land if not to spy for them? Where is she, Megelin? She's not human either, we know that."

"I've not seen her this morning," he answered.

"Where is she?" Adlyn demanded of Eldrida, whose arms by now were gripped hard by two Britons. Adlyn's tone held fear, and because he was afraid the air was full of danger.

"I don't know."

Vivayn had always come and gone as she wished, by trickery if other means couldn't serve her. Eldrida didn't know whether to hope she would return now, or remain away until this was finished.

"Well, we'll find out," Adlyn said.

Eldrida said, "Take Cerdic back to the house. You won't make him watch if any of you are men at all."

"There will be nothing to watch," Megelin said harshly. "Yet I agree, we don't need the boy. Kelda, back to the house with him and look after him well."

"I—"

"Go!" That settled, Megelin looked thoughtfully at the cart-men. "You might send yours home too, Adlyn, if you intend what you seem to be intending."

"I'm not ashamed, and you keep your nose well out of harm's way. There is nothing wrong in a boy seeing how sea-wolves ought to be handled."

"But only their women and little boys, is it?" Megelin answered. "Well, well. I am just wondering how brave you would all be if it was twenty weapon-men. Besides, there are two we should have here if there are questions to be answered. The lady Vivayn and the saint."

Someone clouted him from behind with a cudgel then, and he made the frost crunch under him as he embraced the earth. Then Eldrida was handled back and forth, lifted over heads and carried screaming and kicking to the slaughter-yard while Megelin's younger son stayed by him.

"Here, you," he said to a bondman he had seized by the tunic, heedless of fleas. "Run to the house and bring help, and bring it well armed, look you. Stop, or go another way, and I will pull out your ribs one by one as they were daisy petals."

The bondman set off. Megelin's son wrapped his father in a cloak.

"Which will happen to the weasel who struck you down, once you are walking again," he added to the insensible figure, "for I saw him, receive assurance. It's a shroud he will need, not a warm cloak. But all in good time."

Since there was little one man could do against a mob, he sat and waited. Eldrida was stripped bare to raucous yells of joy from the men and malice from the women, then tied to the slaughter-yard's main post. She shivered, and began to turn blue.

"Ah, she's cold," one harpy shrieked. "Make her a fire!"

"Yes! Roast her!"

"Roast the sea-wolf bitch! Roast her well!"

They had a small fire smouldering before her feet ere-long. Because they had been hasty, she still wore her shoes and the woollen wrappings around her lower legs. It hardly mattered.

"Now," Adlyn demanded, "what's this about sea devils coming to kill us? Speak."

"There's nothing! A baby's anger! You'd do this to me because a boy let his tongue wag?"

Adlyn chuckled. "Come now, whore. I was lately in Aleth. I heard the tales about Gudrun Blackhair being there, and having two mermen with her. They swam away, it's said. No, there is something to all this, and for our own safety, we mean to know what."

"Aye!"

"You'd better speak!"

Bruised and freezing, Eldrida had about reached that conclusion herself. Surely she must tell them *something* which would satisfy them. She owed little consideration to the Children of Lir; they had broken faith with her and Vivayn. These people were worse, though—much. Cruel and petty. Since they were enjoying themselves with her, they might refuse to believe if she blabbed too soon, and continue hurting her. She knew how that was. She'd heard her brother's pirates talking about it on Vectis. They had forced the hiding-places of wealth from enough victims to know all about it, and *they* said it was hard to stop once they had started, in case there might be more to discover.

She whimpered, "Please . . ."

They grinned and mocked her. Yes. The pigs liked that. Oh, but it was miserable, to be raw-naked and cold before such a gang of stinking yokels! *Play for time and think of a tale.*

"Please . . . there's nothing . . ."

Molofi doubled a fist like a stone and hit her in the belly. "There's any amount, girl! Put her foot in the fire."

Hands in dirty half mittens gripped her leg. They rammed her foot among the coals so that her shoe began to smoke. She stared at it, knowing that soon she would feel the heat. Her foot was warm already through the leather, and *how far would these fools go?* Maybe to any lengths at all, if they urged each other on, and worked each other up to it. Eldrida saw herself mutilated and dead. The stink of burning leather filled her nose, mingling with the whiff of ordure and offal from the slaughter-yard behind her.

She writhed and begged some more. She was more serious about it now, as her foot grew painfully hot. Then, judging the time right, she screamed, "No! I'll tell, I'll tell, I'll tell!"

They took her foot out of the fire.

"It's true," she gulped. "True, about the islands no man can see. They have a glamour over them. They are the sandbanks about one day's sail northwest from your coast. Gudrun Blackhair's raiders live there, hidden from sight by magic, the sea-demons she rules, pirates, monsters, killers all."

She gabbled this because it seemed to be what they believed and what they wanted her to confirm.

"And you're their spy?"

"N-no. I fled from them. I swear it! I dread your sending me back to them. Please, don't do that."

"Huh. I think she lies."

"No lie," Eldrida gasped. She thought of something, a tale of Faerie customs she had heard in Britain. "I fled because . . . they pay tribute to Hel each seven years. It would have been my babies and I."

They muttered among themselves. Molofi put the next question, somewhat less harshly. "What about these sea-demons, girl?"

"Th-they have brown scales, and paws with fishy webs in place of hands and feet." Eldrida had heard this from Hemming the Saxon. "They look like handsome men and women, though, to a mortal's eyes. They eat drowned sailors, or live ones when they can catch them."

There was more discussion, to which someone put an end by cutting her free. She was shaking against the support of the post at which she had, perhaps, come close to dying, when Sulghein strode through the crowd. Who had run to the holy mountain to fetch him she never knew.

He was an appalling sight. His night in the cistern, spent there for reasons best known to, and appreciated by, himself, had left him not so much blue as sullen indigo with cold. He might have been a wood-painted Druid of former times. He walked stiff-legged, and little flakes of ice rustled in his hair. He wore only a long, yard-wide band of cloth, kilted several times about his waist and tossed plaidlike over his shoulder.

"Cover her!"

"Now, lord—" Adlyn began.

Sulghein's fist came across like a hammer. Adlyn went down on his backside to discover, when he came out of his mumbling daze, that he was three teeth the poorer.

"Cover her!" Sulghein thundered. "She offends me!"

Eldrida struggled into her torn clothes and accepted a cloak. Sulghein's eyes blazed yet with visions of the world's destruction, and she felt more afraid of him than she had been of all his flock, with their crude torments. She had to repeat her story now, telling of the sandbanks which were truly enchanted islands. She had also to stand by her fabrications. Sulghein, with fervor seething in his brain, believed it all. It fitted well with the apocalyptic visions he'd been having.

"The wickedness of the Sidhe, and it nearby," he marveled. "Now I will go. I will travel to the coast, and take a boat, and reach this nest of demons by Samhain Eve. They will show in their true forms then. With God's help I will destroy them wholly out of this world, and obliterate them from the ridge of the earth!"

He was rapt, uplifted, seeing angels and demons and nothing else.

"What are we to do, lord?" someone asked out of the chastened group. "With this one?"

Sulghein looked at Eldrida, not as though she mattered. She knew that her life and her children's hung upon his whim. *Vivayn, where are you? None but you hereabouts can match this crazy man's power....*

"Keep her and do not harm her," he said indifferently. "I'll judge her when I return. If I do not return, you must judge her."

What sort of judgment that would be, Eldrida knew too well. No matter. She was reprieved until after Samhain—and she would not leave Megelin's house again.

"Lord," Molofi said practically, "will you eat before you leave?"

"Bread and leeks only," Sulghein answered. "I touch no meat until my work is done."

Within the hour, he had eaten, warmed himself by a fire and dressed in his robe, gathering it halfway up his legs for easy movement. He wore leggings and stout shoes under it. Then he was away, following the stream which flowed through Lansulcan and the forest, northwest towards the sea. He took with him a book, protected by an inner case of wood and an outer one of silver, and he took also the gold-set saintly skull.

In the meantime, the party from Megelin's house had arrived, and the man himself had recovered from the cudgel-blow. They took Eldrida back. Despite her blistered foot, she walked without complaint, and when she looked at the sky, the pale sun's height told her the morning was only half advanced. A short autumn morning, too. Much had happened in a very little while.

Vivayn walked in at the gate before noon, oblivious of

trouble. She had gone out at sunrise, guided by a man whose forebears had lived in the region for very long, to visit a dolmen which stood in a forest clearing. She had reasoned that if she needed to work an enchantment, the holy mountain would be the most appropriate place, but if she could not do that because of Sulghein's presence, the dolmen might serve. She had spent a couple of hours there, open to the influences of the spot.

When she learned what had happened to Eldrida, and what else had almost happened, she grew ominously still and quiet.

"These neighbors of yours require lessons in Christian charity," she said to Megelin. That was all, and not much of a comment to some which had been bandied that morning, yet it caused Megelin more unease than any bluster would have done. Looking into Vivayn's light-gray eyes, he thought of snowstorms and of deadly hail stripping flesh to the bone.

"Some of them do," he said grimly, "and Adlyn and Molofi first of all. Aye, and at least one other I could mention." He touched the huge glistening lump on his head. "I didn't see him, but Retho did, and I will visit him tonight and give him bloody cudgels from behind."

"So?" Vivayn pressed a smile from her lips. "Then I will gladly leave the matter to you. Strength to your arm, my friend, and strike a blow for Eldrida, if you are pleased to."

It was a trifling thing, anyhow. The mission Sulghein had given himself was enormously more weighty. Vivayn knew about it, had known since the hour she returned from the dolmen. All Lansulcan knew, and was talking about it. The farmyard geese knew. A woman who could understand the voices which spoke in the wind was not likely to remain ignorant.

"Well, my chick," she said, embracing Eldrida lightly, "you had a bad time, I am told."

"It wasn't much fun. Nothing to make a great fuss about, though. Some skin burned off my foot, a few blows, a little shame." Eldrida grinned. "And I never have had much of that! It might have been worse."

"Then it would have been very much worse for those responsible. I should have seen to it." Vivayn ruffled her friend's hair. "Every little thing is magnified beyond reason in this place. It is too small, and ruled by a crazed monk. Maybe we should go to Avranches instead. It's barely three leagues."

"I can't walk it now."

"No. The children would hamper us, too, and then it is nigh to Samhain. I wouldn't traverse the forest then. We might meet anything—phantoms, the Wild Hunt, even a *real* barghest."

"Not to speak of wolves or a stag in rut. They can be just as bad."

"Not to speak of those. Yes. We must bide until Samhain is over, then—and I still trust Megelin."

"So do I."

"As for Sulghein, I don't know whether to hope he succeeds or fails. He may succeed! He has the power, and he knows how to do what he wants to do. It will not end there, mind. The fool doesn't know what he is meddling with." Vivayn reached a decision. "I'll warn the Children of Lir, and Felimid also."

"I thought you would."

Vivayn sat at a loom and began weaving. As she wove she sang, a clear song which pierced like crystal blades, and in a little while an air sprite came to her in the form of a bird. It was white and palest blue, with a spreading lacy tail, the colors and patterns of a clear winter's day. None but Vivayn could see it.

"Child of air," she said, "there is a message I would have you take for me, to Rothevna the Prince of those Children of Lir who dwells in the Veiled Isles, and to the bard with the gold-strung harp who has the love of Gudrun Blackhair in Sarnia. And these are the words..."

XVI

I come with a message, not mischief only.
    —The Lay of Thrym

Felimid's head sang pleasantly with wine. He felt that brotherhood of liquor which suits the inconstant human spirit better than most other kinds. The long hall of Sarnia was a wondrous place. All its splendors, like the varied weapons shining on the walls, the gold winking on Gudrun's captains, and the trophies of white bear and red ape flanking her seat, were tenfold more splendid. Any sleazy aspects were dissolved in the liquor.

Gudrun had abandoned her high seat to drink and laugh with some of her men. Felimid, of course, was one, and Decius the Spaniard, whose tough, sardonic practicality she loved, and Hemming the Saxon, who still had a faraway look now and again when he remembered Eldrida, and Turo the otter-man, her hostage from the Children of Lir. There was Giguderich, too, cadaverous and gloomy-looking, but one of the best fighters even in that company, and chestnut-haired Sigar, whom she had recruited in Jutland.

"Nay, but tell me," Giguderich said earnestly to Turo, "what is it . . . like . . . to be a shapeshifter? I've heard of such things. I've seen wonders, understand! You do, when you sail with the lady, but I never spoke with a shapeshifter until now."

"You may have done, without knowing," Turo told him. "They are born now and again among your kind, as among mine. Among yours they are usually killed, most strictly in Christian lands, but sometimes their mothers conceal the truth. Then they live to grow. It's hard, though, for them to hide the beast-skin or bird-plumage which is part of them and gives them the power to change."

"Ah. Ah." Giguderich nodded. "You said *born,* though. Does that mean they come from the womb as—"

"It does, so," Turo confirmed. "I was born in the shape of an otter cub, fur and all, Giguderich, from out the womb of a sea-woman, and then I squirmed out of the skin and went to her breast as a boy shapen like any. But that skin is part of me yet, and I must keep it near me."

"Wonnerful. *Hic.* But suppose," Giguderich said, choosing the words of his hypothesis with care, "suppose a man was to steal this skin of yours?"

"Then I could not change until I had my skin back. I might have to do whatever the man asked of me that he would return it." Turo smiled wickedly. "He might desire to turn shape himself, and the pelt of a shapeshifter born is the most certain way for a man to achieve that, by putting it on. But then he must risk not being able to take it off."

"But my question, lad?"

"Question?" Turo was somewhat drunk, too. He felt his position as a hostage, and had not spared the flagon. His strange eyes glowed. "Oh. What it's like?"

He spoke not in Gothic, but in Saxon, one of three tongues he knew, and which Giguderich barely comprehended. It mattered little. Any misunderstandings could be lubricated.

"That is like asking a bird what it is like to be a bird. It has never been aught else, so how can it know? But I'll tell you as best I can. It is like having the freedom of two worlds, and belonging truly to neither. Oh, diving and gliding through the green, Goth-man! Hunting a fish, spurning the water with webbed paws, alive to the end of every hair, anticipating your prey's twists and turns, and sinking teeth into its live flesh! Coming up to the shore, the way it feels to writhe out of the skin and stand as a man, and captain a ship! To love a girl! Yes, and I've done that sometimes without shedding the otter-skin first, let me tell you. Human girls do not confess everything in church. What is it like to be a pirate, and follow the lady?"

"Damnation!" Giguderich said. "Now *you* are asking! I

can't use words as the bard, there, can...no...not even
as you can, otter-man. No...What's it like? I'll say this.
On land, for me, there is nothing except a gibbet, and if I
'scape that, pig dung on my feet every day. Bowing and
scraping. Fear. Now here on Sarnia I'm as free as the likes
of me can be. I swagger, I stand tall. I'm one of Gudrun
Blackhair's men. See? I, I'm 'fraid of nothing...except
the lady...and no man has to be ashamed of fearing her.

"In a fight, I kill a man or he kills me. Sea-fight or land-
fight, when we win, I look at them we've killed and I think,
well, it was not me...this time. It might've been, though.
And one day, it will be. That's what. You take the risk and
know the end. It's better to take the risk and know the end
than cringe, otter-man. You asked me. Now I've told you,
the best I can."

Turo clapped him on the back and refilled their horns.

He did not wear his otter-skin. That lay in Gudrun's
chamber, against the day he was free, no more a hostage.
To hold Children of Lir against their will on an island was
impossible, short of chaining or enspelling them, so Gudrun
had chosen Turo, because his skin-turning nature meant that
he could be contained. The man of Gudrun's who had gone
to the Veiled Isles in exchange was young Rowan; he had
offered. Indeed, he had been determined. He was Gudrun's
man to the depth of his young heart. There was nothing he
would not do for her, and be pleased to do.

"Let's have a song, Bragi!"

"Yes. One about the lady!"

Felimid played a bold, simple tune. "One about the lady?
Here's a thing that befell in the north."

He sang:

> "A miller lived in Wendish lands,
>   And the worst of men was he, o,
>   Nine young girls there he drowned and slew
>   To please the water sidhe, o.

> "Gudrun Blackhair passed one day
>   When summer's growth was green, o,
>   And she was clad as a fine young man,
>   The match of any seen, o.

"*Gudrun Blackhair stopped and stayed,*
  As the miller's guest she tarried, o.
He neither knew her by her hair,
  Nor the snake-backed sword she carried, o.

"*He knew her in his stable-yard,*
  The mare and colt obeyed her, o;
The stallion stamped and ramped and reared,
  And his loud neigh betrayed her, o.

"*They dragged her to the water-marge,*
  Five men could scarcely hold her, o,
By the clacking, clamouring water-wheel,
  The miller he starkly told her, o:

"*Nine young girls have I drownéd here,*
  Yourself the tenth must make, o.
Remove your clothes now, wanderer,
  You must die beneath my lake, o.

"*Then Gudrun reached for her jerkin-lace,*
  But she grasped her sword instead, o,
Two of the men she flung from her,
  And a third struck suddenly dead, o.

"*The fourth she slew with her snake-backed sword,*
  She sundered and hewed him well, o,
The fifth she fed on his own broad knife,
  And there by the marge he fell, o.

"*She pinned the miller with sharpened stakes,*
  She weighed him down with stones, o;
'Now there in your own lake bide,' she said,
  'Till the fish swim through your bones, o.'

"*'Die there, die there, you worst of men,*
  Aye, sink and drown,' she cried, o,
'Sith nine young girls you have murdered here,
  Go tell them how you died, o.'"

The men roared, delighted by their chief's deed. She was delighted by the song. The bard received a kiss. Then, as he was wetting his throat after the ballad, the impalpable bird with lacy wings flew through the hall and alighted on his knee.

It spoke to him in Vivayn's voice.

Being happily in drink, Felimid was not at his most quick-witted. He looked and listened unthinkingly while it greeted him and began to tell him things. Gudrun noticed him staring at what, to her, was the void air, and felt her skin prickle. She was closely acquainted by now with her man's ability to see things others did not, and believed in it fully, but it hadn't ceased to disconcert her.

"Bragi, what's toward?"

"We have a visitor, and there's news. A moment, Gudrun. I haven't understood it yet."

The bird repeated its news, and Felimid, carefully listening, felt himself grow a deal soberer as he grasped it.

"Our alliance with the sea-people may end when it has hardly begun. Listen."

He described the situation.

Gudrun didn't find it urgent.

"What is it to us if some fool of a monk decides to die?" she asked. "The Children of Lir have stronger magic than his, surely? If he sees their isles at all he will not live long. They can deal with him."

"Maybe not. The power this madman carries is the power that kills magic. He may destroy the glamour over those isles for all time, and expose them to the world, which means the end of Rothevna's folk."

"Then let them stop him before he reaches the Veiled Isles! Let them drown him a mile from his own shores. That is simple, and if Rothevna cannot deal with one crazed priest, he is not the man I reckon him."

"True for you, Gudrun. Rothevna—or the least of his folk—would deal with this priest right briskly, did they know that he's coming. They do not! The sprite has flown to Rothevna's hall with a warning, but it went unseen and unheard. I don't know why. Rothevna and Idh should be skilled enough in air magic to see such an elemental. Or perhaps just Idh. Probably the sprite lost patience before it found either of them. Its kind is fickle and light. I'm astonished that it came here instead of forgetting its errand entirely, once disappointed."

Gudrun yawned in the firelight. "Whatever is to happen will have happened before we can forestall it, Bragi."

"No!" Felimid was eager and Gudrun the laggard, for once. "This priest, this Sulghein, set out this morning. He'd some four leagues of forest to be passing, as the crow flies, Vivayn says; once he reached the sea, he'd still have to obtain a boat; and then he'd have six or seven leagues of tricky water to cross, even after he caught a favorable tide. And the tides are very fierce in those parts, as I know who have been to Aleth but once! He can't reach the Veiled Isles before tomorrow night, but we can."

"This truly matters to you?" Gudrun asked slowly.

"Indeed, and I'll be telling you why! If the monk succeeds it will mean one more triumph for the powers that shrivel magic. They have had too many as it is, and to that I take oath. Now I am for warning Rothevna, and intercepting this monk in his little boat, and . . ." He hesitated, then went on firmly. " . . . if he can't be silenced or his danger averted in any other way, I am for slaying him."

"By the high seat of Hel!" Gudrun was astonished. "This does matter to you."

"I think it right," Sigar affirmed. "This fellow has appointed himself their enemy. Well, when a man comes uninvited to supper, he must just take what he finds in the pot."

"Agreed," Decius said succinctly. The Spaniard was orthodox; he did not think highly of Celtic churchmen in any case.

"You say nothing, Turo," Gudrun observed. "These are your folk."

"I? I'm your hostage, lady. I did not know I had anything to say. Since I am asked—yes! Wasn't this your agreement? That we help you, and you help us? That you keep our secret, and aid us to keep it from others? Why else am I here, and why else is Rowan in the Veiled Isles?"

Giguderich grunted assent.

"Yes," Gudrun said. "That is true, and it shames me that I did not think of it first. All right, then. In the morning we will go. Now, with that settled—do you know any good drinking songs, Bragi?"

"A moment." Felimid stood, with the sprite's impalpable form on his outstretched arm like a falconer. "All thanks for bringing this word, child of air. I'll repay you as I can, with harp-music, poetry and song, and you will ever be welcome where I am."

The elemental ruffled its wings, very like a bird of flesh and blood. Then it leapt from Felimid's arm, with a brief gust of air, and flashed white through the ale haze.

"Now, about that drinking song—"

He gave them "Kvasir's Blood," and "The Sea of Ale," and "The Shore Wife." They joined in, roaring, and more casks were broached. Decius climbed on a long table and imitated a Hun with piles attempting to ride down fleeing fugitives, moaning, flinching and cursing the maker of his tough wooden saddle. Two of the women in the hall fought tooth and nail over a man, first informally and then in a circle to Gudrun's rules. All in all it was quite a night, and it did not end until the little hours of the morn.

XVII

I am the wind which blows over the sea,
I am wave of the sea,
I am lowing of the sea,
I am the bull of seven battles,
I am bird of prey on the cliff-face,
I am sunbeam,
I am skillful sailor,
I am a cruel boar,
I am lake in the valley,
I am word of knowledge,
I am a sharp sword threatening an army,
I am the god who gives fire to the head,
I am he who casts light between the mountains,
I am he who foretells the ages of the moon,
I am he who teaches where the sun sets.
> —The Song of Amergin

It was unfair, some would have said. The mighty serpent-ship had eyes which saw clearly in fog and rain, a hull which slipped through the sea as though water offered no resistance, its timbers flexing like live bone and sinew with never a normal, natural creak to be heard, and could sail better to windward than a ship had any right to. Withal, it could speed before the lightest breath of a breeze, and a mere dozen oars propelled it faster than forty would do for another vessel. In a contest with that was one struggling man in whatever boat he had been able to find; a leaky fishing craft, probably.

Felimid mac Fal could not have been better pleased that

it was unfair. He wished it were even less fair. The unfair advantages would be all on Sulghein's side if he ever reached his goal.

"Easy, my man," Gudrun said, noting his urgent stare southward past the high serpent-head, and the grip of his right hand's fingers on the gunwale. "You fret too much. You used to be lighter-hearted."

"I did, didn't I? And I promise you, I will be again when Samhain has passed; but it is *tonight*."

Samhain. The most dangerous night of the year.

The gods seemed to be aiding the monk. As the previous day, the dawn had been frosty, the morning a clear, pale, tender blue. There was not even a trace of mackerel cloud to promise rain. The gray sea's waves made no threat, but rolled steady and sedate. Well, they would reach the Veiled Isles all the sooner for that. They, speeding from the north while Sulghein sloshed and lumbered from the south.

But he did not have so far to go.

Felimid would have been worse troubled if he had known the sort of boat Sulghein had obtained, and was using. No inshore skiff, no craft of heavy, waterlogged, leaking timber, did the saint sail on his mission, but a swift two-man curragh used for setting lobster pots, nimble and seaworthy. When its owner had protested, Sulghein had left the silver outer case of his book with the man, in case he failed to return.

The greased leather hull skimmed through the troughs and crests like a seabird.

Sulghein rowed tirelessly with the narrow-bladed oars, and when the wind served he raised the sail on the light mast, adjusting it constantly. He knew this work. Born to a royal clan in Erin, converted young he had gone to Britain and become a monk at David's monastery in Mynyw. His master's ruthless discipline had agreed with Sulghein; he wholly abstained from liquor, drew carts and ploughs like an ox with his brothers, and practiced austerities which would have killed a man not made of seasoned oak. Sulghein had grown even stronger. He had sailed small boats on many errands in those western waters, and fished them well, fish being a great necessity as David's monks never ate meat at all.

Learning had not come as easily. Sulghein had furrowed

his brows many a night over letters and grammar, and never truly mastered them. A prodigious memory aided him there, for often he had only to open a book and look at its illuminated pages to *remember* what was written thereon. He could recite without actually reading, and seldom made a mistake. This was not dissimilar to the training of the Druids, who learned by word of mouth; and in many ways Sulghein was more like them than he realized.

He would have denied that with hot fierce pride.

Eight years previous, he had crossed the sea, navigating his own boat like many another monk, and had come to the holy mountain. After fasting for forty days on the crag, he had consecrated it to his god and church and Saint Michael, and founded his parish. Lansulcan bore his name, altered somewhat by British pronunciation, for he had done much to create it.

No longer one monk among many, he bowed to neither abbot nor bishop. He ruled his community, prince and priest in the same flesh. Because of that, it was for him to protect them. They were in his care.

"When he prepared the heavens, I was there," Sulghein chanted. *(Bend! Row!)* "When he set a compass upon the face of the depth *(Bend!)*, when he established the clouds above, when he strengthened the fountains of the deep *(Row!)*, when he gave to the sea his decree that the waters should not pass his commandment *(Bend! Row!)*, when he appointed the foundations of the earth then I was by him, as one brought up with him, and I was daily his delight, rejoicing always before him *(Row!)*; rejoicing in the habitable part of his earth; and my delights were with the sons of men." *(Brace! Bend! Row!)*

"And these who are not sons of men," he added to the lucid sky, "with your help, Lord, I will destroy from your earth and banish even from your sea! Never shall devils despoil my people, body or soul."

Brine gurgled below his curragh.

Ormungandr came to the Veiled Isles in daylight, and as Felimid scanned the lagoons and woods he saw to his relief that all appeared safe. Turo stood nearby, in kilt and sandals. His otter-skin had been left on Sarnia. Gudrun wore her mail and helmet, a white glitter in the sun, and the wind spread the black wings on her helmet wide, as a raven spread its black wings across her crimson sail.

"Take down the serpent-head," she commanded. "I do not wish to offend any powers here."

The ship which met them this time had a white swan for a figurehead, while its sail bore a stylized pattern of waves in blue and purple. Around the sail's edges were curling, intertwining maroon stems representing seaweed. It beat *Ormungandr*'s dress sail hollow, for complexity of design, anyway. For vivid color they were about equal.

"Aidan!" Turo called, recognizing the ship and knowing her "husband."

"Aidan it surely is. What has brought you back so soon, and with your host?"

"It's news of danger we're bringing," Felimid said, "and of how it can be averted. A priest is coming to ban your isles."

"Follow me in," Aidan said abruptly.

Rothevna received them gravely. With Idh to translate, he heard their story, sitting motionless, mantled to the throat in a cloak sewn all over with minute shells. He remained so still that the shells never rustled, and it was as though he had expected to hear this for a thousand years and was not astonished.

"It comes now, then."

"What? Lord, this priest means to destroy your place, the home of your clan, and he has the means! We brought the news so that you may prevent it! Is one mad Cross-worshipper to ruin all this?"

Idh replied in his own voice, not for Rothevna. "But one mad Cross-worshipper can. That is our weakness. Besides, this place was never a home, but an outpost, a guarding fortress. Surely you guessed that?"

"*I* did not," Gudrun cut in. She glanced suspiciously at the bard. "What is it you guard, then?"

"Tonight you may see for yourself," Idh answered. "What must be done is for the prince to decide, no other. The charge of our clan has been to maintain the Veiled Isles in secret for so long as it can be done—and when, in spite of everything, they are made naked, to save them from conquest. This may be the time or not. I think it is."

"The time—for what?"

"I would not offend, lady, but I may not say. If I am right, you will soon know. You delivered your warning in friendship, and I am grateful."

"Do not be grateful to me! There stands the one who argued for it, and brought you word. I would rip the truth from you if you stood in my hall."

"No doubt," Idh said.

Gudrun snorted, and left in a temper. Her disposition was not improved by her finding Felimid, a little later, in deep conversation with a green-haired daughter of Lir.

"Secrets and mystifications!" she complained.

The sea-woman said soberly, "There will be no secrets left after tonight. Too many know now. Urbicus knew, but kept his own counsel, and he is dead. You know; Vivayn knows, and she is free in the world; the people of the holy mountain know, because of her; there are rumors in Aleth; this priest Sulghein knows. The bubble has burst, the key has been taken, the well opened. The only wonder is that it did not happen before."

"Gudrun, this is Niamh, Rothevna's sister."

"Huh. I remember you, I think, from the day we killed Urbicus. You should be yonder, now, tearing a hole in this nitwit's boat. We wasted time coming here if you will not defend what is yours."

"Enough!" Niamh raged. She bent forward, her fingers spread into claws, and absolutely hissed. "The secret is known! You broke it yourself when you escaped. A secret broached cannot be made secret again, any more than goslings can be put back in the eggs, or dead leaves restored green to the trees. If it was to be kept at all, Vivayn and Eldrida should never have been brought here, and you and your men should all have been slain. I argued for it. Idh backed me. We did not have our way. How do matters stand now? Your pirates know, the yokels of this place Lansulcan know. We would have to wipe them all out. We cannot do that and remain unknown." She breathed violently, her spired breasts jumping, her hands shaking. "No. Useless it would be to kill you now, but I would like to do it anyway. *Do not tempt me!*" she yelled.

There were sudden, grief-stricken tears in her eyes, rising

and sparkling like the tide. She did not try to hide them.
For a moment she glared through the hot bright flood, then
abruptly flung away.

"She's right, you know," Felimid said ruefully.

"Surely she is right." Gudrun shrugged. "She knows *now*
what they should have done *then*. That bakes no bread."
There was a certain sympathy in the look she cast at Niamh
where she now sat brooding on a couch, but no pity. "The
gods know they must have killed often enough to guard this
secret of theirs in the past. Maybe they have gone soft this
last hundred-year."

Or is it only Rothevna? she wondered. *Is he maybe a
weakling, for all that splendid appearance and noble manner? Has he much behind it?*

She whispered to Felimid, "Do you suppose they are
acting and not telling us?"

"I'd not be amazed," he answered in a normal tone.

The afternoon drew on.

Sulghein in his curragh peered over the gray rolling sea.
There lay the peninsula, far to his right, and that headland
to the north must be Angia—aye, but the southeastern extremity of the island. The woman Eldrida had said that the
Veiled Isles lay due south of Angia, and had the appearance
of sandbanks a few miles in extent. So, then. He would
take his boat due west, and watch for shoals.

Dolphins rose out of the water, sporting around his curragh. They appeared to be laughing. Then they rammed his
boat from beneath, making it lurch and roll dangerously.
He grabbed a thwart.

A blue-black dolphin a fathom and a half in length leaped
before him. Clinging to its back was a sea-woman with
streaming purple hair and a wet body white as royal salt.

"Greeting, Sulghein, scion of kings," she said. "Abandon
the death you go to. Let me come aboard and love you.
Drift to Angia with me and find a house to guest in, before
sunset."

"Demon! In the name of God, the Mother and the Christus, go! I know your right shape."

"This is my right shape," she declared, arching to show
it. She spoke only the truth. Sulghein did not believe it.

"Turn aside, or turn back. Go with me."

"Demon! Trickster! Accursed of God!" His fanatic's vision saw her as scaled and fanged, with slimy fins breaking through the white skin. It was the reverse of the bardic sight, seeing only what one was determined to see, of which bards themselves had always to beware. "I bid you go!"

He invoked his unconventional Trinity again, and for good measure held forth the gold-set skull. The Daughter of Lir shrieked, threw her arms high, and slid from the dolphin's back to vanish beneath the water. Some of the dolphins paced him for a while in friendly innocence, blithe to his curses.

Bubbles of bright cruel laughter streamed below his leather hull. It is doubtful that Sulghein ever thought he was, perhaps, being cunningly lured ahead rather than feebly, ineffectively attacked. The woman might have overturned his boat in a moment, sending skull and book to the bottom of the sea. But what then? There were numberless saintly relics, and other books. Of righteous fools there was no end.

A more convenient wind blew. Sulghein trimmed the sail, and as the curragh skimmed onward, he chanted the *Biait* over and over.* His purpose flamed ever more exalted, more intense, as he stared hungrily westward. He chanted louder.

The sun went down.

In the sea-people's hall with its eerie, smokeless lamps, Felimid, Gudrun and Rowan sat together. Something was happening in which they had no part. The hall's outer doors stood open, and the doors of the foreroom, so that they could see down to the jewel-colored lagoon, now a lake of rosy fire on which *Ormungandr* floated. Tables bearing delectable food and wine stood within the doors.

"Touch none of that," Felimid warned. "I know not if your people have the same custom, but that food is for the clan's dead, if they should happen to come home. The doors are open to let them in."

The sunset was fading. Now Samhain began, the night between summer and winter, the old year and the new, when Gates were opened and uncanny beings were abroad. Even

*Psalm 118.

the distinction between life and death blurred at Samhain.
The dead rode out of their tombs and barrows to make free
with the earth. Magic flooded like a river in spate. The
Otherworlds could be entered. (It was another thing to leave
them.)

Above all it was the night when the world died into
winter. Always there was the chance that summer might not
be renewed. They had entered the night of no limits, of
wild, tragic, ungovernable events.

The lagoon became a lake of dark-blue shadow.

Out of that lake, a woman came naked and dripping into
the hall. She knelt before Rothevna, her purple hair streaming. She spoke to him. None of the Sarnians were close
enough to hear what was said, although Niamh did. Without
a word, Rothevna rose, dropping his cloak, and went out
with the newcomer. Niamh followed. As she passed Felimid, Gudrun and Rowan, she said:

"Go down to the shore and rejoin your men. It's in my
mind that you will soon see a thing you will remember until
you die."

"A friendly little thing, is she not?" Rowan muttered.

"Amiable," Gudrun agreed. She was decidedly fond of
Rowan. Her fondness had begun when he had tried to win
a place in her ship on her northern voyage by fighting two
men for the right, beating the first but losing to the second.
Nor was liking him any more difficult for her because he
was young, merry and well-formed. "Still, she is right. This
is a time I should be with the crew."

Out in the evening, a voice came ranting hoarsely across
the sea. Its sound carried far, as sound will at night and
over the surface of water it recited maledictions with steady,
systematic venom.

"Sulghein," the bard said softly. Then he raised his head
high, startled, sniffing through his recently broken nose.
"Do you smell—?"

He stopped there. It was the smell of another world, as
surely as he was a bard. First there was an odor of mud,
sleek fecund mud on briny sea-flats with a trace of pungent
spices in it, and then came a whiff of mingled warm growth,
of nameless trees, vines, parasitic water-plants, swamp and

a great river and somewhere beyond it all an open sea, a thousand scents he had never known before, teeming and commingling in his nostrils.

And there was warmth. A slow wind caressed his face. No such wind as that ever blew in autumn on the Narrow Sea. Yes, warm and moist it was, a wind not of his world. When it met the crisp air of October with its tang like frosty apples, it condensed into white, rolling fog which streamed across the lagoon from side to side. Sulghein's excoriating voice was muffled, but it remained audible.

He'd begun his cursing in the name of the Father, Mother and Son, as before, but this time, in honor of an entire island filled with devils and a few smaller isles around it, he had then proceeded through the troop of heaven's archangels led by Michael, the ancestors, the prophets, the patriarchs, the apostles, the virgins, the martyrs, the high saints and the monks, his revered skull was lifted high and the book held secure in the bend of his other arm as he thundered and itemized. Having listed the authorities by which he condemned the sea-people, he was now cursing in careful order all the parts of their bodies, from head to foot, within and without, before and behind.

Something overwhelmed the oration, although too briefly. From a seemingly vast distance there came a bellow which was certainly made by nothing human.

"By the tree of the nine worlds!" Gudrun said in sudden comprehension. "A Gate is out there now. It has opened!"

Felimid remained silent.

"Into *Ormungandr!*" Gudrun cried, her voice vibrating with desire. "Aboard, every man of mine. Tiumals, Hemming, raise the serpent-head. I will count while you do it! As many gold coins to you both as the count is below a hundred!"

"Lady! You don't know what's out there."

"I know that I want it."

The pirates scrambled into *Ormungandr* and ran out their oars. Rhychdir took the tiller-handle. Rowan, his position as a hostage forgotten, was among them, as was Felimid. They heard Gudrun counting eagerly.

"Three score three! Three score four!"

"There's light in this fog," Rowan said, awed.

There was, a pale purple shimmer, very faint. The warm slow wind from nowhere seemed to excite it, for it glowed occasionally brighter in drifts and curls. Felimid wondered what sort of unseen world produced it. A warm world, warm and wet and voluptuous, or his nose lied.

"Three score eighteen!"

"It's done!"

"Reckon what I owe you and dun me afterwards!" Gudrun rubbed the curving serpent-neck with her palm. "Show me the way now, best of ships," she pleaded. "Find me this Gate and take me through, and you shall have gore to drink. Where is it? Where, in this fog?"

The skin of Felimid's back and hands prickled as the great ship seemed to swing back and forth like a hound questing. A trick of the wind? Of warm water meeting chill below the keel? Yet the carved wooden eyes forward and above now seemed to hold a live blaze.

Then the oars were fouled. As once before, dripping shapes swarmed aboard, but this time they were not nicors, mottled and ray-tailed; they were the hot-blooded Children of Lir. Nor were they attacking to eat. They wielded short cudgels, used their hands, knees and feet with skill, and flattened rowers from bow to stroke. Women and children followed the men, not to fight but to do something more simple and effective while the rowers were stunned. They pulled out the thole-pins and threw them into the sea as swiftly as they could. Now half of *Ormungandr*'s oars had nothing to work against, now more than half. Then the boarders vanished, back into the fog and the roiled lagoon. They had come and gone so deftly that even Gudrun's pirates, busy at the oars, had had small time to respond. Those oars now trailed limp. Most of them.

Gudrun screamed like a gyrfalcon. For pure, raging frustration, that scream set records. Felimid, characteristically, chuckled. Even Gudrun Blackhair had to learn someday that she couldn't have everything she wanted.

Somewhere nearby, Sulghein was still pronouncing his anathemas. Having finished his anatomical dissertation, damning the lights, hearts, livers, reins, bowels, stomachs

and much else of the sea-people, he now cursed them in
every imaginable situation and condition: walking, swim-
ming, standing, sitting, running, eating and drinking, sleeping and rising, staying at home, traveling by night, by day
and throughout all four of the seasons. He included the men,
the women, the children and the babes unborn. He gave
particular, vitriolic attention to their halls, their houses, their
tents and any structures which might conceivably shelter
them. He damned, banned and execrated any and all kinds
of food which might find a path to their mouths and save
them from starvation.

Then he drew a long, necessary breath and devoted to
destruction the Veiled Isles where they lived.

The fog eddied along *Ormungandr*'s strakes, glowed,
parted—and they saw Sulghein in his boat. The bard could
have spat a plum stone at him, and hit him. But it wasn't
a plum stone he desired to propel at the monk. His detes-
tation of Sulghein's mad venom towards folk who had never
harmed him in the slightest had reached an intolerable pitch.
He drew forth his sling and reached into his pouch for the
last of his silver balls.

Then, as Niamh had said, he witnessed a thing he would
remember until he died.

With a rush and surge, Rothevna came out of the lagoon,
gripping the curragh's oak gunwale and drawing himself
up, over, within, in one fluent movement. His vast right
hand snatched the gold-mounted skull from Sulghein's grasp;
his left pushed the saint the length of the boat. The saint's
strength to his was like a salmon's to a whale's. With mas-
sive grace, Rothevna turned, looking, seeking, the skull
balanced in his hand as he stared through the writhing fog.

Then he threw the relic, straight and far.

Felimid saw it glitter, saw it stir the fog as it passed and
leave a trail of pale purple cometary light. Somewhere ahead,
by daylight diffused and faint, he saw muddy beaches bor-
dering a milky sea, fronded trees, a river flowing sluggish
out of a swamp, tiny water-dragons feeding along the shore,
and a harbor in which rode ships like those of Rothevna's
clan. He was looking through the Gate, and *Ormungandr*
drifted straight towards it.

The skull passed through first.

Between one breath and the next, as swiftly and undra-
matically as some people die, the Gate was destroyed. It
vanished; it was gone. Not closed, but gone.

Amazed, Felimid looked back at the curragh. Little had
changed; Rothevna still stood hugely tall. Sulghein had come
back from the stern and crouched at the prince's feet, holding
out his hand. Was he pleading?

No.

The handle of Sulghein's ritual knife showed black against
Rothevna's white-skinned stomach. A rivulet of dark blood
ran down towards his loins. The prince stood unmoving for
a long, long, dreadful time.

The given death, the royal sacrifice. The prince of his
people had been killed by one who was also a prince, and
a priest withal; killed with a sacred knife. Felimid understood, then. This was why Sulghein had been allowed to
reach the Veiled Isles; this, all the time, had been the purpose.

Rothevna fell like a crashing menhir in the bottom of the
boat.

XVIII

*The dumb ass speaking with man's voice forbad
the madness of the prophet.*

*These are wells without water, clouds that are
carried with a tempest; to whom the mist of darkness
is reserved for ever.*

— 2 Peter 2: 16-17

No longer fed by warm air from the Otherworld, the mist
cleared slowly. *I can do that,* Felimid thought, his harp
riding on his back; the harp of Cairbre which could alter
the round of the seasons. *I have done it. And what befalls
now?*

The events he'd witnessed had made him lightheaded.
Used to strangeness, he moved, thought and spoke, calming
the pirates who were more than lightheaded. They were
close to terror, for none of them had seen a Gate between
worlds open before.

"It's ended, lads," he assured them. "The Gate has disappeared, and the mist is going. The enchantment is over.
Now there's only that mad priest to be settling with."

He believed the words while he uttered them, for he was
still not thinking clearly or deeply. Not yet had it occurred
to him that the dreads of this Samhain night might scarcely
have begun.

"Gone!" Gudrun was fulminating. "My road to new
worlds, gone!"

Briefly, Felimid thought of Myfanwy, the goddess's
daughter in the shape of a black mare, who traveled between
worlds as she willed . . . but she was free now, and could

173

no longer be constrained, and moreover had had all she wanted of serving the desires of violent mortals. He put her lovely image out of his mind.

"Rothevna's dead," he told Gudrun. "Sulghein slew him."

"Ah, no! Are you certain, Bragi? I would have looked for the other outcome."

"I'd have preferred it my own self. But I saw Rothevna fall with the priest's knife in him, and short of feeling his pulse that's as certain as I can be. I think he allowed it."

"Ha?" She was startled anew, but she understood. Nor was she one to be greatly shaken by sudden death. "Yes, it may be. Well, it is the Children of Lir's affair, not ours. The priest is theirs to judge."

No torches burned by the lagoon. All fires were put out before sunset on Samhain eve, and kindled anew before dawn. Felimid saw little, therefore, but as he waded ashore the lagoon water was only cool, not flesh-nipping cold, and he smelled the fertile mud the river had carried into that otherworldly sea. Its waters had mingled with the lagoon, as the airs of the two worlds had mingled. A sea-spider moved away from him near the marge for further proof. Soon it would probably die in the cold.

Some Children of Lir were dragging Sulghein's curragh ashore. The priest, pinioned and roughly handled, was there too.

"You killed the prince, my brother," Niamh said to him, her stare incendiary. "Do you understand, clod-man? Do you know what that means? *You have killed a Son of the Sea.*"

"I failed," Sulghein groaned. Very clearly, he did not understand. He expected to die. "God receive my spirit."

Niamh struck him, violent in her loathing. "Fool, babbler—you know nothing! That you should be the instrument we had to use! I will let you find out what you have done."

Six men of her folk had lifted Rothevna from the curragh. She pointed contemptuously to the empty craft, holding Sulghein's gaze the while. He did not clamber into it at once, for he did not grasp that he was free to go.

Niamh turned her face to her brother and began a lament in the tongue of the Children of Lir, stately, rhythmic, ritualistic, yet for all that charged with intense grief. The women by the shore raised a wordless moaning and slashed themselves with knives, while the men voiced a deeper mourning-chant.

"By my advice," Felimid said to Sulghein in the tongue of Erin, "you'll depart while you can."

"You're from Erin!" Sulghein said in the same language. "What do you among these devils?"

Felimid might have said that he was seeking better company than that of monks, since the earth grew overfilled with them, but he was in no humor for sallies, or to avail himself of easy openings. He said:

"I'm from Erin, indeed, but no friend of yours on that account. You had better be on your way, fellow. The Children of Lir are forbearing for some reason, yet I tell you that the Sarnians won't for very long. Some of them would slay you just to see which way you fell. And it's not I would be stopping them now."

"That ship is Gudrun Blackhair's," the monk said slowly, looking at *Ormungandr*. "It's true, then . . . all of it was true. No, I will not go. These isles defy men and God by existing, and I will ban them."

"Ban them from your curragh, then," the bard said wearily, "or you will not live to finish. Niamh had the right of it. You understand nothing."

Sulghein looked at him, and although the night obscured his face, the monk's voice was now completely serene. "I understand more than you," he said. "You think I am in your hands, or theirs. I tell you we are all in God's, and the day of the sea fiends has come to its end. Can you not see?"

He swept his arm seaward. A foot-high wave surged through the lagoon, crashing on the beach and sweeping up to Rothevna's feet. A second followed, reaching higher.

"It is done!" Sulghein cried in triumph. "I have cursed enough, and God has heard my cursing. The sea rises in obedience to him! Kill me now, if you care to. It matters not at all."

Felimid agreed. He ran for *Ormungandr*, wasting no more words on the monk. Gudrun came to meet him, halting him with unceremonious body-to-body impact and gripping his shoulders hard.

"Not in my ship," she said between her teeth. "Go with your friends."

"What?"

"How big a fool do you think me? You knew!" she raged. "You knew there was a Gate in this place, and you did not tell me! Had I known before—but now it is gone!"

"Gudrun, we can talk of that later. The sea's a-move!"

"That I know well. I am leaving now. You go with the Children of Lir, since you prefer them to me. By Odin!" she yelled above the sea's noise, reverting in her anger. "Were you any other man I would take off your head! Try to board *Ormungandr* and I may take it off anyhow!"

"This is mad talk," Felimid said. "It's Samhain, girl! Samhain! You may not wish my presence, but you may be needing my bardic sight as you never did heretofore! And you owe me—"

Kissing Viper came out of the sheath with a hopeful rasp. Gudrun struck at the bard in her fury, but he had drawn the instant he saw her begin. The two swords rang together, and he leaped back before they could cross again.

"Put up!" he shouted. "Have your will, then—and if you decide later it was not what you wanted, it may be too late!"

He sheathed Kincaid again, and was running to the Children of Lir before the hilt had met the scabbard-mouth.

"Has your ship space for another?" he asked. "I'm not welcome in *Ormungandr,* it seems."

Thick dark rage clotted in his throat as he spoke. Gudrun, the stupid, arrogant hellcat! She was entitled, maybe, to be furious. She was not entitled to cast him off like a worn mantle at a moment like this. If Niamh refused him, he would be in bad trouble.

"You had best go aboard, then," Niamh said. "We have work to do, bringing babes and infants out, but you cannot help us with it."

Although brusque, she did not seem unfriendly, and it was surely no time for formal speeches. A wave surged higher than any yet, to hiss around their calves where they stood, and by the cold starlight he saw yet another break across the bar of the lagoon at a different angle, whitely seething. Storm-driven water might behave so, but there was no storm, or more than a gentle wind. The sea was aroused and threatening all by itself.

Lurching and stumbling in a rush of yeasty brine, Felimid reached the nearest ship. He dragged himself aboard, soaked to the waist. *Ormungandr* slammed and bucked its way out of the lagoon through a mess of colliding waves. The bard's anger simmered hotter as he watched it go.

Then he saw that the waves now ran the whole way up the shelving beach. The ships in the lagoon stood in stark, immediate danger of being driven ashore and broken aground by this unnatural tide. Men worked desperately to prevent it. They poled and rowed. They secured long lines to the prows and gunwales of their ships, and odd-looking harnesses to the other ends of the lines, before dropping them into the sea. Felimid could not see details enough in the moonless dark to guess what that was meant to achieve. He could only suppose the Children of Lir knew what they were doing.

He didn't even know whence the furious tide came. It raged among the Veiled Isles in twenty conflicting channels, cutting new paths for itself as it surged and ravened. It ate through sandbars like hot water corroding salt. Crashing ever higher up the shore of the main island, it surged at last into the naked oakwood by Rothevna's hall.

Water hissed across the tree-roots, a scum of dead leaves rising to cover its surface. It slid between the trunks and invaded the ribbed, hemispherical leather huts in the wood. One wave had not started to ebb before another burst after it, reaching higher. The sea roared unendingly in sorrow and wrath—the wild sea itself, rolling immense around the world, not some god of the sea comfortingly imagined in human form. The first tents came apart like hammered shells.

Blown conches from far seas roared the alarm. Women with small sea-children fled through the oakwood to somewhat higher ground, not in helpless panic as earth folk would have done, but to be in the open where help could reach them when their kinsmen organized it. They had all been taught from childhood that this day must come. They knew what to do.

In the ship with the figurehead of a swan, Felimid felt

the lines grow taut. Something was pulling the vessel seaward. Sleek dark heads showed in the maddened water
before the ship, and the white figures of merfolk could be
glimpsed there, at equal risk of battering, dazing and drowning. The latter drove constantly, to feel out the shifting
channels and cry the information to their fellows in the ships,
who worked like demons. The best thing Felimid could do
was to stay out of their way. He did.

The sea continued to boil and rise. Now the waves were
spilling through the open doors of Rothevna's empty hall.
They swirled across the foreroom, spilled down into the
sunken central floor and covered it from side to side, shining
under the luminescent yellow globes. None was there to see
the murky water rise, dark with dissolved soil a scum of
leaves, twigs and rubbish floating on top. The biggest wave
yet burst in, wrenching a door awry as it came, surging
over the first of the wide steps leading to the exquisite booths
built against the wall. Rothevna's cloak of shells, lying
where he had dropped it, was snatched into an ale-brown
eddy and sucked to the bottom.

Outside, the sea rushed by the walls, dragging, pulling,
undermining. Huge posts began to lean and creak, tearing
away from the timbers they upheld. Roof-beams shrieked
on the rack. The leaning door was wrung from its housing
completely and, dragged back and forth by the rising waves,
it battered the foreroom to pieces.

The white ship struggled through seething water until it
won around the northern point of the island. Then it ran
along the eastern shore in relatively sheltered water, drawn
by creatures Felimid now recognized as the big golden seals
of Rothevna's hall. Released from their harnesses, they swam
back the way they had come, barking. The white ship plunged
alone into a murderous tide-race between two isles. The
bard shut his eyes and considered himself dead. Any vessel
which went aground here would simply be ripped apart in
minutes.

It amazed him to look and find that they were through
the race.

The white ship's crew now rowed it. In time they reached
the shore near the island's highest point, a bare forty feet

above the sea, where the white fountain gushed in the star-light. They took forty children and youngsters aboard. Fif-teen men went ashore to make room for them.

"Now you will have to grip an oar," Aidan told the bard.

"That's not one of my best skills. Nonetheless I will pull till my muscles rip. What of the seals and the men? And all the women I saw yonder?"

"They have more work. By the god my people swear by! There will be work for all the ships which survive, for man and woman, seal and dolphin—and it will be more than they can do. In the morning we will know how many of us are left."

Felimid nodded. A tightness in his throat would not let him speak, and as he rowed through the endless haunted night he wondered many things. Was this in part due to him? Had Sulghein escaped? Had *Ormungandr* escaped, and where was Gudrun now?

The wild sea moaned. Gazing at the stars through spin-drift from time to time, Felimid gathered that they were headed south and from the resistance to his oar he estimated that the mounting, powerful tide ran southeast. Felimid bent to his oar and tried not to think about that; about the depth, the width, the unbelievable weight of water channeled to-wards this tiny part of the world. Simpler to think of the oar that bucked and fought him, the naked sea-child who sat and solemnly watched him.

The false dawn turned the sky gray. An endless while later, it lightened for the real sunrise. Felimid fell away from his oar without even a groan. Two slim youths took his place on the bench.

"You will live," Aidan told him.

"And was that meant to reassure me?" Felimid stretched his knotted muscles. "Cairbre and Ogma! Where are we, husband of ships?"

"In a bay some miles west of Aleth. Here we will bide, I think. If any earth-folk pass they will not see the ship."

"Tell me if there's news of Gudrun, will you?" Felimid mumbled, before he rolled over and slept.

When he awoke, he stirred like a man of seventy. His left hand, with its sword-toughened palm and calloused harper's fingertips, was no more than a little tender. The right had blistered and bled before all the skin wore off the palm. Elsewhere, every muscle he had throbbed like a boil. Riding hard all night would not have wasted him so.

"Upright, sluggard," Aidan said.

"Why?"

"Because you might improve with food in you, and none here is going to feed you morsel by morsel, as you were helpless."

Thinking about it, the bard discovered that he was starving. After he'd applied fish-oil and razor to his face, and eaten and drunk, he felt better. Samhain was over, too, he remembered. That made him feel better yet.

They rode at the end of three anchor-cables in a deep bay. The cables hummed with tension as they held the white ship offshore, for the waves were still running endlessly up to the land. They had advanced all that long night, and Felimid saw no sign that they would now retreat.

He shook his head, finding no words.

"You should see the mouth of the Rance," Aidan said. "All Manannan's white horses are crowding in there. A tide half a hundred feet high has gone up the river, striking like rams. The folk of Aleth are all on their knees giving thanks that their city is built on a promontory. East of Aleth—" The ship-lord closed one fist. "You would not believe me if I told you."

"How did this come to you?" the bard asked.

"The dolphins told me. They talk through the sea, and they can be heard from afar if you know their language. I've been listening below the water."

"Did they speak of Gudrun?" the bard asked, because he had to.

"No."

Felimid, again, found nothing to say. The terse negative was not encouraging, and if any sea could have driven *Ormungandr* to destruction, it had been running the previous night. Aidan had something to add, though.

"Sulghein survived. He's reached the shore he set out from."

Felimid did not greatly care. Still, it puzzled him that

Aidan should impart such news with satisfaction.

"What will we be doing now, then?"

"Doing? We'll be awaiting Lir's pleasure, and hoping our anchor-cables hold. And putting out nets to take fish and our sail to catch rain, for the sky promises that we'll receive some. You will fear for Gudrun Blackhair, I for my people . . . and both of us, it's to be hoped," Aidan said, bitter-softly, "will keep our dreads to ourselves."

XIX

Do you not see the course of the wind and the
    rain?
Do you not see the oaks beating together, the sea
    corroding the land?
Do you not see the sun vanishing and the stars
    falling?

           —Gruffyd ab Yr Ynad Coch

The tides ordained by God rose and fell twice a day.
Sulghein had no difficulty in believing that this one came
from some other quarter.

How he'd won clear of the Veiled Isles he never knew.
He fervently thanked his god that he had, as he turned his
curragh for home with the drowning islands of the sea-fiends
behind him, and assumed as he went that the power of that
god had intervened on his behalf. Why else would Niamh
have spared his life?

"The Lord destroys the wicked and the enemy," he gloated.
"The Lord gave the prince of the Veiled Isles into my hand
to be slain, and now he destroys his realm utterly. The Lord
has triumphed and the fiends of the sea are made nothing."

The sweeping flood-tide which carried him home had
also delighted him, at first. It bore with it the wreckage of
the Veiled Isles; a mangled tent, a shred of netting, leaves
and acorns afloat, a carved wooden toy, a dead man of the
Children of Lir who kept pace with the curragh for a while,
his flesh gleaming like new ivory in the sun, wide eyes ill-
wishing his murderer. Little Sulghein cared. Once he saw
a broken beam with its end shaped like a fish's head drift

forlornly by. Ruined, all destroyed, the foulness of their heathen pride!

The first little specks of tarnish appeared on the luster of his triumph when he noticed that the tide which drove him onward was still increasing. Hadn't the anger of God achieved its object? Well, perhaps the Veiled Isles were not wholly ruined. Sulghein left oars and sail untouched and concentrated on merely steering his boat. This miraculous tide was taking him unerringly back to Lansulcan. He'd be ungrateful, even impious, if he fretted.

Later that morning, he came in sight of Lansulcan's coast. He felt no mere misgiving then, but chill fear. Under the leaden sky with its rain clouds, the endless waves poured over the shore, into the forest, as they had poured into the oakwood by Rothevna's hall. The pounding, battering, hungry roar of them could be heard a league out to sea, and Sulghein felt their impact in his appalled flesh.

It will stop, he told himself. *It's merely an aftermath of the Veiled Isles' destruction. It will abate. I have faith that it will.*

The seething waves, undeterred, carried him over the beach that had been, and hurled him among the trees. Drowned underbrush clutched his hull with a hundred thousand ripping fingers. The curragh slammed into a moss-grown, brine-drenched oak; its slim mast caught in the branches and snapped. The next wave drove it twenty paces on. Sulghein tried desperately to stay inboard while guiding the curragh between trees with an oar.

A new wave kicked it. As it sprang wildly forward, a snag burst through the leather hull and ripped a yard-long rent through which water gushed. The curragh revolved around the impaling snag, to strike a tree sideways. Its ash frame crackled like birds' bones.

Sulghein snatched a leather satchel which now contained his book. As the curragh tilted, he climbed into the branches of the tree and clambered through them to the other side, where they intertwined with the limbs of a southern neighbor. A score of trees later, he was able to descend to the wet ground. Rain was falling heavily by then.

The trees in the Forest of Dol grew far bigger than those

on the Veiled Isles. Between their trunks, underbrush was tangled to form a nearly solid wall spreading for leagues. This broke the force of the attacking waves, yet they came without end——and even when their force was broken, the water spilled through. Sulghein was delayed more than the marching sea. He struggled through the brush, pursued by something vast and tireless, like a man who flees in a nightmare. He was sobbing when he came to the blessed freedom of a game trail.

It meandered widely. Sometimes it led back towards the sea, and once Sulghein trod in brine from which he recoiled as from a wriggling adder. Retracing his steps, he found a spot where the trail branched, and hurriedly took the southern fork.

The beasts were also a-move, fleeing inland. A red hart and two hinds came down the trail after him. Sulghein, afraid, hungry and tiring, did not become aware of them until nigh too late. He almost died on the hart's antlers, and had to crawl through a thicket to save his life. It seemed to him by now that earth, sky and sea had all sworn themselves his enemies.

Lost and bewildered, he spent three days and nights finding his way back to the holy mountain. In all that time the sea never ceased encroaching on the doomed Forest of Dol. Some trees fell, the earth washed and sucked from around their roots. Most remained standing, but were killed where they stood none the less, poisoned by salt. None would put forth green buds in the spring. And still the sea roared and battered in all its tremendous power, its endless fury.

Sulghein saw the crag of Saint Michael against a watery sky on the morning of the fourth day. Filthy, weary, scarcely having eaten and with fever making itself felt in his body, he staggered to the mountain's foot. Step by dogged step, he climbed the path. Before the shrine to Saint Michael which he had raised, he fell prone and entered a trance of delirious prayer which lasted moments, or hours.

Afterwards, he looked north from the mountain. At a careless glance all was much as before. The sea had risen perhaps twenty feet, and mile upon mile of low-lying country was now submerged, but all that victorious water lay below the treetops yet. The dense forest roof, obscured by rain, lit by occasional lightning, seemed inviolate—yet below it, the waves ravened.

"God!" Sulghein cried. "Halt the sea!" His voice held agony. "Turn back the devourer, the gray destroyer whose demons mock your might, I beg of you! You established the ocean and set the bounds it may not pass. Will you suffer the fiend Lir to defy you now? Can his revenge touch your servants?"

He received no answer but the sea's steady advance.

At Megelin's farmstead, Vivayn stood listening to the voices in the wind, rain and thunder. Some tidings are too huge for a response. One hears and understands, and cannot but believe, yet the knowledge will not sink beneath the skin, or go deeper than the ears. The mind does not accept it.

It had been that way for Vivayn when the sea-wolves took her father's kingdom. Nothing astonished her after that, until in an obscure corner of Lesser Britain she learned that the sea was overwhelming the land. For the second time in her life, then, her mind refused what it knew.

Vivayn was too relentlessly clear a thinker, though, to enjoy that luxury for long. She lifted her head from her hands and went searching for Eldrida. The Jutish girl looked once at her face and left the flour she was sifting.

"What? Fire of the gods, what?"

"The fool!" Vivayn said, whitely furious. "That righteous, blighted fool! Oh, he has done what he so proudly set forth to do. The Veiled Isles are a waste and Rothevna is dead by his hand. Now the sea comes to avenge its son. We will see salt waves rolling past Saint Michael's Mountain before nightfall, and on across these fields—and as always, it will be the women who take the blame. This time I should not be surprised if Megelin kindles the fire."

"What can we do?"

"Save ourselves! Now it's useless simply to flee. We don't know how far or fast the sea will follow. I think we should do two things; go to the highest ground hereabouts, taking plenty of food, and hide a boat against our need."

"The boat sounds good. But the highest ground hereabouts—"

"—is the mountain. I know, Eldrida. It's the mountain,

and Sulghein has returned. Nonetheless, that is where the nearest thing to safety can be found, and where I mean to go. Should it make it needful to have some overdue words with that sacerdotal madman, I shall have them—and I think I'll take more pleasure in it than he."

"Fine," Eldrida retorted, "but you must get there. We're supposed to stay at this farmstead until Sulghein comes back to judge us, remember? If what you say will happen, happens, I know what his judgment will be! So do you! You said it. He won't blame himself for the results of what he's done."

"Leave Sulghein to me. For that other difficulty, you know it is not much. We have come and gone as we pleased in a royal dun. Are you afraid, after what happened here before?"

Eldrida nodded, slowly and definitely. "I am. I'll do it, though."

Then Vivayn took her aside, marked an intricate quincunx about her feet, and walked sunwise around her, thrice nine times, singing a complex song once each nine circuits. When she finished the song the third time, the yellow-haired girl had taken the appearance of a young loon whose rags scarcely held together. This was Claud, Lansulcan's fisherboy, too simple to work steadily, or else too cunning to appear to have all his wits. None would wonder to see him poking about the river.

The illusion would last until sunset.

And . . .

Packs of gray wolves came out of the forest, running across the fields of Lansulcan. Deer, red and roe, fled in bounding, explosive leaps. Hares pattered and sprang; owls flew by daylight. Creatures less canny, visible to Vivayn's eyes only, passed under the weeping sky. A wraith drifted through the air and a shaggy, goat-legged urisk loped along, both avoiding the mountain. Behind them, a soughing grumble grew to a thunder.

Out of the forest came a yard-high wave, miles wide. It divided around the mountain's base and swept unresisted across the stubbly fields. It poured into houses and well-filled barns, rushing gray and yellow for half a mile before it dissipated in dun froth. Before it retreated, a second wave almost as high followed it, roaring.

Vengeance had come to Lansulcan, the aroused, insensate retribution of Lir. Past the barrier of leagues of ancient forest it had reached, through matted, piled, uprooted and compressed walls of undergrowth, between a million trees, hammering and driving to its destination, these first waves the mere vanguard of a host whose ranks stretched out past Erin, advancing for a thousand miles.

The helplessness caused by a sudden flood is complete. Against encroaching water, little can be done. Walls or dykes can be built if there is time, but here there was none. Some folk ran. Some mounted horses and rode. Some turned their livestock loose, gathered their families and made for the mountain, wading through knee-deep water.

Sulghein saw his people toiling up the holy mountain. He saw the vast sheet of spreading water far below, stippled by cold gray rain. Soon it would swallow the river, obliterate the fields, make the cleared ground one with the surrounding forest, and in time destroy the forest. The holy mountain would stand as an island in an immense tide-marsh.

"Why, Lord God? Why?"

He was answered. A blaze of bright sunlight fell about him. He saw a tall warrior with shining hair and a fiery spear, an ornate, exquisite torc of gold around his throat. From his shoulders flowed a cloak embroidered with golden sun-wheels. In the stranger's face was more than human beauty, more than human justice.

"This is your work. Do you now ask why? You destroyed the Children of Lir without cause, and God has permitted them to unleash the sea against you. As you did to them, Lir will do to your folk. Have you warned them of their danger, or have you crawled to my shrine and prayed to soothe your own soul, while the sea covers their land? Look down, Sulghein. What you see is your own work. Does it please you now as it did when the Veiled Isles drowned?"

A ghastly sound came from Sulghein's salt-raw throat. His reddened eyes stared and stared at the stranger, whose aspect was like that of the pagan sun-lord Lugh and Michael the Archangel. Behind him were two unearthly horses harnessed to a blazing chariot.

Sulghein looked down, as he had been instructed. He

saw the upward-turned faces of several dozen of his folk. All saw the stranger; all had heard him. His dazzling light flamed over the mountain peak.

Sulghein did not look at him again. He looked outward, to the foaming water that surged from the north, through the devastated forest. Then he threw himself from the ledge and hurtled through thirty fathoms of air with the wind shrieking past him. He vanished in the turbulent water breaking about the mountain's base.

"Lansulcan is finished," the stranger declared. His voice rang. "Not again will seed-time, harvest or the hunt be known here. You must depart, and build your homes elsewhere—and go swiftly, lest the sea swallow you all."

The people saw him enter his chariot. He drove it glowing to the peak of Saint Michael's Mountain. A gust of wind, a concealing flurry of rain, and he had gone.

None saw a smaller, slenderer figure among the rocks on high, with a drab shawl covering her bronze-red hair, as she waited for sunset. None observed, in the fearful confusion which ruled, that there were two perkily vacant fisher-boys in the crowd, or saw one steal away with Eldrida's children. The renewed drizzle hid much.

The water had become thigh-deep by the time they reached the clump of alders between mountain and river where Eldrida had hidden a skiff. Then they waited, until Vivayn could make her way back down the mountain, less swiftly than Sulghein had done, and join them after wading through water which by then was waist-deep—or only hip-deep if one happened to be tall.

The signal Eldrida had used when they escaped from the Veiled Isles proved useful again. Hearing the shearwater's cry, Vivayn struggled into the flooded alder-thicket. Eldrida, still wearing the semblance of a fisher-boy, helped her into the skiff.

"Well, my swan, it looks as though we're running again," she said.

"Yes."

"What befell Sulghein?"

"*Befell* is an excellent word. He promised us his judgment; I gave him mine instead." Something of the stranger's dispassionate awesomeness showed in Vivayn's face for a moment. "He might have seen it was an illusion I conjured, if he'd had his wits about him, but they were scattered as far as the Children of Lir by then. He threw himself from the crag."

"Good!" Eldrida said positively.

"It is good. He brought this disaster, he made it—and with Sulghein gone, there will be less, let us say, unanimity of thought around here. Megelin may be the strongest man left. I think we should go back to his farmstead and help him to leave."

"The water hasn't reached it yet," Eldrida said, peering through the wet. "His home's on a rise, anyhow. Carts could get away along the southern track if they're loaded quickly. Two miles poling this skiff should bring us to sunset, and I will look like myself again before anyone but us has to see me change. There, Nye, stop howling. Your mother will return, we'll have her back for you, there, croodle-doo... *Oh, shut up or I'll give you reason to bawl!*"

Vivayn took off her soaked skirt and wrung it over the side of the skiff. Young Cerdic regarded her bare white legs with an interest which, although years away from being active yet, was real enough. Nye continued screaming.

The waves rolled on around the towering crag.

XX

*Is it not absurd to suppose that a whole people
could be driven from their homes by resentment against
a natural and continual phenomenon which recurs
twice a day? In any case, this extraordinary tide
appears wholly fictitious, since variations in the level
of ocean tides are quite regular and seasonal.*

—Strabo, VII; 2

Three brilliant, strangely shaped sails came flying across
the sea, first on one tack, now on another. Dolphins accompanied them. They spoke through the water in their
strange, carrying language as they came.

"It's Niamh," said Aidan.

"Is there word of Gudrun?"

"They gave none. Soon they will be here and you can
ask Niamh face to face. She is the clan leader now. Rothevna
named her his heir years ago. Idh, I suppose, will be her
spokesman and advisor as he was her brother's."

That could be more than interesting, Felimid thought.
*Those two counseled slaying Gudrun and me, and Rothevna
it was who refused.*

Gently, he put Golden Singer aside. But when the ships
drew near and Niamh hailed them, she did not appear hostile, only dog-weary.

"Greetings, Felimid," she said. "Your woman is safe."

"Only until I meet her again," Felimid said, disguising
his relief. "Do you know where she is?"

"Surely. She reached a well-sheltered bay near Cout-
ances. Two ships of ours went with her. We'll all tryst soon."
Niamh smiled wryly. "She stayed awhile on Samhain Eve.

190

Her pirates saved fifty of my people, and so I no longer have the pleasure of hating her." Niamh swayed drunkenly back and forth as she spoke. Clearly only determination kept her from sinking to the deck and lowering her face into her splayed fingers. "Lir, I am tired!"

"Then sleep." Aidan spread his cloak on the deck for her. Every man of the Children of Lir did the same, until she had a pallet thick as twenty quilts. With a sigh deep as the sea she sprawled upon it. For hours thereafter she scarcely twitched.

Gudrun had come safe through Samhain, then. She had also risked filling her ship with Children of Lir before she departed. There was no predicting her. She would display arrogance, ruthlessness, temper, and then do something like this. Yet Felimid was glad she had. He felt proud of her.

When Niamh awoke and ate, the tide at last showed signs of slackening, after booming relentlessly landward for days. She assessed the sea with the glance of one who belonged to it, and her eyes were somber in her drawn face.

"Thus it ends," she said.

"Lady, how did it begin?" Felimid asked.

"You are a bard, and descended from the Tuatha De Danann. Surely you know, or have guesses? Were you so simple, Felimid, as to have none, I'd never have been for killing you."

"Oh, aye, I've guesses! And since Samhain I have been sure. The Children of Lir had no more a place in this world, so, like the rulers of the Tuatha De Danann, they retreated to others. But Gates remain by which those worlds can be reached, and one of them was in the Veiled Isles. It opened each Samhain, and maybe each Beltaine, too. Your clan had the trust of guarding the gate, and—once you could no more hold it—of seeing that it was destroyed. Your brother died to achieve that."

"Your guesses are very near the bone. There is little else for me to tell you. The Gate could not be destroyed but from this world, with the help of one such as Sulghein. The power was in him. Because he came alone, he was perfect. We fooled him, lured him, and Rothevna ... did what his rank asked. Sulghein played his part, but he thought only to injure us, and so to my mind he did wanton, brainless murder." She showed her teeth. "I might have killed him. I wasn't that merciful. I let him go, to discover for himself that his god does not rule the sea. I hope he lasted that long."

"I rather hope so myself," Felimid murmured. "What will you do now?"

"Nothing. There is no more a secret to keep or a gate to guard." Niamh clamped her small jaw like one forbidding herself to weep. Between set teeth she said, "You needn't fear."

"Good, then, for I wasn't fearing. Nor was I meaning that. You have answered the wrong question, lady. I meant, what will you and your people do? Not to me, but for yourselves? You're homeless, and it is winter, and there was a certain guarded friendship pledged between us before all this happened. Sarnia is still a strong holding."

"Oh," Niamh blinked. "That was a good thought, cousin. No, we will thrive. There is time for us to go south to warmer waters, and the sea feeds us. Maybe we will see you again in the spring."

South, through the winter storms? Felimid thought. But he did not question her. The dolphins could guide them past rock and reef in the blindest weather, and there might be other communities of the Children of Lir in more remote parts. If Niamh thought they could survive, it was likely they could.

The tide no longer ran onshore. It was receding slowly, with seeming reluctance. The Children of Lir spent the rest of that day tacking out of the bay and sailing east past the Rance. In Aleth the church bells were pealing, and masses being sung with fervor, as they had been for days. The masses had been effective, or the precipitous banks of the Rance estuary had, for in that region the monstrous tide had done small damage even though the water stood higher than it had ever done before. Aleth might indeed give thanks that it was sited on high ground.

The four ships spent the night on a sheltered beach. In the morning they fared on. No human eyes watching from shore saw anything but dim patches like the shadows of moving clouds.

They passed a headland which had been part of a continuous coastline a nine-night before. Now it marked the beginning of a bay fifteen miles across, scoured from low-lying country by the wild sea's unimaginable strength. Felimid looked in fascinated awe.

Trees had been uprooted and heaped together. Brush in huge swathes had been piled around them to form islands like immense, sodden birds' nests, over which the waves broke creamily. Beyond these, most of the forest yet stood, and the trees more than thirty feet high showed above the surface. There were many such. The squirrels could still travel for miles from treetop to treetop, twice and thrice as high above the water as the water rolled above the roots, but they traversed a dead realm.

"Cairbre and Ogma! How far does that go?"

"As far into the land as it's wide, or thereby," Aidan said. He did not explain how he knew. "In ten years there will be nothing to see but silt and tide-sand all the way."

"Yes," Niamh agreed with a certain satisfaction, watching the waves. "One day, maybe, the Cross-worshippers and their sort will own all the wild world, and there will be no place for us . . . or for bards, or for the likes of Gudrun. But until that day comes, there is a price for offending faerie, and yonder you see it reckoned and taken."

Felimid looked away. Thus he was first to see *Ormungandr* and two smaller ships of the Children of Lir approaching. Within the hour, many who had been separated at Samhain met again, and Gudrun came aboard Aidan's ship.

"Bragi! You came through safe."

"I did, so. Small thanks to you. You barred me your ship and drew sword against me while Lir was doing his utmost to drown the world! With all there is between us and the meager cause you had, I say that must be the pettiest, meanest thing you have ever done."

"*Meager!* You lied and cheated me of my strongest desire—with all there is between us. Your own words! And you did it for—" Gudrun stopped, and looked around her. "For a people never to be belittled, I admit." She gazed at the devastated shore with, there was no doubt about it,

distinct admiration. "But you gave me cause to believe you
would be true to me first."

"What I did, I would do again—and maybe that's untrue
to you, as you say. Yet I never did lie to you. I guessed,
and as it turns out I guessed near to the truth, and didn't
tell you, because it wasn't my right to be telling. Nor did
I wish to. My love you are, Gudrun, but ruler and owner
of my entire soul you are not. If you find that cause for
complaint, you have loved the wrong man.

"*My* complaint is that you left me. You abandoned me
on a flooding shore to drown, for all you knew. Had the
Children of Lir not taken me with them, my body would
now be tangled somewhere in that." He pointed vehemently
to the ruin of the Forest of Dol. "You were less than Gudrun
Blackhair then, no matter what cause you had to quarrel
with me."

Gudrun looked long at the miles upon miles of inundated
wreckage before her. In her mind she saw other things;
Felimid beside her in the dwarf king's hall, the reddened
beach on Rugen, the obscene mass of vampire-weed sent
to her as a gift horse by Urbicus, and herself in the bard's
arms. Her eyes held the unfocused gaze of the blind when
she looked at him again.

"I did wrong. I am ashamed. But it never even came to
my mind that the Children of Lir would reject you. They
did not, either, did they? Don't leave me."

"Until the next time I do something that angers you? I
know well it never entered your mind. It should have! Look,
Gudrun. Look at that. You were for crashing into an Otherworld without a notion of what was there, and in that you
were like Sulghein. That, yonder, is what is apt to happen
when you meddle with Faerie, as Niamh says."

"I care nothing about that!" Gudrun suddenly knelt before
him. She drew her sword and held its viper-backed blade
across her palms. "I raised this sword against you. May it
turn against me and destroy me if I ever do that again in
anger. May it do the same if I abandon you to danger again
for any cause. Demand what reparation you like, Bragi. But
don't leave me."

Felimid raised her and kissed her mouth long. "I tried

that, once. I couldn't make it stand, and trying it again
would be an idle gesture. But I may leather you with a
scabbard until you howl like a hurricane."

"So? I give you leave—if you can." Gudrun's smile
invited and challenged. "Provided it is private."

They had spoken in Jutish. The Children of Lir did not
know that tongue—at least, none who were present in Aidan's ship. Niamh interrupted with some resentment in her
voice; resentment of earth-bred folk who could indulge their
disagreements and affections at such a time, with nothing
more desperate to trouble them.

"We had better depart, for the tide will soon turn. I don't
wish to be here when it runs landward again. Gudrun, have
we your leave to camp for a few days on Brechou?"

"Brechou is yours for the winter if you require it."

"Thanks."

They gazed again at the devastation of Dol and Lansulcan, awe of the god blending with morbid wonder.

"Do you suppose," Niamh asked thoughtfully, "that Vivayn and Eldrida survived?"

"You hope they did not. Myself, I would wager gold that
they did, but we would have to go beyond that mess to
learn. No ship could penetrate it. Even *Ormungandr* would
be ripped apart on snags fit to impale a kraken. Live or
dead, they are beyond your reach and mine."

The seven overloaded ships rowed north, and were joined
by two others as they fared. They passed the Veiled Isles.
Nothing was there now but shoals and sandbanks, just what
had appeared to be there to the untutored eye, a nine-night
before. It seemed like a thousand years.

Felimid sighed for the loss. Lansulcan and the monk were
no payment for the Veiled Isles. Worship of the Cross was
a tide as irresistible as the sea which had torn down Rothevna's hall. There were always more monks, and the slaugh-
ters and tortures of them and their dupes produced ever
more holy relics, but there would not always be more enchantment.

"We have earned a winter of ease, I think," he said.

"Yes. And when summer comes, my man, I will go to
Erin with you as you desire. I will divide the ships and loot

among my men and disband the pirates of Sarnia. Pascent will have his desire, a ship to resume trading and his pick of some very useful sailors. I will take as many as we need to crew *Ormungandr,* no more."

She snuggled against him.

"Bragi?"

"Yes?"

"What did you say, once, about magic and otherworldly Gates still abounding in your land?"

AFTERWORD

Again, the background to this novel is largely accurate. The setting of the Channel Isles and the neighboring coasts, with their rocky shores, swift currents and strong, treacherous tides, is much as described, though I may have understated. Little is known of the chieftains who held Sark, Jersey and Guernsey in the post-Roman period. Nominally they were no doubt under the Frankish kings, while in practice it passed between pirates, wreckers and monks, Saxons and expatriate Britons.

Invaders, colonists and refugees from Britain had taken over Armorica so completely that the peninsula was known as Lesser Britain . . . in later times, Brittany. The rest of Gaul was divided between four Frankish brother-kings, successors to Clovis, the Burgunds of the central massif, and the Goths who held small coastal areas in the south.

Some of the characters are known to legend and history. Cynric and his father Cerdic appear in the *Anglo-Saxon Chronicle* a few decades after Hengist. They are credited with founding Wessex. Cerdic's name is British, so I have made him half British, half Jutish, and the founder of Jutish settlements in Wight and southern Hampshire, which fits the archaeology of the area. The *Chronicle* says that he conquered and slew a British king, Natanleod, in that region.

Nothing else is known about Natanleod (and what the *Chronicle* tells us isn't certain), except that his name seems to be Pictish. There is no record of his having a daughter. The daughter I've given him, Vivayn the sorceress, is the Viviane of Arthurian legend, also (and confusingly) known as Nimue. I've assumed that the latter name is a corruption of the Celtic Niamh, and that legend combined the sea-

woman with the British princess in the way that legend often
does. There's another Niamh in Celtic legend, Niamh the
Fair, but she has nothing to do with the green-haired mermaid of this novel.

Her separate identity—if you care to take the idea of her
seriously—may be preserved in the character of King Ar-
thur's supposed sister, Morgan le Fay. A "morgan" or "mu-
rigen" is a type of Celtic mermaid, and a "fay" is simply a
fairy. Morgan was supposed to rule a magical island in the
western sea, lovely and immortal. Later stories tell of her
carrying Charlemagne's paladin, Ogier the Dane, to her
home and keeping him as her lover for centuries. Maybe
Niamh and her people did find a new home beyond Erin.
It would be pleasant to think so.

The monks and missionaries depicted in the story belong
not to the orthodox Church of Rome, but to the native Celtic
Church of the early sixth century. The superficial differences
between the two, such as variant tonsures and ways of
calculating the date of Easter, were only symptoms of the
real difference; the Celtic church did not accept the su-
premacy of Rome. In this as in other matters, the Celts were
fiercely independent and individualistic.

Celtic monasteries grew out of tribal societies with their
own royal clans. In Ireland particularly, where there were
no towns or even villages of any size, the local monastery
was often the largest community in the *tuath,* including the
royal stronghold—and the abbot, as often as not, was a
cousin or younger brother of the king. The Celts conceived
of their monastery as a mission to the tribe that sustained
it. The buildings were of timber and thatch within circular
earthworks, and the rules varied from place to place depending on the convictions of the local abbot.

David, the patron saint of Wales, was about fifty years
old at the time of this novel (late in 512 A.D.). His rules
were exceptionally severe, and I haven't exaggerated them.
He allowed his monks neither meat nor alcoholic drink at
any time, and enforced the other austerities described. My
fictional Sulghein, who trained under him, seems to have
outdone his master in horrible holiness, although he did eat
meat—whenever he wasn't fasting. Sulghein's fanaticism

and unconscious semi-paganism were probably traits of many real Celtic monks of the time, especially in such isolated communities as the one described.

The young monk named Samson, one of the two who brings Cynric's message to Sarnia, may have been the famous Breton saint of the same name. His mission to Brittany took place years later, but he may well have made an early journey there, subordinate to a senior monk.

Those monks who lived in monasteries rather than as hermit-saints on mountains were less dismal. The art and scholarship of the Irish church which flowered in the sixth century became famous throughout Europe. Celibacy was not a rule. In some monasteries, Celtic monks lived with their wives and children and saw nothing untoward in that. Roman churchmen took to calling these women "concubines," denying them their legitimate title, which the Celts saw as a presumptuous insult. The orthodox churchmen of Gaul were even outraged by the *conhospitae,* or female deacons, who formed part of the Celtic Church in Brittany. The letter from the bishops of Tours quoted is real.

Saint Patrick (Padraigh) studied on the continent and followed orthodox Roman principles. He established sees and bishoprics on the Roman model before his death, the date of which is still in dispute. They didn't suit the pattern of Irish society, though, and by Felimid's time the first great Irish monasteries had been founded and the functions of abbot and bishop had begun to be combined in one man. If distinctions between abbot and bishop, monk and priest, are sometimes treated carelessly in this novel, the distinctions were sometimes vague in real life, too.

The conflict of Roman with Celtic practice went on for centuries. It ended in the twelfth century when Pope Hadrian IV authorized Henry II of England to conquer Ireland, on condition that a silver penny a year was squeezed out of each inhabitant of the country for the See of Saint Peter.

The above is wide open to argument. I've studied and researched the matter as best I could, and the wide range of opinion on the subject is, uh, interesting. For instance, the Reverend D. Davies, in *The Ancient Celtic Church and the See of Rome,* strongly takes the view that the Celtic

Church was independent. The Reverend John Campbell McNaught, in *The Celtic Church and the See of Peter,* takes the view equally strongly that it was subordinate, and never disagreed with Rome in any fundamental way.

The various supernatural creatures are authentic—authentic legends, that is. Some stories about the barghest describe it as resembling a monster hound, others a monster bear. They are told both in Cornwall and Brittany. Stories concerning the sea-people, dreadful and otherwise, are much more widespread. Celtic lore is filled with merrows, selchies, lake-women, kelpies, sea-hags, Fomors, and creatures like the horror of Scattery Island.

Being afflicted with a tidy mind, I've tried to sort this into some sort of order without losing the substance of Celtic legend. I've assumed that the sea, surface, depths and fringes, was home to many kinds of faerie creatures, few of them what they appeared to be to humans. Of them all, the Children of Lir were closest kin to human beings, and like their magical cousins the Tuatha De Danann, they were conquered and ousted by the iron-using, sun-worshipping Celts. Their situation later became much worse with the growth of the Roman Empire, and later of the church which may have aided it to collapse. Certainly the lunatic proliferation of sects, cults and heresies did little to hold it together. Arian, Sabellian, Donatist, Orthodox, Nestorian, Monophysite—Christianity came in more flavors than ice cream. I've taken the (not very original) view that most of them were poisons to magic and faerie.

Besides the warm-blooded, air-breathing Children of Lir, there were scaled, fishlike monsters. In the story they are commonly described as "sea demons," but as someone mentioned, "real" demons are much more formidable, being able to change their shape and size physically within limits so broad as to be, from the human point of view, unbounded. They can assimilate or discard mass at will as they transform, and are vulnerable to few manmade weapons, of which Felimid's sword Kincaid is one.

The "sea demons" or Cold Ones, on the other hand, cannot even change their appearance through magical illusion, unless they have the help of a human wizard. Nor

can they survive out of water for more than an hour—
unless, again, a spell cast by an air-breather allows them
to. But they can stimulate human emotions and passions
from a distance through the medium of the sea, direct the
activities of sharks, rays, sea-snakes and octopi, and control
schools of fish in such a way as to ensure record catches
of fish for fishermen who oblige them with human sacrifice.
Sometimes they associate themselves with humans like
Urbicus the wrecker, who commit evil on a bigger scale.

The kelpies or water-horses *(eać uisge)* are among the
most dangerous creatures in Celtic folklore. They lure the
unwary to ride them, then carry them into the sea to devour.
It seemed logical to associate them with the Cold Ones.

The more sympathetic selchies or seal-people are yet
another race of magical seafolk. The Children of Lir have
only occasional born shape-shifters like Turo among them.
The golden seals in Rothevna's hall were probably not selchies, as it's said that these generally take human form on
land.

The "Gate" between worlds is another concept widely
used in Celtic stories. The magical Celtic Otherworlds are
more fanciful and less precisely located than the "nine worlds"
of Norse myth, linked by the branches and roots of the
universe tree Yggdrasil. Celtic gods and heroes pass in and
out of enchanted realms freely. My twentieth-century pes-
simism convinces me that it couldn't be that easy, therefore
by Felimid's time most Gates have ceased to exist, those
remaining open only at certain times like Samhain, and even
they are vanishing one by one.

The climactic event of the story—and one of the most
unlikely in it—is genuine. Until some time between the
fourth and eighth centuries, Dol and Mount Saint Michael
stood within a huge forest. A rapid encroachment of the sea
overwhelmed it all, and left the high places like the holy
mountain standing as islands. This created the present Bay
of Mount Saint Michael between Normandy and Brittany,
but the area submerged was originally much larger. The
waters did not recede until the twelfth century, and did so
gradually even then. The supernatural trimmings are mine;
still, they fit the many Celtic inundation legends in which

an area is drowned because some taboo is broken or a curse invoked.

The quotation from Strabo dates from centuries before Felimid's time. That supercilious Roman had heard a similar legend and dismissed it with a snort, even though he lived within the Mediterranean himself and had no experience of what Atlantic tides could be like. He wasn't the first or the last to assume he had adequate knowledge of a matter of which he was in truth dirt-ignorant. I couldn't resist using his words as a chapter epigraph.

—Keith Taylor

Stories

~ of ~

Swords and Sorcery

Prices may be slightly higher in Canada

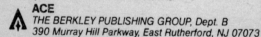